"I'm not ready to say goodbye."

"What are you suggesting?" Saafir asked.

"That we do what feels right and that it stays between us."

He thought a secret affair was perfect, and yet sad, too. It highlighted the fact that love came second to duty.

He pulled her tight. "You should know that while you are mine, I will treat you like a princess. I will spoil you for any other man. You will think of me long after I am gone." Then he kissed her.

He laid her back against his desk, until he heard a sharp knock at the door. His security officer stepped into the room. Of all the times to be interrupted, this was not it. From the look on the guard's face, Saafir knew it had to be life or death.

He reached for his gun and pulled Sarah behind him. He hated this. A man should provide safety for his woman...but he had brought peril to her doorstep.

Dear Reader,

I have a close friend whose parents arranged her marriage. She was satisfied with her parents' choice until she fell in love with another man.

Not having a choice in love can be devastating. In this book, the new emir of Qamsar is to have an arranged marriage for political reasons. Saafir first appeared in my third book, *Protecting His Princess*. Strong, quiet and loyal, Saafir's future has been decided for him, except he's not sure he wants the life he's been offered.

Recently divorced and disillusioned with love, Sarah Parker feels her heart has been broken and trampled. She wants a fresh beginning, and meeting a mysterious and exotic stranger seems like a good start to a new chapter in her life. Even though Saafir can only be temporarily in her life, there's something about Saafir that makes him hard to resist.

As for my friend, while it wasn't easy and required a lot of compromise, she got her happily ever after with the man she loves.

I hope you enjoy reading how Sarah and Saafir's story turns out. I love hearing from readers and can be contacted through my website, www.cj-miller.com.

C.J. Miller

UNDER THE SHEIK'S PROTECTION

C.J. Miller

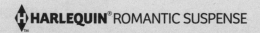

Recycling programs
for this product may
not exist in your area.

ISBN-13: 978-0-373-27883-1

UNDER THE SHEIK'S PROTECTION

Copyright © 2014 by C.J. Miller

All rights reserved. Except for use in any review, the reproduction or
utilization of this work in whole or in part in any form by any electronic,
mechanical or other means, now known or hereafter invented, including
xerography, photocopying and recording, or in any information storage
or retrieval system, is forbidden without the written permission of the
publisher, Harlequin Enterprises Limited, 225 Duncan Mill Road,
Don Mills, Ontario, Canada M3B 3K9.

This is a work of fiction. Names, characters, places and incidents are
either the product of the author's imagination or are used fictitiously,
and any resemblance to actual persons, living or dead, business
establishments, events or locales is entirely coincidental.

This edition published by arrangement with Harlequin Books S.A.

For questions and comments about the quality of this book,
please contact us at CustomerService@Harlequin.com.

® and TM are trademarks of Harlequin Enterprises Limited or its
corporate affiliates. Trademarks indicated with ® are registered in the
United States Patent and Trademark Office, the Canadian Intellectual
Property Office and in other countries.

Printed in U.S.A.

Books by C.J. Miller

Harlequin Romantic Suspense

Hiding His Witness #1722
Shielding the Suspect #1770
Protecting His Princess #1777
Traitorous Attraction #1801
Under the Sheik's Protection #1813

C.J. MILLER

loves to hear from her readers and can be contacted through her website, www.cj-miller.com. She lives in Maryland with her husband, son and daughter. C.J. believes in first loves, second chances and happily ever after.

To my mom, Jane, who taught me to "play something with imagination."

Chapter 1

Saafir hated secret meetings. They reeked of corruption and backroom deals that had no place in Qamsar's government. At least, not anymore. Saafir's brother, the former emir, had abdicated the throne when it was revealed that his fiancée was allied with a terrorist network. As the second oldest male of his father's recognized lineage, Saafir was next in line for the throne. He'd been thrown into the position of emir, and he had made it his policy to be open and honest. Anything less and he would break the already shaky faith of his countrymen and be ousted.

"These are the files you requested, your excellency," Frederick said, handing Saafir a folder thick with its contents. "There are a number of them to go through."

Saafir opened the folder. His advisor and friend's

assessment was an understatement. Dozens of profiles to review, and he had to pick the right one.

Saafir's position was precarious, holding together the three political factions of the Assembly with the Conservatives, the Progressives and the Loyalists. The Conservatives, with Rabah Wasam leading them, believed Saafir and his entire family should be cast out of the ruling seat they had held for over two hundred years for taking a reformist stance on culture and the economy. Saafir's personal history with Wasam didn't help matters.

The Progressives were distrustful of Saafir, viewing him as no better than his brother, who'd tried to keep social change from taking hold in Qamsar. Only members of the Loyalists party stood steadfast at his side, although Saafir had heard murmurs of dissension. Threats of violent revolution were a weekly occurrence. Saafir didn't want civil war, and he was working against extreme rhetoric, polarizing positions and unrealistic demands.

Saafir had never wanted to be the emir. He had been raised to believe that position would belong to Mikhail. Saafir had made decisions about his life based on not being in the spotlight. But the laws of Qamsar were clear. Saafir had inherited the throne, the title and the responsibilities.

He sat in his private library inside his compound in Qamsar with two of the country's most powerful men, both members of the Loyalist party, discussing a bizarre and uncomfortable topic: his wife. Or lack thereof. His lack of wife presented a political opportunity. Once a trade agreement with America was in place, a marriage to one of the daughters of a leader of the Conservative party would seal the trust between them and the royal family. With the Loyalists and Conservatives united, and if Saafir could forge a successful trade agreement with America to please the Progressives, they'd move the small desert Middle Eastern country in a forward direction and give the economy and the culture a chance for growth.

The candidate list was long, and the profiles were detailed. Frederick laid out each one, a photograph and a written profile, like resumes from job applicants. Each was pretty and from a prominent Qamsarian family. Saafir hated to choose a wife this way. A picture and resume spoke nothing of who each woman was, only of what they had done and their credentials, as if being his wife were a job. In some ways, he supposed it was. He hoped whoever was chosen was happy with the match. Being the emir's wife came with benefits—wealth, power and prestige—but in the current environment, many drawbacks. The uncertainty swirling around the royal family, a husband who was busy and traveled often and little privacy weren't part of the hopes and dreams of many women.

Saafir didn't know a single one of them, and he knew none of them would have his heart. Frederick pressed on, oblivious to Saafir's discomfort and unhappiness.

"We've arranged the women in order of preference. Some women provide benefits over the others," Frederick said.

Benefits. Not love. Never love. As long as he could form an amicable, mutually beneficial relationship with a woman and they could tolerate each other long enough to have children, it didn't matter to Saafir who was selected. The best woman for the position was the one who provided something his flailing country needed.

"You don't have to do this, Saafir," the third man said. "You should not do this."

The third man did not sit at the table with Saafir and Frederick. He stood in the shadows near the doorway, leaning against the wall with a lazy sense of ease. Saafir knew nothing was further from the truth. Saafir had known Adham since their time together in the military, and his head of security was anything but lazy and never at ease. He could explode into action at a moment's notice. He'd already thwarted four assassination attempts on Saafir's life since Saafir had become the emir.

"I have to do this," Saafir said. "Qamsar needs me to do this."

Frederick nodded his agreement. "The people want to see a married emir with a growing brood of children. It will give them a sense of security and clarify the line of succession."

"Only a fool marries for anything other than love," Adham said. "You will resent any woman you choose for not loving you. She will resent you for using her as a political tool. You will only find sorrow in this."

"I will remind you that you are speaking to the emir," Frederick said to Adham, glaring at the larger man, trying to silence him. Saafir gave Frederick points for courage. Few had the mettle to openly disagree with Adham.

"I am glad Adham speaks his mind, but in this case, it doesn't change the facts. Love is a luxury an emir cannot afford," Saafir said.

"Did your father love your mother?" Adham asked.

The words were daggers to Saafir's chest. His parents' arranged marriage had resulted in a love match that had lasted until his father's death. His mother and father had been lucky to be given to each other.

Saafir's thoughts were interrupted by the sound of shattering glass. Something had been hurled through the large window on the far side of the room. Saafir dropped to the ground, pulling Frederick with him.

Adham raced to Saafir's side. He and Saafir turned the table on its side to create a barrier against whatever may follow. In the process, Frederick's organized files scattered like party confetti. Adham covered Saafir with his body.

Saafir craned his neck to look at the object that had come through his study window.

It was a brick, not a bomb. "Move, Adham," Saafir said, pushing his friend aside.

Adham was speaking commands into his comm device as he moved to investigate the brick that had come through the window, peeling a piece of paper from around it. "Nibal, take the south side. See if you can catch the perpetrator. Jafar, check the security footage."

Saafir raced to the window, taking cover to the side, and peered out. A black hooded figure was racing across the grounds. Adham reached for his gun and Saafir touched Adham's arm, stopping him. "We will not respond with lethal force." Escalating the situation by killing the perpetrator, likely a member of the Conservative party, netted them nothing but higher tensions and added more fuel to the fire.

"We have to strike back and show strength," Adham said.

"I have no interest in starting a war," Saafir said.

"Then let me start it," Adham said.

Adham's response time was fast, but he needed to let cooler heads prevail. Striving for peace wasn't a weakness. "Let me see the note," Saafir said.

Adham handed it to him. What was it this time?

The attached paper read, "True sons of Qamsar will take the throne back from the unworthy one!"

Another threat. It was worrying that they had penetrated the royal compound grounds, getting close enough to fling something into the second-story window. A threat this time, but next time it could be a bomb.

Saafir let his head of security's drone drift off along with Frederick's curses. A woman's picture from the folder, one he vaguely recognized, was lodged under his foot. Her profile had remained attached.

He bent to pick it up. "This one," he said. His words silenced both Adham and Frederick. "She will be my wife."

"Alaina Faris?" Frederick asked. "She is a difficult woman. She has had many disparaging things to say about you and your family."

Saafir didn't like hearing that, but what did it matter? It seemed everyone had an agenda and a criticism. Saafir turned the photo over and scanned the paper. "Her father is Mohammad Faris, prominent member of the Conservative party. By marrying Alaina, I can bring the Conservatives to our cause. That is what we've decided is the best course of action."

Adham looked as if he wanted to say more, but he kept his mouth shut.

"Do you want to meet her?" Frederick asked.

It was the next logical step, even if Saafir had no desire to forward this along. "Please invite her family to the royal country home for dinner on the Saturday following my return from the summit. I will make myself available from seven until nine in the evening. If both parties are amenable, I will speak with her father about the appropriate arrangements for our courtship." The word courtship stuck in his throat. He wasn't skittish about a commitment, but choosing a woman in this way left him cold.

Frederick nodded, bowed and left the study. As soon as his advisor left, Adham clapped him on the back. "She will never love you, Saafir."

Saafir nodded. He knew it. "She does not have to love me. She only needs to love Qamsar."

One problem down, an infinite number remaining. He needed to stay one step ahead of those who wanted him dead and to prepare for the trade summit that would restore his nation to economic prosperity. And yet his mind wouldn't let go of his impending engagement. His father had ruled Qamsar and found love. Why couldn't he?

Sarah Parker pulled open the door to the liquor store. She needed a bottle of wine to take the edge off. She blew by the aisles filled with the cheap stuff and the aisles of expensive stuff that tasted cheap. Her job had trained her to tell the difference at a glance, and she kept going until she made it to the aisles that had something worth the calories.

The really expensive stuff.

It was more than she could afford to spend on a bottle of wine, but today, she needed it. Today, she had received her finalized divorce papers from her lawyer. While she hadn't been living with Alec for more than two years and their relationship had been on the rocks for the three years before that, the final nail in the coffin of their marriage had struck her hard.

It was over. She was no longer a missus.

If only Alec had stayed clean, they could have worked it out. If only one of his first three stints in rehab had worked, they might still be married. If only, if only, if only. Maybe his current stay would help him. This time, Sarah wasn't holding herself responsible for his sobriety except for agreeing to foot the bill from the clinic. Just this one last time, she would pay for Alec's rehab and hope it worked. It was money she didn't have to spare, but she would find a way to pay. She had to do everything possible to help him and then she could move on and live her life without the nagging guilt that she hadn't tried hard enough.

After paying for her wine, she walked the remaining ten blocks to her apartment in high heels. She'd had back-to-back meetings since 8:00 a.m. Organizing details with the florist, the caterer, the hotel manager, the media and the security team were her responsibility. Thanks to the kindness and amazing connections of her former brother-in-law, Owen, her fledgling business had secured a huge contract. The new emir of Qamsar, Sheik Saafir bin Jassim Al Sharani, would be arriving in America on Monday morning to begin work on a trade agreement with the United States. For months, Sarah had been preparing, conferring with the sheik's advisors, keeping lists and agendas, and ensuring she was prepared to play hostess to the leader of Qamsar.

She had her orders: keep him comfortable, wine and dine him and roll out the red carpet wherever he went.

The United States wanted the petroleum readily available in Qamsar and Qamsar wanted favorable trade arrangements with the United States. It should be a straightforward exchange; however, nothing involving money was ever simple. Politics, culture, economics and ego played a role in every decision made in Washington, D.C.

Sarah entered her apartment and put the bottle of wine on her recently installed granite countertops. After she and Alec had separated, she had moved out of the apartment she'd shared with him and downsized into this one, a small space in a converted stone townhouse that was now three units. It had made her happy to look at the gleaming cabinets and countertops for a few days. Then it had made her feel pathetic. In the last five years, she hadn't invited her friends over and cooked them dinner—not once. They always met at a bar or restaurant. Sarah planned events for other people, sometimes pro bono, but she didn't make time to plan any for herself. Not even for her birthday.

All that would change. Sarah had to think about her new life, now that her marriage to Alec had ended. She made a mental note to invite someone over for dinner in the next month.

She peeled off her suit and tugged on a T-shirt and stretchy yoga pants. She wasn't planning to exercise, but she would be comfortable while she drank her overpriced wine and stared at the television screen.

Two reruns of her favorite comedy later and deep in a funk, Sarah received a text message from her good friend Molly.

"Krista & I at Palazzo lounge. Stop sulking. Come play. Happy Birthday!"

Sarah smiled. Her two closest friends had remembered her birthday. She texted them that she'd be there in twenty minutes, and changed into a knee-length blue dress with cap sleeves and a pair of black heels. The weather had turned warm enough that she wouldn't need a sweater. A night out with friends and some good food would turn her mood around. Besides, everyone deserved a slice of cake on their birthday.

Twenty-five minutes later, Sarah was sliding into a booth beside Molly.

Her friend gave her a hug. "Happy Birthday!"

Krista pushed a drink they had ordered her closer. "Relax. Have a drink. You seem tense."

Sarah didn't want to rain on her friends' cheerful moods by dumping on them about Alec, so she sipped her drink and listened. As the conversation turned from work to men to apartments, Sarah followed the flow. This was what she needed. A break from her work, even if it was only for a few hours.

"Why are you in a mood? It can't be that you're a year older," Molly said.

Sarah's advancing age didn't bother her. Should she tell her friends about the divorce? They'd held her hand through the ups and downs of her marriage. They knew the official end of her marriage was coming. "I got the finalized divorce papers today from my lawyer." Several long moments followed.

"At least you're free now," Krista said and winced. "Sorry, I don't know what to say to that. 'Congratulations' seems out of place."

Sarah didn't blame her friends for not having the words to salve the hurt. She didn't think words existed to take the edge off the pain. That's why she had had wine tonight. "There's not really much to say about it. I was married. Now I'm not." She touched her bare ring finger where she'd once worn a plain gold band. Her friends had been at her wedding and now they were beside her after her divorce. With her mother dead and her father estranged, Sarah had found family in her friends.

Molly rubbed Sarah's hand. "He has problems. There's nothing you could have done."

Sarah held up her hands and shook her head. "Let's not go over this again. It'll bring down the entire night. Alec is sick. I can't help him. You guys have listened to me talk about it for five years. Let's talk about something else." She'd spent too many sleepless nights mourning her relationship with Alec and far too many hours complaining to her friends about it.

"You need to get laid," Molly said. "You need to throw yourself into a one-night stand, have a great time and use that as the jumping-off point for your new life. Forget the past and give yourself a birthday present. One eligible bachelor, even for just a few hours."

Sarah shuddered. She had been with Alec since she was nineteen. She didn't know how to date anymore. She didn't have one-night stands. "I wouldn't know how to approach a man in a bar. I wouldn't know what to say."

"You work with men every day, all day," Krista said. "You approach people all the time and invite them to fund-raising events. You can do this."

When she invited affluent families to a charity dinner or dealt with a contractor for an event, nothing personal was involved. "I work with strangers, not sleep with. Very different," Sarah said.

"Look around the room. Find a guy without a woman and without a wedding ring and go talk to him," Molly said.

"What should I say?" Sarah asked, squirming at the idea. She could talk about her work or dealing with a drug addict's many issues, the two topics she knew the most about. Who wanted to hear about those things?

"Ask him what his favorite TV show is," Krista said.

"Lame," Molly said. "But you're cute enough that it doesn't matter."

Could she approach a man? Sarah smoothed her dress and finger-combed her hair. She could do this. Or at least try. A little liquid courage and the idea of growing a year older alone spurred her to action. Her first step was to talk to a man. She could always flee the conversation if it was too awkward. It was a bar. Bars were filled with awkward conversations. "I'll start by trying to talk to someone."

Krista squealed and clapped her hands.

Looking around the room, Sarah tried to pick someone. As her eyes landed on the men around the room, she dismissed them one by one. Too young. Too old. Not alone. Drunk. Sarah sighed. This wasn't easy. She was about to tell her friends to forget it when her gaze dropped on a dark-haired man sitting at the corner of the bar. He had a drink—it looked like coffee, perhaps of the Irish variety, on his right. His back was to the wall. He was talking to two men standing to his side. His posture was relaxed and he was immaculately groomed. His pressed suit was a far cry from how Alec dressed during their marriage. She couldn't make out the details of the man's face in the darkened room, but he was handsome and seemed familiar somehow.

A woman in a short red dress strutted in his direction and blocked her view of Mr. Gorgeous. Sarah's heart fell. Another woman had beaten her to the punch. No way would he turn away the thin blonde with the curves. Though she had only just spotted him, disappointment streamed through her. Sarah would have to pick someone else. Looking around the room, Sarah was about to call off her plan when the woman in the red dress stalked away from the man Sarah had zeroed in on a few moments before. Red Miniskirt looked disappointed and a touch annoyed. Had she been rejected?

After witnessing that, Sarah knew she couldn't approach him. If he'd said no to Red Miniskirt, he'd shoot her down and she didn't need that tonight. As if sensing her watching him, he met her gaze. She turned away before he realized she had been staring.

After looking around the room twice more, she returned to Mr. Gorgeous. Not only was he exceptionally handsome, but something about him was compelling and mysterious, too. If she was going to make a fool of herself, she may as well do it for someone sexy. He wasn't looking her way and she took the opportunity to stare at him a little longer. She made up her mind. If he rejected her, at least she would have been turned down by someone like him.

"I'm going to talk to him," she said pointing.

Her friends followed her extended finger.

"Oh, yes. Good pick. Delicious," Molly said, nodding her approval.

Krista gestured for Sarah to go. "You can do this."

Taking another sip of her wine, Sarah strode across the room to him and tried to mimic his relaxed posture pressing her shoulders down, tilting her chin up and adding a swagger to her walk.

Three feet away, his gaze met hers. His eyes never left her face and something came into them, something dark, deep and sensual. The look was so heated, she stopped, stumbled and grabbed on to a nearby stool to steady herself.

Thanks to her clumsiness, he would think she was drunk. Wonderful. She righted herself and straightened, hoped her cheeks weren't too red with embarrassment and continued forward, undeterred. He was watching her, his friends were eying her and she felt her friends' stares at her back. She couldn't turn away now. His buddies turned toward her, staying close to Mr. Gorgeous.

Sarah's gut told her she was missing a key piece of information. Something about him, about his midnight eyes, his patrician nose and his perfectly shaped mouth was familiar. An actor? Musician? Politician? Someone she should have recognized?

It felt like minutes had passed while she stood gawking, though it had likely been milliseconds.

She couldn't be too aggressive, yet caginess would come across as unwelcoming and she was the one approaching him. Sarah stopped in front of the three men and gave them a small smile.

"Hello. I'm Sarah."

Would he introduce himself? Mr. Gorgeous stood and extended his hand. "I'm Barr. It's nice to meet you."

He was handsome. Too handsome. Dark hair and

polished good looks. Strong and confident. Oh, she was not prepared for this. First impressions were everything. Would she blow it her first time hitting on a man post-divorce? Making a fool of herself was always a possibility, but this colossal screw-up could send her back into social seclusion for another few months.

But he was speaking to her. This gorgeous man was speaking to her. Sarah focused. What had he said? Why were his friends staring at her? She realized she was shaking his hand, clinging to it entirely too long. His clasp was firm, his skin cool and soft, and she pictured his hands running over her. It would feel amazing to have him touch her.

She shivered and pulled her hand away before she let her imagination run further. "I'm sorry, with the noise of the bar I couldn't hear you." She waited for him to repeat himself.

"Sarah, it is a pleasure to meet you. May I buy you a drink?"

He had a beautiful accent. Sarah had already had enough to drink, but she felt silly asking for an iced tea. "A glass of red wine would be great."

He motioned to the bartender who practically raced to serve him. The man had presence. He requested a specific year and vintage, one that she recognized as expensive, though not from personal experience, only through catering lavish affairs. Barr wouldn't do that if he had no interest in her, right?

Her confidence ticked up a notch.

He held out his hand. "Please join me." The cadence in his voice weakened her knees and his words cut through her anxiety.

He was sweet and that surprised her. Men who were

too attractive for their own good didn't need to be kind to seduce a woman. But she was getting ahead of herself. Buying her an expensive glass of wine didn't mean he wanted to sleep with her. Her worries about pursuing a man and remembering what to do and say melted away with every word he spoke. Something clicked into place and she felt a thrill she'd been missing for years. A simple conversation had awakened a long-slumbering part of her libido.

"My birthday is today," she said, feeling like she needed to explain why she was in a bar. What if he thought she routinely came here trolling for men? She re-questioned her approach and wished she had thought this through. What else could she talk about now that she had his attention? If she didn't keep the conversation going, he would walk away. Red Miniskirt had been a good example of the other options available to him. On the heels of those thoughts, she wondered why it was so important to her to keep his attention. The bar was filled with other men yet it was this man who'd captivated her.

"Happy Birthday, Sarah," Barr said. He smiled, his teeth flawlessly white and his lips full.

"I'm not here alone."

"I noticed you were with your friends," he said.

Had he been assessing her the way she'd been assessing him? "They told me to talk to you," she said.

"Why's that?" he asked, not unkindly.

She wouldn't slam the truth down on him. Her drug-abuser ex and her divorce were among the least sexy topics of conversation she could think of. "It's my birthday and I wanted to meet someone new."

Barr smiled. "Would you like to invite your friends

over? I've been traveling all day and haven't eaten yet. The restaurant is preparing a private table for us to enjoy a late meal."

Sarah looked at him and then his friends. They were quiet. Why hadn't they said anything? They were looking around the bar, but if they wanted to give their friend pseudo-privacy to speak with her, why not take a few steps away?

She made the decision that she would invite her friends. It wasn't safe to leave the bar—even to move to a table—without letting her friends know her plans. "I'll ask them. Please give me a few minutes."

"Of course."

Sarah hurried back to her friends, her neck and back hot imagining him watching her leave.

"That man at the far end of the bar invited us to eat with him. His name is Barr and he has an accent." She half expected he would disappear in the time she'd taken to return to her friends.

Molly looked over at him and smiled. "Nice. You need us to be wingwomen to the friends?"

Sarah hadn't thought about that. "The friends are strangely silent."

"They're probably trying to stay out of the way if you two are making nice," Krista said.

Perhaps. Sarah still felt she was missing something about the three men. "Does he look familiar?"

Both Molly and Krista craned their necks to look at Barr at the same time.

Sarah blushed. "Not so obvious, please."

"He knows we're talking about him," Molly said and rolled her eyes. "The one right next to him is cute. Did you get a name?"

"Nope. I forgot to ask," Sarah said. It wasn't like her to forget basic social graces, but once she had started talking to Barr, she had fixated on him and the rest of the world had seemed to disappear. Was that what having a crush was like? It had been so long, she couldn't recall.

"We'll join you, enjoy and provide backup if anything gets weird. We're your excuse if you need to leave," Krista said.

Even if Barr was perfectly charming, Sarah didn't know how ready she was to spend the evening with a man she found attractive in a situation that had the potential of leading somewhere, like a bedroom. Putting on an air of confidence at work was easy. Talking to him had been more pleasurable that she'd imagined. Was she ready to take it to another level?

Sarah drummed up some extra courage. Sharing a drink and a meal with a man was a good first step. A simple step. But if it was so simple, why did she feel light-headed?

Sarah felt daring as she and Barr walked across the street and entered the golden doors of the most expensive hotel in D.C. She hadn't wanted to return home when the restaurant closed. She'd accepted Barr's invitation to his hotel because she'd wanted the night to last as long as it could.

His gaze lingered on her like a promise of more to come. More that she wanted and more that she craved.

His friends followed behind them and Sarah knew Molly would be disappointed. She and Adham had seemed to have some chemistry, but he'd cut the evening short when Barr had mentioned they were leaving.

Excitement shot down Sarah's spine as the elevator doors closed. Her knees went weak when Barr hit the button for the penthouse suite. Barr was traveling in style. He didn't just have a hotel room. He had the top-level hotel floor complete with a view of the White House. Everything about the night since she'd met him felt surreal and magical. Even if it was only a fleeting fantasy, she would enjoy it.

One night with Barr wouldn't turn into a lifelong romance and she didn't expect it to. He'd mentioned he was from the Middle East traveling on business with his associates, and while he didn't elaborate, Sarah figured the specifics didn't matter. She was entering into a brief fling with no future, but she needed to lose herself in a man's arms. Tonight, she needed to feel wanted and cherished and decided to play along with the fantasy.

Tomorrow, she returned to her life as it was and to the responsibilities and problems and loneliness that awaited her.

Barr ushered her inside and closed the door behind him. His associates didn't follow him inside and she was grateful for the privacy.

"Can I offer you a drink?" he asked.

No small talk. She might lose her nerve if this didn't happen quickly. She threw her arms around his neck and kissed him, long and hot and hard.

It took him a millisecond to respond. Barr was masterful with his mouth. His lips were firm and soft and hot. Very hot. His hands slid from her shoulders, down her back and to her hips. He held her tight enough for her to feel desired and loose enough to move and sway.

The sense of rightness and the depth of the connection shook her. Her heart tripped and her pulse sped up to keep pace. She found herself confronting a fantasy. Mysterious foreigner, luxury hotel suite and one romantic evening she would dream about for years.

She tugged at his tie, struggling to remove it and tossed it to the floor. Then his jacket. With his arms more free, he banded them around her. Clutching his biceps, she felt the muscles flex and she held back a giggle of delight.

This was what she needed. Two strangers, no complicated history and no judgment.

She unfastened the buttons of his shirts, shoving the satiny white fabric off his shoulders. He flicked the shirt away.

"You're wearing too many clothes," he said.

Barr spun her, lifted her hair and kissed the back of her neck. She let her head fall to the side, giving him complete access to the sensitive skin at her nape. Everything he was doing ignited her senses and made her hotter. He smelled of soap and spice and the caress of his hands was hungry for more. She wanted to be the woman to satisfy that hunger. He slid her zipper down her back, brushed the sleeves across her shoulders and the blue dress fell to the floor. The sharp intake of his breath let her know he liked what he saw.

Sarah didn't have Krista's model good looks or Molly's boundless confidence, but her confidence shot higher knowing this man—this sexy, handsome man—wanted what she had to offer.

He muttered something in a language she didn't understand. She whirled to face him and for the first time in years, she felt powerful. Her femininity had been buried under work and problems and stress. In the hands of this amazing man, it came roaring to life.

"You must hear this from men all the time, but I must tell you that you are beautiful." He said another word in his native tongue.

"What does that mean?" she asked.

"Goddess. You have the body and face of a goddess."

That was a word she had never heard spoken about her. She reveled in it and swallowed every iota of flattery he was feeding her. If she was having a fantasy night with this man, she would enjoy every over-the-top moment of it. Sarah didn't want to be the doubting, questioning person she had become during her marriage and worry about the future.

She unbuckled his pants and in a flurry of motions, his trousers fell to the ground. He lifted her into his arms as if she weighed nothing and carried her to the bedroom.

The sleigh bed was covered in a maroon-and-gold comforter. Holding her with one hand, he flicked it away to reveal crisp beige sheets. He set her down gently and slid over her on the bed. One fluid motion. The man had practiced moves. He knew what he was doing in the bedroom.

The lean strength of his body indicated he must work out. Probably had a personal trainer or a gym in his house. She was no fan of exercise, but to keep up with him, she could be talked into it. She ran her hand down his chest where a long scar reached from his shoulder to his abdomen. A tight, muscled abdomen.

"What happened here?" she asked, tracing the line with her finger.

"Military training injury from my youth," he said.

A military man? He had the body for it. Her curiosity about him heightened. He had a tattoo on his biceps.

"What is this?" she asked, tracing the small dragon.

"Another remnant of my time in the military," he said. Sarah wondered about it and sensed it had deep, personal meaning to him.

He set his hands on her sides and inhaled, letting out his breath slowly. "Is this moving too fast?"

She shook her head. Fast was good. She was afraid reality would catch up to her and she would realize some great flaw in her plan to sleep with this man. They would be safe about it and she would preserve her heart. She wasn't a virgin. She knew the mechanics of sex and how easy it was for a woman to fall for a man once she'd slept with him. But that wasn't what this was about.

Barr hadn't lied to her about what he could offer or made promises about the future. He was traveling from some place halfway around the world. This was about tonight and making each other feel amazing. As turned on as she already was, she knew this would be incredible.

He slid her panties down her legs and tossed them over his shoulder. He reached under her and with a snap of his fingers, undid her bra. It came free and he rid her of that, too.

He pulled a foil packet from the bedside table, opened it and rolled it on. "To make sure you are safe," he said.

Despite the preparation, he didn't rush to push inside her. His mouth explored her body and his hands worshipped every inch of her.

It was her that wanted more, faster. "Please, Barr, please hurry."

He laughed low in his throat. "I want to take my time with you. Every moment is already too fleeting and precious."

His mouth dropped to hers in a long, lingering kiss. His lips trailed south along her body to her breasts. He took them in his hands, using great care with her, sucking each pert tip into his mouth. As he slowly explored her, she strained against him.

She lifted her hips in invitation and then clasped both sides of his face. She wanted to feel him moving inside her. Making her wait was driving her wild with lust. "Please."

Surrender in his eyes. He wanted this to be good for her, but he couldn't say no to her plea. He tilted her chin to look at him. Their eyes locked and then he came into her. She was on the brink of release and went off the moment he was inside her. Mind-blowing, soul-shaking tremors rocked through her.

He stilled as her climax eased. She was embarrassed by her quick finale, but Barr didn't give her a chance to apologize or explain. He kissed her and then began moving again, long, slow glides of his body inside hers.

She accepted him as part of her, meeting his thrusts and undulating her hips. More. Longer.

Only when she came apart again in his arms did he crash with her in a tangle of limbs, panting breaths and racing hearts. The room was utterly still and quiet. The crisp sheets were now tangled and damp, the pillows in disarray. The single bedside light in the room cast a glow across Barr's face, illuminating again how handsome he was.

She had a hard time believing this had happened. It was so unlike her to meet someone and have an instant connection with him, but it had been so great, she didn't have room for worries. Sarah accepted the night and Barr for the gifts they were. After the last several years, she figured the universe owed her some good luck.

Barr didn't speak, though his breathing was deep and still and his eyes were closed.

What now? Did she get up and leave? Thank him? Wish him well?

He was still inside her and she was thinking of an exit strategy. Not because she was eager to leave. Sex with Barr was the best she'd had in recent history. Well, he was the only man she'd slept with in recent history. She didn't want to overstay her welcome or worse, mar the night by him asking her to leave. Sarah wanted to walk out of this room on her terms, her head held high. She shifted, extracting his body from hers.

"What are you thinking?" Barr asked, running a hand down her hair.

"Nothing much. Just going over my agenda for tomorrow." A lie. She was watching him and he had every ounce of her attention.

He laughed and opened one eye. "That stings a bit. I hoped you were basking in the afterglow of our lovemaking."

What man called it lovemaking? This was most assuredly a fantasy. Was she asleep? "I'm not sure what I need to do now." She wished she had said something smoother and practiced, some witty response to his comment or to allude she was more worldly and confident than she was.

"You don't need to do anything except tell me what you'd like to eat or drink or if I can get you anything. And then you lie here with me and let me take care of you and hold you."

He'd confirmed it. This was make-believe to the nth degree.

"I'm not hungry really," she said.

"If I didn't exhaust you, at least a little, that means I didn't do it right. Give me an hour and I'll try again."

She laughed. "You did everything very, very right." She kissed his forehead. She lay in his arms for a few minutes and closed her eyes.

The phone on the bedside table rang. "I need to answer that." He pulled away from her slowly and picked up the phone.

Was this his exit strategy? Tell her to stay, give her the royal treatment and have one of his associates call with an emergency. She refused to think about how many times he had done this before.

She hated to be made a fool of, so she stood and searched for her underwear and dress. She was still wearing her shoes. She refused to let her awkwardness post-sex ruin the memory. That she was holding close and preserving.

He was speaking into the phone in another language and he sent her a questioning look. He hadn't dressed, nor had he made any attempt to cover himself. Not that he had anything to be ashamed of. He was the most ripped man she had ever seen naked in real life.

Barr shook his head, one corner of his mouth lifted and he pointed to the bed. He wrapped up the call quickly, never taking his eyes off her.

"Please don't leave so soon," he said, sincerity in his voice.

How could she say no to that? If he'd wanted her to leave, he hadn't needed to stop her. "I'll stay. For a little while."

She returned to the bed and he pulled her into the crook of his arms and held her. Sarah rested her head against his shoulder and found sleep tugging at her. She'd rest for a few minutes and then she would say goodbye.

Saafir cursed inwardly. Sarah Parker. Her name was Sarah Parker and she was the event coordinator for his trip while he was working with the Americans on the trade agreement.

It had been Adham who had encouraged him to take the night off and enjoy some time in an American bar. As one of his last weekends as an unattached man, Saafir would forget his responsibilities for an evening. Adham had implied it would do Saafir good to have a fling with a woman. Flings were more complicated than the word implied and Saafir had learned to be careful both with a woman's heart and with jumping into bed with her. Saafir hadn't been sold on the idea until he'd seen Sarah, spoken to her and listened to the warmth in her voice. Her dress fit close to her body, showing off her curves, the right amount of softness and strength. They'd had a sense of connection, that rightness that came when two people clicked on a level beyond first impressions. Something primal had stirred in him and he'd known he'd needed to have Sarah in his bed.

Having a drink and a meal in the bar had been a last-minute decision, like many of his social plans. Last-minute didn't allow for security preparation, but it also limited anyone knowing where he was scheduled to be and using that information to plot an assassination. Though he didn't like it, he had to think in those terms to protect his life.

Though Saafir had told Adham not to, Adham had dug around and found out more about the woman who had approached him in the bar. Saafir would have connected who she was when she'd shown up at their meeting Monday morning.

Did she not know who *he* was? The Americans wouldn't try to manipulate him in such an obvious way. No one could have predicted the chemistry he had with Sarah. No one could have known he would desire her as strongly as he did. Even holding her in his arms a few minutes after sleeping with her turned him on.

Her long brown hair hung over his arm and her skin was soft against his. She was different from the women in his country, no less sophisticated or beautiful, but more free and uninhibited. She hadn't waited for him to take the lead on their meeting or remained passive when they were alone in this hotel room. Fire and passion simmered inside her and Saafir wanted to be close enough to share her heat.

If it was a setup, he would have expected an Arabic woman or someone who spoke his native language. Still, he'd never had this combustible attraction with a woman before and he wondered if any part of their relationship had been architected. She hadn't been the first woman to approach him in the bar, but she was the first woman who he'd been interested in talking with.

"You never said what you did for a living," he said. A test. Would she lie?

"I'm an event coordinator," she said, sleep heavy in her voice.

Was she evading his question? He didn't detect anything in her voice. He didn't want their connection to have been a fraud. He wanted her to like him for him. The thought was desperate, perhaps a remnant of the relationship he had wanted before becoming the emir. "Do you focus on certain types of events?"

Sarah yawned and rolled over to face him. She opened her eyes and he was caught by the shades of brown in her irises, flecks the color of sand and of cedar.

"Do you really want to hear about this? Most people find what I do boring. Unless it's a bride and it's her wedding. Those conversations last well over an hour."

He found nothing about her boring. But if she was here to pry information from him, he wanted to know it now. "Tell me about it. I bet I won't find it boring."

She tilted her head up to look at him and brushed some of her long brown hair away from her face. "I started my business about four years ago. It's still small, but we're growing every year. I take any contracts I think I can do well. I've done dog birthday parties, a Pi Day event and a divorce party where the client wanted every menu item to include strawberries, which her ex had been allergic to."

Saafir laughed.

Sarah drummed her fingers on his chest. "I've done some charity events to raise money for a local substance abuse support group." She brought her hand to her mouth in thought. "I've turned away a few elaborate weddings, but I did take an important contract recently. If it goes well, it will be great to have on my resume for other jobs. It's already been a wild experience."

She must be referring to the trade summit contract. "What was the contracted event?" he pressed. He could have dropped his line of questioning, but he wanted to know if this was a happy coincidence that they'd met and not that she was a spy. He expected a spy to lie, flat out and without so much as a blink.

Sarah shifted, appearing uncomfortable. "I've been asked to keep the details private. It's an important client."

Unless she was a world-class liar who could lie even while naked, she didn't know he was the important client.

Saafir couldn't stand the thought of her showing up with breakfast Monday morning and realizing he was the emir of Qamsar. Being fastidious about security, Adham had booked this hotel under Saafir's mother's maiden name, Barr, the name Saafir used when he wasn't representing himself as the emir, two days earlier than he was expected to arrive in the United States.

"Is your client someone famous?" he asked, wondering how trustworthy she was. He hated testing her. If she admitted something, it was akin to entrapment.

"I can't discuss that," she said, her tone serious. She slid her leg off him and he grabbed her thigh.

He didn't want to lose the closeness and his questions were making her uncomfortable.

He gave her credit for integrity and discretion in not revealing his name. Another woman might have bragged about the connection or caved under the pressure and given away more about the event.

"This is Washington, D.C. You have me thinking it's someone infamous," Saafir said.

Sarah laughed. "Isn't everyone in D.C. infamous?"

Saafir smiled, pleased she hadn't given away any details of the contract. He didn't want to ruin the moment. He would tell her in the morning who he was and hope she forgave him.

Sarah was walking on air as she entered her apartment building and tiptoed up the stairs. She didn't want to risk the neighbors complaining about the early morning disturbance. The sun had begun to rise and though she'd had little sleep, she wasn't tired.

For the first time in months, she'd had fun. She was awake and alive and she'd had a wonderful time with a man. A handsome man who had treated her like a queen. His sexual appetite had been insatiable and she'd been as surprised about her response to him. She'd wanted him as much and as often as he'd wanted her. It had been the best birthday she'd had in years. Maybe this was the beginning of a new chapter in her life.

When she told Krista and Molly about the night, she felt confident she had done everything right. She hadn't lingered too long or created an awkward morning situation. A quick kiss on his forehead and she'd dressed and bolted.

She pulled her keys out of her handbag and froze when she found the door ajar. Had she forgotten to pull it closed behind her? Another more distressing thought raced through her mind. Alec had bailed on rehab and had broken into her home. It wouldn't be the first time.

Sarah pushed open the door and turned on the light, expecting to find her ex-husband passed out on the floor.

If Alec had been here, he had been in a rage. Her home was destroyed. The stuffing from her couch was bursting from the cushions, papers were strewn across the floor and dishes and glasses were smashed on the ground. Her granite countertops were scratched and chipped. Red spray paint covered her furniture and the carpet. A nasty word was scrawled across the wall in blinding orange.

A sob caught in her throat. She didn't want to look, but she couldn't turn away, either. Who had done this? Another thought tripped her shock into fear. The person who had done this could still be inside.

Why would someone do this? She had nothing worth stealing, except maybe her computer, a five-year-old laptop she used for work. Her jobs! She would be lost without her lists and spreadsheets. Had they been destroyed, as well?

Torn between wanting to run inside and to run away, she hesitated for a moment. But then logic prevailed and she rushed out of her apartment and down to the street level. Fumbling for her phone, she took four tries to dial 9-1-1.

Chapter 2

Sarah held her cell phone and listened to the caterer apologize for the tenth time. She didn't need to apologize. She needed to get to the meeting so Sarah would have the breakfast spread ready when the trade committee arrived.

Months of preparing and rechecking and confirming—and yet the meeting room was in a state of chaos. She blamed whoever had ransacked her apartment. She had located some of her printed documents on the event, but some were missing in the mess. Her laptop had been smashed. It was with a computer repair and data recovery company, but they'd told her it was unlikely they'd recover anything since the hard drive had been removed and mangled.

Alec's whereabouts had been confirmed as still in the rehab facility, and Sarah felt guilty for suspecting that he could have vandalized her place. Holding him accountable for her problems wasn't fair. She had to take responsibility for the successes and failures in her life. The way the day was shaping up, the first meeting would be a big check in the fail column. She couldn't let Owen down. He'd stuck his neck out getting her this job.

Without the benefit of her notes, Sarah was relying on memory for the event details. She'd decided to temporarily stay with Molly who had helped her reconstruct what she could remember. Sarah was missing huge chunks of information that would be needed at the worst possible time. This was the biggest event she had ever planned: a week-long series of meetings, hotel accommodations, meals and entertainment.

Her resume-boosting event was quickly turning into a reputation smasher.

Sarah needed to stay unemotional and think on her feet. Handling a late caterer went with the territory. Could she find a local donut shop and buy some holdover food? Getting off on the right foot with the trade agreement committee—in other words, having something to serve more than coffee and tea—was crucial.

"My GPS says I'll be there in ten minutes," the caterer said.

In D.C. morning traffic, that meant thirty. Sarah reminded herself that losing it on the caterer wouldn't make the food arrive faster. "Come directly to the back entrance. I'll meet you there."

Sarah disconnected her call. After sending someone to buy muffins and donuts at a nearby shop, Sarah turned her attention to the meeting room.

Owen, the chairman of the committee, had arrived

and was sitting at the end of the conference table, his leather binder open in front of him. Happy to see a familiar face, Sarah hurried to greet him.

"Good morning, Owen," she said, slipping her arm around his shoulder and kissing his cheek.

"How's everything going?" he asked, looking around the room with a scrutinizing gaze.

She wouldn't let anyone see her sweat. She hadn't told him about the break-in at her apartment, and she wouldn't burden him with it now. Her personal problems did not enter this space. "The caterer is running a little late, but I have coffee and tea ready. I sent someone to pick up donuts to tide us over. Do you know if there were any problems at the hotel? I called the front desk last night to confirm everything was set for the emir, but he hadn't arrived yet. Is he planning to check in before this meeting or later?"

Owen touched her shoulder. "Relax. If there was a problem, we would have heard about it. I am sure the accommodations will be fine."

Sarah's tone must have given away her anxiety. She relaxed her shoulders. Coming off tense and edgy wouldn't accomplish the job she'd been given.

"I heard from the rehab center early this morning," Owen said, lowering his voice.

Her anxiety shot up again. "Did something happen?" she asked, regretting immediately that she had. She'd wanted to close the door on that part of her life. If Alec had left rehab, if he had run away or had gotten into an altercation with the staff or one of the patients she couldn't afford another place. As it was, she was counting on the payment for this job to cover most of the expense.

"He's refusing to take part in the group therapy. If he doesn't cooperate he'll be kicked out of the program," Owen said.

This time, rehab had been court-mandated thanks to an assault charge from a barroom brawl. If Alec left rehab, he was headed to jail. The idea of it made her feel sick. Alec couldn't see how serious the consequences for his actions had become. Either that, or he didn't care. Their marriage, his job and his relationships with his siblings had been damaged or broken. It seemed nothing mattered to him except his next fix.

"I'm sorry, Owen. I can't get involved." She forced away the guilt that crept over her. It had taken her a long time to understand she couldn't help Alec. In fact, sometimes, she wondered if she had enabled him to indulge in bad habits more by covering for him. She had believed Alec's lies and after a while, everything he said was a lie. He was quick to claim he was trying, that he just needed another chance and that he was doing better, and she, wanting to believe it would get better, had been quick to accept what he'd said. Every time it had been a lie, and every time her heart had broken a little more.

She, Owen, Alec's twin sister Evelyn and Alec's therapists had agreed Alec had to face the consequences of his decisions without any of them swooping in to fix it. Especially her. She had been the weak link, being the safe place for him to land.

"I'm not asking you to." Owen covered his face with his hand. "I'm sorry, Sarah. I didn't mean to bring this up. We agreed to let Alec handle this. I just don't have anyone else to talk to who understands him the way you do."

Owen's marriage was on the rocks. His wife, Chelsea, was the daughter of a prominent state senator, and some assumed his position was a result of nepotism. Sarah knew Owen had earned it. "I know," she whispered. How many times had she called Owen and Evelyn over the years when they were trying to help Alec? When he hadn't come home at night and she was terrified for him. When he was in a stupor for days and she couldn't get through to him.

Several more people entered the room and Sarah introduced herself as the hostess and escorted them to the hot drinks.

"Do you have black coffee?" Virginia Anderson, the representative from the American oil company, asked. She had barely looked up from her phone as she typed with her thumbs.

Sarah was struck by how svelte and refined she appeared. From her perfectly done hair and makeup, to the thousand-dollar designer handbag on her arm to the expensive shoes, she was the image of success and power. Sarah wished she had spent a little more time on her appearance that morning. Her clothes had been destroyed and she'd borrowed something from Molly. Used to blending into the background at events, Sarah had known she would have more visibility during these small, frequent meetings. Wishing she had a closet of designer outfits to hold a candle to the attendees, she brushed aside her self-conscious reaction and turned her attention to her arriving guests.

The door opened and a familiar man stepped through it. It was Adham, one of Barr's companions. Had Barr tracked her here? She cleared her throat where emotion was building and strode to the door.

This wasn't the time or place for a reunion with her one-night stand. How had he found her?

Then Barr stepped inside and her heart and movement stalled.

"Good morning, Sarah," he said. His voice was firm and commanding, loud enough for the room to hear him. The words were warm and gentle like a caress and images from the night they'd spent in each other's arms flashed to mind. His gaze raked over her, and she felt his desire in her core. Her body responded instantly. He'd given her that same look the night they'd met and she could interpret exactly what it meant. He wanted her naked beneath him. If history could predict the future, she wouldn't say no.

Everyone in the room turned and Sarah panicked. She couldn't cause a scene. She'd be fired. She strode to him and kept her voice low in response. "Barr. What are you doing here?"

His hair was neat, his suit fit him well, as if it was custom-made, which it probably was. Maybe he had a meeting in the area and had glimpsed her when the door had opened. He would say hello and wouldn't stay for more than a moment.

"Sarah? You've already met the emir?" Owen asked, coming to her side.

Like the final puzzle piece snapping into place, understanding slammed into her and Sarah saw the whole picture. The men who accompanied him, the expensive hotel suite, the accent and the name. Barr was Saafir bin Jassim Al Sharani, the emir of Qamsar. She had read that his mother's maiden name was Barr.

Had he realized who she was the other night? No surprise registered on his face now, so he must have.

"Welcome," she said, injecting confidence into her voice. Should she pretend as if they were meeting for the first time and that she hadn't been writhing beneath him, screaming his name Saturday night?

Was that hurt in his eyes? Or pride? How did he expect her to react? "It's a pleasure to see you," he said.

Nervous energy churned in her stomach. The word "pleasure" felt punctuated with innuendo, or was it just her imagination? She wouldn't say anything, not with the members of the trade agreement committee staring at the emir and at her.

Barr introduced her to his colleague Frederick, a man who served as one of Barr's advisors.

Somehow, Sarah managed to give her practiced greeting and offer both men drinks she hoped they'd enjoy. Why hadn't Barr told her who he was? He'd had the opportunity.

"Please excuse me, I'm meeting the caterer in a few minutes," Sarah said, fleeing to the back entrance. She would do the job she had been hired for and not think about her one-night stand reappearing in her life.

Needing to get some fresh air, Sarah stepped outside to the alley where the caterer should be arriving any minute. It was early enough in the day to be cool in the shadow of the building.

The caterer was twenty minutes late. Sarah's hands were shaking from the encounter with Barr and she needed to get ahold of her emotions and calm down. Her one-night stand was turning into a situation she would have to live with for the next week. Her stomach tightened. This was a professional complication she didn't need in her career. Had her liaison with him been the reason her apartment had been ransacked? Did everyone already know she had slept with him?

"Sarah."

Sarah jumped and turned, meeting Barr's—or Saafir's—dark eyes.

"Sarah, I owe you an apology."

Standing in the alley outside the office building between the Dumpster and the street was the strangest place for the emir to be. He shouldn't be out here. He belonged in the meeting. Adham lingered near the door, looking around.

She should have told him it was fine, even though it wasn't, and that he should go inside, but she had one question. "Why didn't you tell me who you were?"

"I didn't figure out that you were the trade summit event coordinator until my security told me."

"At what point was that?" she asked.

"After we had slept together," he said.

Sarah folded her arms across her chest. "This job is important to me." She didn't want to be fired over her decision to sleep with him. If it was awkward between them, would he want her replaced?

"I know it is and I will not do anything to interfere with it," Saafir said. He touched her upper arm. "You look gorgeous this morning. I was disappointed that you left without saying goodbye."

Her pulse beat erratically. "I wasn't sure of the protocol. What should I have done?"

He smiled and ran a finger lightly down her cheek. "You're asking me? I don't know the protocol for how to behave when I meet someone who brings me to my knees with a look."

Her? She had that power over him? "This hasn't

happened to you before?" Or all the time, every time he traveled.

"Never before. Do you have this lure over all men?"

She had to smile at that. "You're the first."

"The first. I like that." He winked at her.

If she entered into an ongoing affair with him, she wouldn't come out of it unscathed. Her professional ethics and her heart were vulnerable.

"Have you been thinking about that night as much as I have?" he asked.

His open flirting was something she wasn't accustomed to. He was playful and fun and almost made her forget she was working. She remembered her apartment. "I should tell you that my apartment was broken into Saturday night."

His face registered shock. "I'm so sorry. Were you hurt?"

"It happened while I was out with you." Was there a connection?

"Why didn't you call me?" he asked.

Was he serious? Why would she have called him? They didn't know each other well enough for her to expect him to come running when she had an emergency. "I called the police. They're investigating."

"You believe I had something to do with it."

She wasn't good at hiding her thoughts. Never had been. "It seems like a strange coincidence."

"I have my share of enemies. If you believe your association with me was the reason for this crime, please allow me to make reparations and look into the matter."

He seemed sincere and honest. "Don't worry about it. I called the police and my insurance will cover it." The insurance company wouldn't clean up the mess, but they were sending her a check so she could replace some of her items. It wouldn't cover everything she'd lost. Some things couldn't be replaced.

"That's unacceptable. I will send someone over to—"

Adham stepped closer. "They're waiting for you, Captain."

His guard was a good reminder of what they were dealing with and the complications that stood between them. He was more than a traveling businessman and she had a lot at stake with the trade summit meetings.

Saafir held up his hand. "One minute more. Please, Sarah, let me take care of your apartment."

Sarah shook her head. "That's really not necessary." If she relied on him, it would make it harder when he left. "I'm handling it. I'm not sure why I brought it up."

"You brought it up because you were concerned," he said. "We're friends. You can talk to me."

Friends? An interesting word and not the one she would have chosen. "What happened this weekend puts us in an awkward position. But we can keep our distance so it doesn't happen again." The words made her sad, but she had to be clear about her boundaries.

The corner of his mouth turned up. "How can you stay away from me when you're the coordinator for the event?"

His smile could have disarmed her, but she would stay strong and stand behind her principles. "From now on, we're keeping this professional."

Saafir frowned. "I'm disappointed to hear that."

Sarah jammed a hand through her hair. "I'm sorry. I don't want any more trouble for either of us."

* * *

Saafir felt like a perfect idiot. He could pinpoint a number of moments after learning Sarah was the event coordinator for the trade summit when he could have told her who he was. The emir of Qamsar. Four simple words. She had slipped out early in the morning while he'd been sleeping and neither of his guards had stopped her, although Adham had trailed her home to be sure she'd arrived safely. He hadn't mentioned anything about her apartment. He must have left before she'd discovered it.

Saafir had made the mistake of thinking he could step out of his role as emir for a night and that being the emir wouldn't matter to Sarah. He wanted to be himself—no title and no responsibilities. Of course that wouldn't turn out well. Denial about his position seemed to creep in at the strangest times. Saafir knew his responsibilities, but some part of him clung to his old, inconspicuous existence. Before becoming emir, he had gone about his day-to-day life with little interest from the public. He could focus on those topics that meant the most to him, like prison reform and social progress, without comment from his family or countrymen.

Now he couldn't speak aloud what he was thinking, not without it becoming a sound bite to be used to cause further instability in the country.

He should let Sarah go. She had made it clear that she wasn't interested in continuing their personal relationship. By sleeping with him she had become someone's target. Her home had been invaded. His enemies would stop at nothing to harm him or find a way to exploit a perceived weakness. Saafir wouldn't let them hurt Sarah. If he stayed away from her, his enemies would lose interest in her and she would be safer.

He was disappointed with the conclusion. Spending time with the spirited American had made him feel more relaxed than he had in months. She was fun and beautiful and different from other women he had been with.

Sarah adjusted her black suit jacket and drew his attention to her waist—likely not her intention. "Saafir, I think we need—"

Gunfire crackled into the crisp morning air, sending a loud echo through the alley. Saafir instinctively reached for Sarah, his protective instincts triggering an immediate reaction. He drew her close and to the ground.

"Shots fired!" Adham yelled.

Adham hovered over them, trying to shield them. Another loud burst of gunfire and Saafir tucked Sarah further under him. She felt small in his arms, and his military training roared to life. Protect. Defend. Retaliate. He shoved her behind the Dumpster, hoping it could provide some protection.

His guard Nibal rushed out of the building, pulling his gun and aiming it high. "I don't have a visual. The car's en route. I repeat, no visual on the shooter."

The sound of gunfire continued at a rapid rate. It was either an automatic weapon or multiple shooters. Bullets kicked up shards of asphalt and concrete, biting into Saafir's skin. His choices were to duck back into the building, remain crouched behind the Dumpster or wait for their car. If they ran for the back door, standing would open them up for another attack and staying pinned down wasn't the safest option.

Saafir's rented black town car screamed around the corner and pulled to a stop in front of him. Adham opened the car door and Saafir pulled Sarah to her feet. He shoved her inside the car and then climbed inside behind her. Adham got into the car and Nibal clambered into the front passenger seat. The driver pulled the car out of the alley, tires squealing.

"Sarah, are you okay?" Saafir asked.

Sarah was pale and staring at her blood that covered hands. "I'm bleeding." She sounded like she was in shock. The sight of red on her hands prompted a primal rage in him. He had to help her, shield her. She was his to protect.

"We need to take her to the hospital," Saafir said. He searched her, removing her jacket and finding the source of the injury. Her shoulder was injured, the skin abraded. Was it from the fall or had she been hit with a flying bullet or rubble?

Too much blood to be superficial. Saafir cradled her in his arms and pressed down on the wound. Sarah moaned in pain.

"Where is she hit?" Adham asked, shifting to help.

"Her shoulder. Looking for other injuries. I think she's in shock," Saafir said.

Adham shifted to get a better look at the injury. Saafir contained his fear and anger at the sight. She should never have been pulled into his problems within his country, and this attack had to be from one of his political enemies. Sarah had nothing to do with them.

"Drive faster," Saafir commanded the driver.

His hands weren't staunching the blood flow. "This might hurt. I'm sorry, Sarah." He shed his jacket and removed his shirt, pressing it hard over the wound. Sarah let out a cry of distress.

She was still conscious and that was good. "I know that hurts. It will only be for a few minutes more. We're getting you help," Saafir said. The amount of blood pouring out of her seemed too great. He'd had some medical field-training and knew that stopping the blood flow was priority one.

"It doesn't look good," Adham said in Arabic. "She is losing too much blood. I can't see if the bullet is lodged inside or if it passed through. Captain, are you hurt?"

Saafir's arm stung, but he wasn't loosening his grip on Sarah to check his injury. "She's my primary concern."

"And you are mine," Adham said.

His guard took his duty seriously. He had earned Saafir's unwavering trust. Saafir looked away from Sarah for a moment. Only then did Saafir notice Adham had sustained an injury. Deep red was darkening the front of his black shirt.

"Adham, you're injured," Saafir said.

Adham hesitated a moment. He was the latest in a long line of men who served Qamsar's emir, pledging his life in defense of the emir, dedicating himself to the emir's protection. It was a thousand-year-old tradition with an impeccable history. Every man named a Qamsarian Warrior had served honorably. Adham hid injuries and hurt behind his sense of honor and duty. It was that sense of honor that would force Adham to tell the truth, especially when Saafir addressed him. "I was hit." His face registered no sign of pain.

"Sit back against the seat. Hold this over it," Saafir said, handing Adham his suit jacket.

Adham obeyed the order.

Saafir turned in his seat and noticed a car speeding behind them, aiming for them. "We're being followed."

"Do you have tactical driving experience?" Saafir asked the driver.

"None in the last ten years." The man's anxiety was evident in his voice.

"Keep the car on the road. Don't turn onto any side streets," Saafir said, wishing he were driving. It was protocol for the emir to be chauffeured, but if he were behind the wheel, he could lose the tail.

Saafir looked around for an opportunity. The light in front of them turned yellow.

"Hit the gas," Saafir said. If they stopped, they'd be cornered and shot.

He did as Saafir asked. They sailed through the intersection. Their follower pursued, but was struck by oncoming traffic.

"That should slow them down," Saafir said. "Nearest hospital."

"Change of plans," Nibal said. "No hospitals. No help. I'll tell you where to drive."

Saafir braced for more danger ahead. He looked from Sarah to Adham to Nibal. It was unusual for Nibal or Adham to disagree with a direct command unless they'd identified a security threat. Nibal seemed off and somewhat nervous. Saafir had never seen him that way.

"Tell me the problem," Saafir said. He struggled to keep his voice calm and not overreact. With Sarah bleeding in his arms and Adham injured, that took every ounce of strength.

"We're not going to the hospital," Nibal said.

"Sarah and Adham need medical attention," Saafir said, stifling the urge to yell. If Nibal was losing his cool, Saafir didn't want to escalate the situation. Nibal had never been as rock-steady as Adham under pressure.

Nibal lifted a gun to the driver's head and had a second gun pointed at Saafir. "No hospital. I'm calling the shots and I'm telling you that we are not going to the hospital. We're ending this agreement with the Americans and we are ending your rule as emir."

Scorching anger in Nibal's eyes confirmed his words—he wasn't interested in helping Sarah, Adham or Saafir. "We will take Sarah and Adham to the hospital and then we can talk about the trade agreement. Sarah and Adham are not part of this," Saafir said. His hand crept down his pant leg to his ankle holster, carefully and quietly unsnapping his gun. It had been a long time since he'd used it, but it would be like riding a bike.

"She is part of this," Nibal said narrowing his eyes at Sarah. "They are all part of it."

"They" being the trade agreement committee or Americans? Saafir had heard this extremist "all" speech from too many fanatical groups in Qamsar. Desperate individuals and groups who needed someone to blame and who took action to make a change. Unfortunately, the action rarely led to accomplishing anything other than hurting people.

This new reality for Qamsar wasn't one that Saafir embraced. It made him angry and frustrated. Those emotions were sidelined by the woman in his arms who needed him to remain calm, defuse the situation and get her medical help. Adham hadn't spoken, but his skin was pale.

The driver kept glancing at Nibal and was visibly shaken by having a gun locked on him. The car swerved in the road, left and right, narrowly missing cars parked along the street.

"Keep the car steady. Do not try to alert the American police," Nibal said.

"Please don't shoot. I am not alerting anyone. I want to go home to my wife and daughters," the driver said, fear vibrating his voice.

Sarah's face was unmoving and her eyes were closed.

Saafir tried again. "Nibal, this is not the way to get what you want. Please let everyone out of the car and we'll talk." If he could keep Nibal's focus on him, perhaps Adham, Sarah and the driver could get to safety.

"No," Nibal said. "No talking. Action. I am making a point. You are the wrong leader for Qamsar. You were never meant to be the emir. I am doing my duty and removing you from your position before you destroy everything we hold important."

Saafir understood the sentiment. He had heard it many times from his political opposition.

Nibal planned to shoot him in cold blood. Saafir reached for his gun and slid it along his leg. He positioned it against the seat of the car. Every time he had used his weapon, he had done so because he had no other choice in defending himself or the people he was protecting. This was no exception.

Two shots and shock registered on Nibal's face, his mouth opening in a silent scream. Saafir's aim had been true.

Nibal's body slumped to the side and the driver shrieked and slammed the car to a stop.

Saafir slid his gun back into his holster. He turned to the driver who was staring at Nibal. He had shoved the body against the window.

"I will drive us to the hospital," Saafir said. Of the four of them, he was in the best position. His arm ached, but he didn't feel light-headed and he wasn't losing a massive amount of blood or in a state of shock. Saafir stroked Sarah's hair by her temple. "You will be safe, my goddess. Hold on a little longer. Help is coming."

Adham situated himself to hold a hand over Sarah's arm. Saafir withdrew his phone and called the American police to meet him at the hospital. On American turf, he'd play by their rules.

"We're almost there, Sarah. Stay with me," Saafir said, taking the wheel and praying for Sarah and Adham.

Chapter 3

The moment Sarah awoke, she knew she was in a hospital. A heart rate monitor beeped rhythmically. Her left arm was restrained and covered in heavy bandages. It took her a few seconds to remember what had happened. She had been speaking with Barr in the alley outside the first trade summit meeting. Not Barr. Saafir, the emir of Qamsar. His big, brawny guard, Adham, had been lurking in the doorway. Then, she had been pinned behind a Dumpster as the sound of gunfire exploded around her.

Thanks to the emir of Qamsar, she was alive.

She opened her eyes and saw Owen's concerned face. Owen leapt to his feet. "Jeez, Sarah, you scared about three decades off my life. What the hell happened in that alley?"

Sarah struggled to sit. She felt groggy and tired.

She pressed the button on her bed to raise the back of the hospital bed. Her entire left arm was numb. "I remember to a point, than it goes hazy."

A long pause. "There are reporters everywhere. What do I need to know about this?"

She wasn't hiding anything. She wasn't sure she fully understood his question. "I don't know anything more than you. How is Saafir? I mean, the emir?"

Owen shot her a curious look. "The hospital won't release details, but a spokesperson for the emir said he is in good health. Given the political environment in Qamsar, there's nothing else they could say. The leader of their country being down and out opens the door for a coup and could cause a revolution. How are you feeling?" Owen added quickly.

"I'm a little worse for wear," she said. When the pain medication wore off, she guessed she'd be in a great deal of pain. "What's wrong with my arm?" She couldn't see anything under the mass of bandages.

"You were grazed by a bullet that hit a large vein. You've got a lot of healing to do," Owen said. His face was grim. "I don't want you to worry about anything except getting better. There's a bunch of crap in the news. You've been named as the emir's lover, the emir's mistress and the emir's American bride."

Sarah groaned. "Already digging around for some lurid ties between us. Will this hurt the trade agreement?"

"Obviously, day one has been derailed," Owen said. "I've communicated with every member of the committee and their staff to alert them we might be dealing with a violent extremist. We're organizing increased security measures and will implement them immediately. The emir could be the target, but how could they have known he'd step into the alley? This may have been an attack of opportunity. The target could be anyone on the committee. It's too soon to know what the objective of the attack was."

Though it wasn't the most pressing concern, she worried about her future. "What about my job?" Sarah asked.

Owen touched her arm lightly. "Don't worry about that. Worry about getting better."

Anxiety made her feel sick. "Owen, no. Don't blow me off. Don't feed me a bunch of bull. If you're planning to fire me, tell me now."

He sighed. "Nothing has been decided. The contract is still yours. But Sarah, it's not worth losing your life over this. I want you to consider stepping back."

Sarah shook her head. Her marriage was over, her apartment was trashed, her personal life was being eviscerated by the press and her job was the one thing she had left. She needed the money and she needed the event for her resume. "I wasn't the target. The emir was."

"If you are not around the emir, you will be safe."

She couldn't back down or back away from this job. She needed it. She'd earned this opportunity and she might never get another like it. "I will be fine, Owen. Please don't take this away from me."

Owen sighed. "Until the police or FBI tell me differently, I am taking the threat as directed at us—all of us. If you get hurt again, I'll hold myself responsible."

"If I get hurt, I only hold the people shooting the guns responsible," Sarah said.

Owen leaned forward in his chair. "May I ask you a personal question about you and the emir?"

Unease twisted through her. Sarah worked to keep her composure. Had she given away that something had transpired between her and Saafir? Owen was perceptive and the intimacy she and Saafir had shared had made a permanent impression on her. It could have been obvious to others. "Go ahead."

"I thought I saw something between the two of you this morning. Have you spoken with the emir before today on more personal matters? Is there more to your relationship than you've led me to believe?" Owen asked.

His question was made more awkward by Owen being her former brother-in-law and her boss. She hadn't wanted to speak of the night she and Saafir had spent together, especially not after learning of his connection to the trade agreement. In light of the shooting, was that information relevant? She didn't want her life to be fodder for the gossip rags, but Owen was a friend. She could trust him. "I ran into the emir Saturday night in a bar. We talked."

Owen was too much of a gentleman to push for details, but he could infer the rest. "You have a personal relationship with him."

She supposed relationship was as good a word as any. "I didn't know who he was," Sarah said. "I was feeling bad about the divorce and he's a tough guy to ignore." In a crowded room, Saafir stood out head and shoulders above other men.

Owen was silent for a minute, his eyebrows drawn together in thought. When he spoke, the words came out slowly and carefully. "This is a good opportunity for us. You can talk to him. Find out what he's thinking. Get a read on him to further negotiations. The faster we can get signatures on paper, the better."

Sarah groaned. She was groggy from meds, but even in her half-addled state she knew this was a bad idea. "We've spent time together twice, including today when someone tried to assassinate him. I don't think that puts our relationship into confidante status. I don't have any pull over him." She did not want to insert herself into a political negotiation.

"I'm not suggesting you pull him, I'm suggesting you do what you can for your country and be his friend. If anything relevant comes to your attention, you bring it to my attention."

"I can't do that," she said. She was the event coordinator. Her responsibilities ended at lodging, food, drinks and entertainment. She guessed security arrangements would be passed to Owen now. Her interest in spying was nil. "I won't. From what you've told me, the agreement is good for both sides. You don't need me in the middle. I'll make it worse."

"The agreement is good, but it's not without trouble spots. You can smooth those over. Come on, Sarah, I got you this job. You owe me. You just asked me not to release you from the contract. Do this for me in return."

He wasn't pulling punches. Her choices were to help Owen or lose the contract. If she lost the contract, she had nothing left in her life. Weeks of sitting around her apartment, draining her savings account and waiting for another job. She had turned away a few jobs knowing the trade agreement would occupy most of her time and it was too late to acquire more. Idle time was bad. She needed to stay busy.

If she agreed to help Owen, maybe she wouldn't have to pass on anything because she may not learn anything. Saafir might not want to see her alone again. He might not say anything to her about the trade agreement. If they never spoke of the trade agreement, she'd have zero insider knowledge. "If I hear anything, I will let you know." The words felt like they were stuck to her tongue.

She was spared further conversation by Molly and Krista, who arrived in her room carrying a balloon and flowers.

Owen sighed. "The news is already on the street?"

Molly glared at him. Owen and her friends had never gotten along. "Details aren't in the news. I heard from Debbie about a problem with the trade summit," Molly said, referring to the congresswoman she worked for. "Krista called one of your waitstaff and got the details."

Gossip spread quickly in D.C., especially when it involved international politics and high-profile situations.

"I'll give you a few minutes to talk," Owen said.

After Owen left the room, Krista set the flowers on the table across from Sarah's bed and sat in the chair he'd been occupying. "He is always so uptight."

"That's not true," Sarah said, though she'd had similar thoughts in the past. "He's under a lot of pressure." His marriage, his work and Alec were strains on him.

"Oh, please. He's always been hard on you," Molly said.

Sarah and Owen had a shaky history. They hadn't agreed on the right course of action for Alec's care. "He's protective of Alec and he knows you guys were on my side during the divorce."

The word "divorce" still pained her. It should be easier to talk about it. Maybe one day it would be.

"Of course we're on your side. We're always on your side," Krista said.

Her friends were the closest to family she had. She'd once felt that Alec, Owen and Evelyn were her family, but not recently, not based on how they now treated her.

"How are you feeling?" Molly asked.

"I'm okay," Sarah said. Should she tell her friends Barr's real name? They were usually understanding and nonjudgmental. "It turns out that I accidentally slept with the emir."

Molly lifted her brows. "Accidentally? How do you accidentally get naked and sleep with someone?"

"The guy from this weekend is the emir."

Molly and Krista had matching looks of shock.

"Does that mean you'll be a princess?" Krista asked.

"What does that mean Adham is? His courtier or something?" Molly asked.

"I am not a princess and Adham is in charge of his security. Adham was outside when the shooting started," Sarah said.

"Is he okay?" Molly asked.

"I haven't heard anything about Adham, and Owen says the emir is doing okay."

"What about you? How are you feeling about all this?" Krista asked.

Confused and overwhelmed. "Physically, I'm okay."

Molly chewed her lower lip. "I'll talk to one of the nurses and see if I can get more information. I'll be right back."

Krista touched Sarah's arm. "Excuse her. She's bounced between worry about you and talking about

Adham. She's crushing on him hard. But are you really okay? I was terrified when I heard there was a shooting."

Sarah hadn't had time to process what had happened. "I'm scared, shaken and confused. It happened so fast. One minute, I was talking to the emir and the next I was waking up in a hospital. I have some fragmented memories, but I think I was fading in and out of consciousness."

Krista clasped her hand. "Maybe you should think about taking a vacation."

"You sound like Owen. You know I need the money and my business needs the boost. Alec is counting on me to pay the bills for his rehab."

"Why can't Owen pay for it? He brags about how he's some big-shot negotiator. Let him deal with his brother."

Krista's vehemence was in defense of her. "I promised Alec I would do this. It's the last thing I will do for him." And Owen had indicated he had some financial problems. His wife was running up credit card balances across town.

"I've heard that before," Krista said.

Sarah let her head fall against her pillow. "It's not easy to cut him out of my life."

"Okay, forget about Alec for a minute. You have that outdoor wedding coming up. You'll get some work from that," Krista said. "You can pass out business cards."

Sarah never promoted her business that way. She let the event speak for her. "The wedding is small potatoes compared to the work I'm getting with the trade summit."

"Tell your new boyfriend about your money problems. He owns a country. Maybe he can help," Krista said.

Sarah laughed. "You know I would never ask him to do that."

Krista sighed dramatically. "But isn't it nice for a second to pretend we'd all meet a handsome prince and get swept away?"

"Sure, but you just said it. A fantasy like that is just pretend."

The police arrived a few hours later to ask Sarah some questions. They had pieced together most of the day's events starting from around the time Sarah had arrived at the office building and began setting up for the meeting. She hadn't noticed anyone strange lingering around the building. She hadn't noticed any strange cars, either, but the office suites were in a busy section of town. Why would she have noticed a car?

She hadn't been aware of the gunfire until she was covered by Saafir and his guard. She wasn't part of a conspiracy to assassinate Saafir.

After repeating details as the police dug for an important clue she had left out, she started to feel like she was answering the questions on autopilot.

Sarah's arm was heavy and throbbing. She wanted a break, to get some medication, get into the bathroom to shower or at least wash her face. If she pressed the button for the nurses, they might shoo the police from her room. Her finger stretched toward the call button.

Before she could press the button for help, Saafir entered the room. Flanked by three security guards— Sarah noticed that Adham was missing from the group—Saafir appeared regal and composed. He showed no signs of injury and nothing on his face gave away he was in pain. His PR team may have been right when they'd said he wasn't injured. Though he had said nothing, the room fell silent. One of the police officers, a woman about ten years older than Sarah, was openly gaping at him.

Sarah echoed the sentiment. Saafir was something to look at. Naked, he was even more incredible.

"Do you mind giving us a couple of minutes alone?" Saafir asked, addressing the room at large. Since Sarah was confined to her bed and this was her room, she assumed he meant to speak to her in private. Excitement tickled her insides. He hadn't forgotten about her. He was interested in talking to her. Though his interest might be rooted in this morning's event, perhaps there was a personal aspect to it. Why did that make her feel special and wanted?

Her one-night stand was morphing into something more in her mind. She couldn't help it. If he hadn't shown up that morning or if she had never seen him again, she may have moved on. With him back in her life, how could she pretend she felt nothing for him? Her body was already betraying her, her skin aching for his touch, her breasts tightening beneath her thin hospital gown and heat pooling between her legs. His gaze plowed into her and she wondered if he could possibly know the direction her thoughts had taken.

The lead detective stepped forward. "Sir, this is a police investigation."

"What's your badge number?" Saafir asked.

The man straightened. "What?"

"Your badge number. I need to know who to report

when I call the chief of police to discuss this matter," Saafir said. He barely looked at the police officer. His attention seemed fixed on Sarah.

"But—"

"This is my investigation. I take a personal interest when someone tries to kill me and the people under my protection." He looked Sarah up and down as if including her under that umbrella.

The glimmer of possessiveness in his eyes did crazy things to her stomach.

"Out. Now," Saafir said.

The police officers did not argue further. They left the room with only their perturbed faces giving away how they felt. Saafir's guards followed them out.

Sarah was immediately aware of several things. She wasn't wearing a bra. She desperately needed a shower. Other concerns should be on her mind, like the person who had taken shots at her, but her physical appearance next to Saafir's crisp and clean one made her feel like moldy green cheese in the deli display case.

Memories of the night they had spent together replayed through her mind. Every time she laid eyes on Saafir, she experienced a fresh wave of lust.

"How are you?" Saafir asked, taking a seat next to her bed. His voice was thick with concern, and many times softer than it had been moments before. He seemed to flinch slightly when he sat. "I've been worried about you. It took some coercing to find out where you were inside the hospital. American doctors and nurses are protective of their patients. I consider that good overall, but bad for my personal agenda."

His personal agenda included her. Her skin prickled in awareness and her pulse beat erratically.

Aside from her friends, Sarah was accustomed to looking out for herself. It felt nice for someone to show interest in her. And the emir wasn't just someone. He was a busy, important leader of his country with little free time and yet he was in her hospital room, talking to her as if she were most important in his life. "My arm is numb and I think whatever the doctors gave me is affecting my brain, too." And Saafir was affecting her brain, making her feel overheated and tingly.

Saafir adjusted his chair, bringing them closer. Her temperature rose another few degrees. "Exhaustion and anesthesia will do that. I have to apologize for both of those conditions. Because of me, you didn't get much sleep this weekend and because of me, you're in this hospital."

Blatantly speaking of the night they had spent together. Maybe getting it out would defuse some of the desire simmering inside her. They had already discussed they wouldn't repeat the encounter, but alone in this room with him, even with her arm in pain, she was thinking about pulling him into bed with her. A hospital bed had interesting possibilities she hadn't experienced before. "I don't blame you for my injury."

His dark eyes darted to her arm and back to her face. "Can I get you anything to make you more comfortable?"

If she wasn't almost lying down, his question would have floored her. The leader of a country was offering to play nurse to her. Even if it was only for a few minutes, she was pleased.

If he wanted to pamper her, she'd let him. "It's a little warm in here," she said.

He immediately walked to the thermostat and adjusted it. With his back to her, she had a few minutes to take him in, from the broad expanse of his shoulders to the trimness of his hips and long length of his legs. She undeniably wanted this man.

"It will take a few minutes to cool down," he said, turning to face her.

The room. Not her. When he was close, her body ran a dozen degrees too hot. She had to get her lust in check. Owen had agreed to keep her on the contract and not activate the termination clause. Her professional ethics had to stay in place or she risked losing this job. Her attraction to Saafir was an unexpected and unwanted complication, but she could handle it.

She shook off thoughts of having sex with Saafir again. She had drawn a clear line with him and she wouldn't cross it just because her emotions were out of balance. He had saved her life. He was being kind. That didn't change the circumstances. She turned the conversation to him, the client. Not lover, not sex god, not client with benefits, just client. "How are you?" she asked, expecting the party line that he was fine.

"I have some pain, but it's manageable."

His honesty surprised her. Owen had told her what was at risk if the public learned the emir wasn't in peak condition. Telling her the truth implied a level of trust between them she wouldn't have assumed was there.

"How's Adham?" she asked, thinking of Molly's quest to learn more about Saafir's guard.

"Adham is in surgery. He suffered a gunshot wound to the abdomen that might have killed a lesser man. But Adham is a Qamsarian Warrior and he will be fine."

Sarah heard compassion in his voice and worry below the surface. Sarah had read that Qamsarian Warriors prided themselves on indifference to pain and not allowing injuries to slow them down. Even so, it was clear that Saafir was concerned about his guard. "The police are trying to find who did this. I'm not sure how much help I was. After the shots, my memory is fuzzy."

Saafir filled in the blanks she was missing: the driver being held at gunpoint by Nibal, Saafir killing him and their race to the hospital to stop her and Adham's bleeding. "My guards and investigators from my country are looking into the incident. Nibal may have spoken with someone in the past several weeks who might have orchestrated this. I believe those responsible are members of a political party in Qamsar known as the Conservatives, or at least some far-leaning members of the group. Their leader, Rabah Wasam, has made some statements this morning to the press that imply he was involved." He paused and Sarah wondered if he knew more about the story but was holding it back. "I wanted to speak to you directly, because I brought danger to you and because you were, and perhaps still are, a target."

"Why would I be a target?" she asked.

Saafir set his hand on hers. "The public has linked us romantically."

She couldn't refute it. She had slept with him. Saying "it meant nothing" or "it was over" felt like a lie. "How do you want to handle it?" He must have more experience dealing with the media and the public. She would take her cues from him.

"I insist on providing you protection and security until the men responsible are found and held accountable," Saafir said.

That wasn't necessary. Sarah wondered if Saafir had come to her room out of a sense of obligation. For a moment, she had thought he had feelings for her, but Sarah was quick to reconsider. She was terrible at judging a person's intentions. Her relationship history was marred with disasters. "Owen mentioned he was increasing security for everyone involved in the trade summit. You don't need to provide anything for me."

Saafir stiffened. "Again, I insist. You've been pushed into the spotlight because of me. The men who want to hurt me won't stop with just me. They will try to hurt the people I care about."

A wave of disorientation pounded over her. Again with the implication that he cared about her, but Sarah was reluctant to believe him. "If we don't see each other again, eventually, people will realize there is nothing between us." She was giving him an out. If he was acting on his sense of responsibility, he didn't need to look out for her.

A grave expression crossed Saafir's face. "The media has already named you as my mistress. If someone thinks they can hurt me by hurting you, they will. I will not allow you to be harmed again."

When she thought about being close to Saafir, a strange mix of anxiety and desire crept over her. "We can make this decision another time." Being near him felt too intense, as if every decision could have life-altering consequences.

Saafir shook his head. "I've already made the decision. I am taking responsibility for the hurt and damage I have brought into your life. I'm looking after you and the people I am working with in America. I am concerned about you."

Even if he hadn't implied interest in her as a lover,

how could she say no to that? "It's best if you talk to Owen. He'll be making the arrangements."

"I will do that directly."

Wasn't Saafir concerned that the assassins would return to take another shot at him? "Are you planning to return to Qamsar? Perhaps work through an intermediary?" Sarah asked.

Saafir shook his head and relief tumbled through her. She wasn't sure how to handle him being so close, but she didn't want him to leave. What she had with him didn't feel over.

His face was determined. "I will work through these negotiations until they reach their conclusion. I will not bow to terrorists or political pressure by running home in fear."

The people of Qamsar had Saafir under a microscope. He had to take his actions with that understanding. "Brave."

He took her hand, looked at it and then at her face. "I am not brave. I am a servant to my people." Saafir stood slowly and winced. He released her hand and pressed his hand over his arm. "Thank you for your time. I promised my nurses I wouldn't be gone long. We'll work something out. I can't express how badly I feel that you were harmed."

"Just a scratch," she said.

Saafir touched her cheek with the back of his hand, the lightest of touches. For a moment, she forgot the aching in her shoulder, and the heat and kindness in his touch evoked an immediate emotional response. Tears sprang to her eyes and she blinked them back. How long had it been since someone had touched her with such affection and warmth?

"Are you in pain? Can I do something for you?" Saafir asked.

Sarah wiped at her eyes with her left hand. "I'm just overwhelmed and tired. I need a meal and a shower and a nap and then I'll be fine."

Saafir picked up the phone in her room. He asked to speak to someone and then gave the list of requests. "Food is on its way. Let me help you in the shower."

"You can't help me shower," she said. If someone walked in, what would they think?

"Why not?"

He'd see her naked. He was the head of a country. He had better things to do with his time. "I can manage alone."

"You need help. If you refuse my request, I will have a nurse assist you, but until you are feeling better, you must accept assistance."

Saafir didn't wait for her to argue the point. He helped her stand and led her to the bathroom. A small stool was in the shower. "Please sit. You may direct me in the manner you prefer."

The list of possibilities was long and dirty. Direct him? He meant in the shower, but she could only think of asking for a repeat of Saturday night. "I haven't been bathed since I was a baby," she said.

"Then enjoy this," he said. He removed his jacket and his shirt.

"Oh, my," she said, impressed all over again.

He had a small bandage of his arm near his military tattoo.

"It's a nick," he said, noticing her looking at it.

"I wasn't commenting on the injury. I was thinking about how you look shirtless."

Saafir laughed. "You are good for my ego."

As he was for hers. He could have asked someone to bathe her. He could have given the task to anyone else. But he was doing it himself, for her.

"Were you hit anywhere else?" Sarah asked.

"My leg. It's not the worst injury I've had," he said.

"Does this mean you'll let me help you bathe?" she asked.

"If it means having you close, then yes," he said.

He treated her with great care, helping her out of her gown, arranging towels around her shoulder and arm to keep her bandages dry. He didn't stare at her naked body, but rather focused on his task.

He wet her hair and poured shampoo onto it. He seemed confused for a moment what to do. "I'll need some direction."

She lifted her hand and massaged the shampoo in. Then she lifted his hand to her head and he mimicked her actions. "That feels good, Saafir," she said. Their hands slipped together and suddenly Sarah wanted to forget getting clean and keeping her professional ethics and get dirty with Saafir.

Saafir's body tensed as if sensing how turned on she was. "Please ask your nurse when you will be healed enough to let me take you to bed."

"I can't ask someone that question."

"Why not?" he asked. He ran the showerhead across her body. As the water streamed over her, desire grew heavier. He hadn't touched her and already she felt on the edge of exploding apart.

"Because I can't talk to someone that way. Are you doing that on purpose?" she asked.

"Doing what?" he asked, innocent words with a hint of playfulness.

The water droplets titillated her skin. "You're going to kill me," she said.

"No, my goddess. I am planning to keep you very, very safe."

Chapter 4

Saafir didn't find it easy to concentrate on the meeting. Every time Sarah entered or left the room, he wanted to bolt and find a place where he could be alone with her. Though their relationship had taken a different turn from what he'd expected, he was on board for the ride with no intention of throwing the brakes.

His plans for her were fluid. His night with Sarah was turning into something more lasting. His visit to America was the last time he would be a single man and his romantic interest should be focused on Alaina, the woman who would become his wife. Even so, he couldn't stop fantasizing about Sarah and spending another night with her as soon as she was well. She had gotten under his skin, and when he lay in bed at night, he was unable to think about anyone else. Her delicate features filled his mind and the memory of her soft laughter filled his ears. When he stroked himself to completion and thought of her, it left him wanting, his desire for her sharpening and beckoning to be sated with more than memories.

Despite his lurid thoughts of Sarah, Saafir forced himself to focus on the terms of the trade agreement.

Saafir wanted the agreement to be favorable to the people of Qamsar. He would walk away from the deal if his people didn't net something more profitable from it than a place to sell their oil. The world was filled with places to market their oil. They needed a partnership.

The members of the committee were watching Saafir. They were curious about him, which was natural considering a ratified trade agreement hinged on his final word, among other things. He'd noticed some interested glances between him and Sarah, but he was careful to give nothing away. It seemed important to her that their relationship remain private and he'd honor her wishes. Involvement with him could impact her career, and he was pleased she took her job seriously. He respected a woman with a strong sense of pride in her accomplishments.

Saafir's shoulder was throbbing by the end of the day. He'd refused to take pain medication that morning. While Frederick was watching everything and keeping meticulous notes, Saafir wanted to be clear-headed. At least, as clear-headed as he could be with Sarah close.

When Owen called an end to the meeting, Frederick leaned over. "Your excellency, we have much to discuss."

They exited the conference room and gathered in the room serving as their private office. Three of Saafir's guards followed them. They had flown in the night before, after the attempt on Saafir's life. With Adham requiring time to heal, though he'd refused to step away from his post completely, they needed additional support.

"What is going on between you and the American woman?" Frederick asked.

"Virginia Anderson?" Saafir asked.

"No. Sarah Parker," Frederick said.

Even if Frederick hadn't read the local papers, Saafir knew Frederick would pick up on the heated vibes between him and Sarah. "We have a personal relationship," Saafir said.

Frederick did not appear pleased to have the news reports confirmed. "End it."

Saafir had always liked Frederick's no-nonsense, honest, straight-shooting approach to matters. In this case, he was overstepping his bounds. "My relationship with Sarah doesn't concern you."

"Have you forgotten about Alaina Faris? We need her father on our side. How will he feel when negotiations for the marriage of his daughter are called to question because you want an American in your bed?" Frederick asked.

He was aware of why they needed Alaina Faris. Saafir understood the rules and what rode along with his marriage to the daughter of an eminent leader in the Conservative party. "She and I are not engaged. Her father has not yet responded to my proposition. I have done nothing disloyal to her." It felt strange to be questioned about his loyalty to a woman he had never met. This was his new life as the emir. Loyalty and commitment to a woman he didn't know. Saafir stamped out his dismay. He was duty-bound to behave in a manner that was best for Qamsar.

"Gray area. Extremely gray area. We can't risk her getting upset about your relationship with an American woman," Frederick said.

"Alaina will not get upset about my relationship with Sarah. It has nothing to do with her," Saafir said.

"I do not approve," Frederick said. He wasn't in a position to command the emir, but he had made his stance clear.

"So noted," Saafir said. He didn't need approval from his advisors for something that couldn't last, but Saafir wondered if he was playing with fire by pursuing Sarah. Even if it would end badly, he couldn't walk away. Sarah needed him and he couldn't deny that something in him needed her.

Dr. Henry Verde, the committee's environmentalist, and Thomas Nelson III, the committee's financial specialist, were having drinks in the lobby bar of the hotel where Saafir was staying. Along with the other members of the trade agreement committee, they'd been displaced from their homes. Henry, or Hank, as he preferred to be called, had been amicable about it, but Thomas had complained endlessly at every opportunity throughout the day. He didn't like being moved from his suburban Maryland mansion and the luxuries it provided.

Hank lifted a hand in greeting as Saafir approached, his guards on his heels. He was running late for his dinner plans with Sarah, having been caught in the meeting with Frederick strategizing their next step. Ignoring the two men would be rude even if Saafir was anxious to see Sarah. What would she be wearing? Saafir thought she'd wear something comfortable for her shoulder, but he found himself wishing for Sarah to wear an elegant dress with a plunging neckline.

"Gentlemen," Saafir said, pushing aside thoughts of Sarah's cleavage.

"I'm surprised to see you here," Thomas said, a slight slur in his words.

"Oh?" Saafir asked.

"I figured you and Owen were bunking in someplace nicer," Thomas said.

Hank's eyes widened slightly as if shocked by Thomas's words.

"We're all in the same situation and following the same security protocol," Saafir said. Though the hotel wasn't the nicest he'd stayed in, it was safe, clean and comfortable. His guards had checked it out and had approved of the security—the lighting, the door locks and the front desk staff on shift around the clock. It lacked the opulence of the penthouse suite where he had stayed his first night in America, the suite where he had made love with Sarah. He had slept in far worse during his training in the Qamsarian military. A soft mattress was a luxury.

Thomas took a swig of his drink. "Same? Sure. That's what I keep hearing."

Saafir guessed the man had more to say, but Hank jumped in. "Making any progress on finding who's behind the shooting?"

Though he had some leads that implicated Rabah Wasam, Saafir wasn't allowing anyone to be privy to their investigation. "Nothing concrete yet." When he had the evidence he needed to convict Wasam, the man would pay for his crimes. This time, his jail sentence would be lengthy.

"Too bad," Hank said. He tossed some bills on the bar. "I need to get going. See you both tomorrow."

Thomas made no attempt to get up from the bar. He signaled the bartender for another drink.

"I'll see you in the morning," Saafir said, and didn't catch whatever Thomas mumbled under his breath in response.

When Saafir entered his room, dinner was waiting in take-out containers and the world news channel was tuned on the television. Keeping tabs on the news had become part of his life, but Saafir shut the television off. He wanted a couple of uninterrupted hours with Sarah. If he missed anything critical, he'd receive a report from Frederick.

Sadly, most events that were brought to his attention were negative, and that depressed him. His father had carried so much on his shoulders and yet he hadn't shown signs of weariness or fatigue with his position. He had been strong and confident. His mother had been his father's confidante. Saafir remembered them talking together in his father's private study late at night.

His father had also had the necessary outlets for his frustrations and disappointments. He'd been an excellent swimmer and runner. To date, Saafir used every ounce of time and energy he had to get his hands around running his country. Political theory learned from his formal education fell short of real life. He had wide gaps in knowledge and big shoes to fill. Little time remained for hobbies or regular exercise outside the training exercises with Adham.

Adham was posted outside Sarah's room and

planned to escort her to Saafir's suite when she was ready. A strong knock sounded on the door. Adham's knock. His lead guard wasn't happy about being assigned to watch over Sarah, but Adham was the one person Saafir could fully trust in America to look out for her safety. He was recovering from his injury and while Saafir knew he wasn't at his best, Adham wouldn't admit he was weaker while healing.

Saafir was nervous about seeing her, the same way he'd been as a young man the first time he'd talked to a girl he'd liked. "Come in," Saafir said. Anticipation over seeing her singed his blood. It had been years since he'd felt this way about a woman.

Sarah entered first, with Adham behind her. Adham's eyes swept the room, perhaps habituated to looking for a threat.

Sarah had changed from the black dress and heels she'd worn during their meeting into a cotton shirt and pants. She looked relaxed, like a cool glass of water on a hot day, and entirely too appealing.

He wanted to tell her how amazing she looked without coming on too strong. She was struggling with their relationship, worried she was crossing professional boundaries. When it came to Sarah, he didn't want boundaries of any kind. How could he convince her she could have her work and him in her life? "Welcome, Sarah. Adham, thank you for escorting Sarah. Would you like to join us for dinner?"

Adham declined, as Saafir expected he might. He would have loved for Sarah and Adham to get to know each other better. They had an unconventional relationship, but Adham was family and Saafir wished to relieve the aggravated tension between him and Sarah.

While he and Adham ate together occasionally, Adham preferred to keep his distance and maintain boundaries when others were around.

"I'll see you later then," Saafir said. He and Sarah would be alone. He loved that. It was an unanticipated gift of another night with her.

Adham nodded and left the room. When his shift ended in a few hours, he was off for the remainder of the night. Saafir hoped he would use the time to rest. Adham had been quieter than usual and Saafir worried about the injury he had sustained in the shooting.

Sarah glanced around the room. "This room is larger than mine, although not as nice as the penthouse."

The mention of the penthouse again brought steamy memories to mind. "Living in a hotel leaves much to be desired." He had never liked living out of a suitcase regardless of how fancy the room that had the suitcase in it was.

"Something smells good. Did you cook?" she asked.

Saafir shook his head. "Even with the best tools and equipment, I wouldn't risk poisoning us with my food. My mother tried to teach me and it was a skill that I did not master. When all I have is a microwave and hot plate, I'm even more useless in preparing a meal."

"Darn," she said. "I wanted to tell my friends that I finally managed to date a man who cooked."

Date a man. Saafir was familiar with the American term, if not in practice, then in its definition. Is that how she viewed their interaction? It was better than how she had previously classified their relationship, as something that had been fleeting and was over.

"I didn't mean to say date." She swallowed. "I meant spend time with."

They were both circling the characterization of their relationship.

Saafir sought to be clear about his feelings. "I've been watching you all day, counting the moments until we could be alone."

"You are supposed to be paying attention to your meetings," she said and smiled. She unbuttoned the top button of her blouse. Was she too warm or was she playing with him?

The blood drained from his head to his lower body. "How can I when you look like this?" He ran his hands down her arms, careful around her shoulder, and took her hands in his. "How is your arm?" He'd felt the bandage beneath her shirt.

"Better every hour," she said.

"I will be exceedingly gentle with you," he said, drawing her close.

Sarah tensed and Saafir worried he had hurt her.

"Tell me what you need," he said.

Sarah pulled out of his arms. "I thought we were having dinner."

Their text messages that day had been about arranging a meal. He'd hoped the subtext was a repeat of their first night together. At least sharing a meal with her meant they were together. "We can eat." He'd let her set the pace. She would be in control. That might set her at ease.

Saafir opened the containers of food and did his best to create a presentable dinner around the small table in his room.

"I thought an emir would eat gourmet food every night," Sarah said.

"There are a lot of misconceptions people have about being an emir," Saafir said.

"Like what?" Sarah asked.

"I'd hate to spoil your view of me," he said. Their relationship had been ignited around a romantic fantasy. Would she lose interest if he grounded their relationship in reality?

"Tell me what it's like to run a country. This is probably the only time I'll eat alone with a leader of a nation."

"Long hours. Little vacation. Mediating problems. Watching everything I say."

"Doesn't sound like a jet-setting life filled with massages and amazing food."

It had its perks. "When I'm home, the food is amazing." If only he could be home more often.

"Nothing like a home-cooked meal," Sarah said.

"I hope my choices tonight stand up against your catering selections," Saafir said.

"Perhaps that's why you've invited me here. To persuade me to arrange your meals around the clock?" Sarah lifted her brow.

Saafir laughed. "You figured me out. But you must know I invited you here because I enjoy your company."

Sarah stopped filling her plate. "I enjoy your company, too."

"But?" He'd heard the hitch at the end of her words.

"But I told you I wasn't looking to get involved with someone, especially not when I know it will be complicated and problematic." She brushed her brown hair away from her face. Her voice was soft.

"Every relationship has its problems," Saafir said.

"This is the first relationship where someone has shot at me," she said.

Boundaries and walls were flying up around her. If she hadn't agreed to share a meal with him, he would have assumed she had no interest in seeing him again. Being here meant something. It meant she had reservations about them, but she wasn't unaffected by their attraction. "I won't coerce you." He needed to make his intention clear. His position as emir sometimes led people to believe they could not say no to him.

She took a seat across from him. "I don't want this to go to a bad place. What we had that one night was so good. It can only get worse from there."

Someone had hurt her. Pain resonated in her voice. "I won't hurt you and I don't think our relationship will get worse. I think it has the potential to be great for both of us."

Sarah set her fork on the table. "It's better if we keep our relationship professional." She echoed her sentiments from earlier.

Her hands were shaking slightly and unless he was misreading her, it wasn't fear or anger. She was nervous. Her heart was at war with her brain.

"I don't want to keep our relationship professional, but I will respect your feelings. Start by telling me how you feel," he said.

"I think—"

He held up his hand. "Not what you think. Tell me what you feel."

Sarah squirmed and set her hands in her lap. "I'm attracted to you. I can't forget the night we spent together. It was, for lack of a more mature word, magic."

He remained quiet. He wanted to hear everything she had to say.

"But what about my job? My business?"

Saafir circled the small table and knelt on the floor at her feet. He removed her shoes one at a time, flicking them over his shoulders. "Your work is yours, as mine is my own. We don't need to bring either into this space."

Sarah watched him as he rubbed the bottoms of her feet. "That feels good," she said.

He moved higher to her calves and the backs of her knees. She let her head fall back and instantly he was reminded of her riding him with abandon. He took a deep breath to keep his libido under control and rose to his feet.

He took her mouth in a long, slow kiss. He sensed she was not ready for more and he didn't push. It was an exercise in control, but he took his lead from Sarah.

By the time they returned their attention to their food, it had grown cold. Sarah didn't seem to mind.

They ate on the couch with Sarah's feet propped on his lap. Saafir loved the way she expressed herself. When she was relaxed, she was less guarded and conversation flowed. Everything about Sarah was both refined and comfortable. She told him about her life in the city and she had recommendations for places to eat and landmarks to see.

She skipped over revealing anything too personal. It was Saafir's experience that people who were intensely private had something to hide. What was Sarah hiding?

He felt strongly about her and wanted to learn more about her. That she'd divulged almost nothing added to his curiosity. "Do you have any children?" Saafir asked. Though it might have come up as a security concern sooner, perhaps she had children who lived with their father.

"No."

No elaboration? She didn't say she wanted any or that she didn't want any or that she had planned to have them, but something had happened to change her mind. Saafir trod carefully. "Have you been married before?"

Sarah froze, her fork halfway to her mouth. The walls he had worked to tear down began to rebuild around her.

He'd hit on the delicate part of her life she'd been shielding. He knew it immediately. A dozen emotions played across her face and Saafir tried to interpret them. Perhaps it had been a traumatic marriage. Abusive? Short-lived? Filled with fighting? He waited for her to answer verbally.

She set her fork down and looked at the floor. When she lifted her head, her eyes were filled with pain. "I was married. It ended recently. I mean, the divorce was finalized recently. Our marriage had been over for a long time."

Her voice contained no bitterness, only sadness. "Do you want to tell me about him?"

Sarah shook her head. "I shouldn't. I need to respect his privacy. He's a troubled man." She paused as though considering if she had already said too much. "Perhaps one day I can tell you more about him, but it's difficult because I know he is hurting and there's nothing I can do. I've tried everything."

Her answer had made him more curious. What had happened to her ex-husband to leave such scars on her?

Saafir wanted to share something of himself with Sarah. To give her a piece of his life in exchange for what she had told him. She may feel better knowing she wasn't the only one who had struck out in love. "I've never been married, although in my position, I will be soon."

Sarah inclined her head. "Soon?"

"My advisors are arranging my marriage." The words were accompanied by heavy disappointment. As much as he had accepted his fate and the fact that this was the life he had been given, a soul-deep part of him struggled against it.

Sarah stiffened and swung her feet to the floor, away from him. "You're engaged?"

He rushed to explain and to clear up any misunderstanding. Americans had different notions of what was appropriate for engaged and married couples. "I have not met the woman who's been chosen for me." As such, it was difficult for him to muster any warmth for her.

Sarah blinked at him. "You slept with me and we were just kissing." The words tumbled from her mouth and he heard the shock and confusion in them.

He could see this diving to a bad place quickly. "What you and I have together has nothing to do with my engagement."

Sarah stood. "I don't understand. You slept with me."

Repeating herself was a sure sign she was upset. Saafir would have told her he was planning to marry another woman, but it hadn't seemed relevant when they'd met. During the night they had spent together, Sarah was the only woman in his life, the only woman who mattered. His engagement, while a topic of discussion and political folly in Qamsar, felt distant and removed from his life. It was a duty and one he would honor, but not something he embraced. "I should have mentioned it, though I didn't think it was important."

Sarah glared at him. A full-on, pissed-off glare. "You didn't think it was important. Will you tell her about me?"

He wouldn't give his future wife a list of the women from his past. "Why would I? My history has nothing to do with her. Just like she has nothing to do with you."

It was as if someone had taken a baseball bat to her chest. Sarah let out the air and for a moment her chest hurt worse than her arm did.

Of course Saafir would have a country of single women interested in him. Probably several thousand if she included other countries. She hadn't thought about it until now, but it was shocking to think he'd be single. The decision to sleep with him had been based on emotion and lust without regard for the future. Now that impulsive decision was coming back to bite her.

For so long, Sarah had been thinking and overthinking, and she had embraced doing something she'd wanted to do solely for that reason. She should leave now and cut personal ties with Saafir before anyone else got hurt. Putting herself in the shoes of his fiancée, Sarah felt terrible.

A sharp rap on the door and then it opened. Frederick hurried in. "Excuse me, your excellency."

Saafir appeared mildly annoyed by the interruption, but gestured for Frederick to speak.

"I received a call from the capital. Rabah Wasam's organized a march of fifty thousand people on the capital and is demanding that you be deposed. There's a petition and social media is buzzing about it."

Frederick was already reaching for the remote control. "It's not on the major news networks since it's, as yet, a bloodless protest, but we'll need a response."

"A response to the same baseless demand we've listened to for months?" Saafir jammed a hand through his hair.

"This is the first time the Conservatives have organized a protest this large. They are putting themselves front and center," Frederick said. "We need a response."

What did that mean for Saafir and the trade agreement? Would he abandon negotiations to go home and handle the protest?

Saafir turned to Sarah. "I'm sorry, Sarah. We'll have to reschedule dinner and finish this conversation later. I will ask Adham to escort you to your room."

He pulled her against him in a quick hug and Sarah could feel the muscles bunched and tensed in his back. Though it wasn't the end to the evening she'd hoped for, it was an excuse to leave. On the heels of his emotional bomb about his fiancée, Sarah was glad for the space, though frustrated to leave the conversation unfinished.

She had told Saafir she wasn't interested in problems. As the leader of a nation, his life was filled with them. She should feel happy to leave, but her heart was too heavy to let her believe she could walk away carefree. "Goodbye, Saafir."

She turned to leave and Saafir grabbed her hand, pulling her to him. "Don't say it with so much finality. This is not over."

Wasn't it? What were they doing if Saafir had a fi-ancée waiting for him at home? Sarah didn't have the words to convey the mix of emotions she was feeling. She pulled away without another word. What more could she say on the matter?

Adham met her at the door and walked her down the hall, toward the elevators.

"Does the emir know about your father?" Adham asked.

Sarah stopped and glared at Adham, not liking that he'd dug around about her. Few people knew about her father. He'd wanted to keep it that way. "I don't discuss my father. As far as I'm concerned, I don't have one and that is none of your business."

"It's my job to protect the emir. That means pro-tecting him physically from harm, but also from com-plications."

"Are you saying I'm a complication?" Sarah asked, not masking the anger in her voice. She took Adham's questions to be openly hostile and she responded as such.

"I'm saying you come with complications and if you stick around, yes, you will be. The emir has money and connections. He doesn't need someone dragging him down because they're needy. What will keep your fa-ther from coming around if he thinks he can get some-thing from the emir?"

Sarah pressed her lips together over the rant that sprung to mind. When she spoke, she kept the frost in her voice. "Like I said, Saafir and I are friends. I guess you think digging around my past for dirt gives you leverage, or maybe you're trying to scare me away. I'm not interested in hurting Saafir or using him or taking his money. That's never been my intention. I don't have an angle. And if my father decided for the first time to acknowledge that I am his daughter, I hardly think that gives him any influence over Saafir. I don't even have any influence over Saafir." Adham must know about the emir's fiancée. He must know that Sarah played a temporary role in his life.

Adham's eyes were black with emotion and she wasn't sure how to read him. She didn't sense a physical threat from him, but she sensed he would go to great lengths to protect Saafir from danger, and Adham considered her a danger.

Finally he spoke. "I don't want the captain hurt. He is a good man and he's coping with a lot. He has women throw themselves at him everywhere we go. Women who think it would be fun to be a princess. I was surprised the emir took you to his hotel room. It was a one-off for him. That tells me I can't dismiss you and if you're sticking around, I need to know who I'm dealing with."

Sarah heard something in Adham's words. A warmth for the man he called captain. Only that kept her from saying something unladylike and storming away. "Don't worry about me sticking around. I know he's planning to marry someone else. When he leaves America, I'll say goodbye and it will be the last you'll hear from me."

Chapter 5

"Please convey to Alaina and her family my most sincere apologies and host their visit," Saafir said to his brother Mikhail over the phone. He felt like he'd been apologizing to most of the women in his life tonight.

Saafir had planned to fly home at the end of the week, but with the delays in the trade agreement committee meetings, his plans had changed and he had to postpone his return. He wouldn't arrive in time for the dinner to meet Alaina and her family.

"What do you want me to tell her?" Mikhail asked, sounding unsure.

Mikhail had been unusually reserved since abdicating his position as emir. It was as if the incident had smoothed the hard edges of Mikhail's personality. Saafir wasn't sure he liked the change in his older brother. He wanted the fire in his brother again. Ideally, that fire would burn in support of Qamsar and for progress and positive change, but anything except the quiet, subservient brother was an improvement.

"Tell her the truth. I am sure she has seen the news reports about why I'm in America. I will meet her and her family as soon as possible," Saafir said. He wasn't being entirely forthcoming about his reasons for staying in America. Part of his reason was the trade summit. The other part was Sarah. If he returned to Qamsar and met Alaina, his life would change. He would be engaged and need to close the door on his relationship with Sarah. He wasn't ready to do that.

He could have delegated responsibilities to Frederick for the trade agreement meetings and stayed in touch over email and by phone, but in person was better. In person made it easier to read body language and tone and watch the reactions of the people around him. They had enough language problems and cultural differences without adding the physical distance of thousands of miles.

"Would you like me to cancel the evening?" Mikhail asked.

It wasn't like his brother to ask questions. Mikhail liked giving directions and was politically savvy enough to maneuver without needing step-by-step instructions. Hosting Alaina's family at the royal family's country home, even if Saafir couldn't be in attendance, was more polite than canceling. Given the purpose of his engagement to Alaina, he didn't want to offend her father.

"What do you think is better?" Saafir asked. He wanted Mikhail to make a decision and to take control of something—anything. Maybe it would boot him out of the misery he'd been wallowing in.

Mikhail let out his breath. "I will invite Mother to dinner, as well. Alaina's family will see we are serious about the match and that we are not insulting Alaina or her family."

Saafir agreed with his brother's plan. "Great idea." Also, it would give Alaina a taste of what life might be like as the emir's wife: interruptions, rescheduling and priority changes. If she chose not to travel with him, they might not have the opportunity to see each other often.

"We've been worried about you," Mikhail said.

An uncharacteristic display of concern from his brother. "I've got things under control." His PR team was doing damage control on Wasam's protest and keeping the media abreast of the trade agreement's progress.

"You can see how easy it is to lose track of problems and how rapidly complications arise," Mikhail said.

Saafir heard something in his voice, as if he were seeking empathy. He and his brother had never directly addressed what had happened to Mikhail. "I never thought it was an easy job. Now, I know it's very difficult."

"I'll handle Alaina and her family," Mikhail said, sounding more confident.

"Let me know how it goes," Saafir said. "I need to go. I have a meeting." His call waiting was beeping, his phone was vibrating with new texts and his email account was filling with incoming messages. Everyone wanted to speak with him about the government's reaction to Rabah Wasam's protest and his campaign to smear Saafir and his family. Though Saafir's staff was fielding most of the requests, he was facing a late night.

The position of emir wasn't glamorous. He hadn't been blessed with the wisdom to solve the country's problems with ease as his father had seemed to. He needed someone to act as a sounding board, someone without an agenda and without biases.

Sarah. The person he needed now was Sarah. She was easy to talk to and speaking to her had a calming and clarifying effect on his thoughts.

But Sarah was out of reach. Her expression when he'd told her about his engagement had been a hundred knives to his chest. She didn't understand the culture and she didn't want to get involved. What could he say to change her mind? They had no future together and he couldn't offer her anything except in the present.

Saafir cursed his luck. He had to keep his distance from the woman he wanted to speak with the most.

Sarah wrestled with her feelings for Saafir. Not see-ing him for the last two days hadn't made her forget and had put into focus an emotion she'd hoped would never rear its head: longing. Sarah missed him. Saafir was out of her league and unreachable in many ways. A king of his nation, an international leader and a crit-ical figure in the trade agreement… His time was at a premium, his resources extensive and his life was mapped out for him. People were counting on him to make good decisions and lead his country into a bet-ter future.

Why was she even considering seeing him again? The only place where they stood on common ground was in the bedroom. The chemistry between them was so right. Those gloriously hot kisses, those fiery touches and the tender way he whispered to her in the dark created a combination she found irresistible. Saafir made her feel like a desirable woman, a description she hadn't used for herself in a long time.

Why had she found those qualities in a man she couldn't have a future with? Saafir was the first man she had dated post-divorce and that had disaster stamped all over it. She wouldn't label their relationship as a rebound, but she was certainly dragging around enough baggage to weigh them both down.

Was she destined to be irrevocably attracted to men who were wrong for her? She needed to find a put-together, uncomplicated, boring man and fall in love with him. Except somehow those safe guys didn't light her fire. Those guys didn't make her feel the heat and burn of desire.

Saafir was engaged to another woman and knowing it hurt more than it should. Getting closer to Saafir would end badly. If she found out anything about the trade agreement, she'd told Owen she would report it, and she didn't want to be in that position. When Saafir left the United States, Sarah would again be alone, and unlike before she'd met him, this time, what she was missing would be plainly in focus: companionship, passion and excitement.

But her reason for staying away was simpler than Saafir's engagement or her promise to Owen. She was staying away from Saafir because she was afraid. Not everything was meant to last forever, but she couldn't be in another relationship that ended in a burning wreck.

Mentally replaying the time she'd spent with Saa-

fir ignited a spark of longing in her body. Lust mud-
dled her thinking and suddenly, she had to see him.
She wasn't a slave to her emotions, but pretending she
could stay away from him when she knew he was in
the same city was futile and would end with her in his
arms. She couldn't help herself.

Saafir was in the middle of a national crisis, but
even emirs needed a break. Perhaps she could convince
Saafir to step away for a few minutes.

Sarah hadn't spoken to him since she'd rushed out
of his hotel room. Making up her mind, Sarah fresh-
ened up in the hotel bathroom and decided she would
drop in on the emir and see if he missed her as much
as she was missing him.

Saafir took another sip of tea and stared out the
window of his hotel room. It had been close to forty-
eight hours since Rabah Wasam had led a protest at
the Capitol building, demanding that Saafir step down.

For the first time since becoming emir, Saafir questioned if it was wise to proceed with the trade agreement with America. He wanted progress for Qamsar.
He wanted the people of his nation to sell their goods
on the international marketplace and have opportuni-
ties to grow their businesses. He wanted the money
from oil sales to improve the country's schools, roads,
prisons and libraries. He wanted public services available to those who needed them. Those things required
money and resources Qamsar didn't have at present.

While he and his siblings had not faced a single day
of poverty in their lives, he knew what life in Qamsar
was like for the lowest economic groups. As a young-
ster, he had once lied to his parents about his plans and

ventured alone into the nearest city. What he'd found there had shocked and angered him.

He had seen children in dirty clothing playing unsupervised on the streets instead of attending school, mothers begging for coins and food, and older people moving slowly in the heat of the day, trying to find shade as they panhandled. The houses in that part of the city were run-down and small and crushed together, windows and doors closed and shades drawn to hinder the heat. Depression and desperation hung over everything and everyone.

Saafir had wanted to observe for as long as he could, but two policemen on patrol had spotted and recognized him. He had been returned to the compound and his father had pressed upon him how dangerous it was for him to leave the safety of their home without the proper security escort.

Progress and changes had been made in Qamsar since then. Those tiny villages had been torn down and more modern apartment buildings constructed in their place. Jobs in factories, fisheries and textiles were more common than herding goats or working the near-barren fields for food. His father had made plans to exploit the oil fields to advance the country's wealth, but he had died before he had seen them to completion.

The task of driving the country forward had fallen to Mikhail and now to Saafir.

Renewed by the memory of his father's vision, Saafir felt the moment of doubt pass, and recommitted to his duties. He couldn't back off from the trade agreement. Too much was at stake. Saafir didn't want his countrymen hurt by destructive acts of protestors, but he wouldn't cave to the demands of Rabah Wasam, whose motives were driven by revenge. Halting the trade agreement would make the statement that the royal family was breakable when pressed hard enough. In its current fragile state, they couldn't afford to show weakness.

Saafir swirled his tea. It had long ago gone cold. His body ached. A doctor had assessed him earlier in the day as a follow-up to the shooting and said he needed more rest. Finding rest was difficult. At night, when he lay in bed, sleep eluded him. He had the welfare of an entire nation sitting on his shoulders. It was difficult to know the right actions to take and it was getting harder and harder to see around corners. The last good night of sleep he'd had was spent with Sarah.

Sarah. She crossed his mind more than she should. She had not returned his calls, at least not to his knowledge. He had been busy and not the easiest to get through to. But he wouldn't press her by showing up at her hotel room or cornering her. If she didn't want to see him again, he'd find a way to accept that.

His phone rang and he answered it. "Yes."

"Your excellency." The words were spoken as a sneer. Saafir's suspicion spiked.

"Who is this?" Saafir asked.

"Don't you recognize your old pal's voice?"

Rabah Wasam.

"I thought we should have a chance to talk directly," Wasam said.

Saafir hadn't spoken to Wasam in years. How had Wasam gotten his number? It was a temporary one while he was staying in this hotel. Wasam had resources and this phone call was a show of how much he knew about Saafir's movements and how extensive his network was. "What do you want, Wasam?"

"I've made it clear what I want. I want you to cease bargaining with a country of infidels and step down as emir."

"For someone without a lot of power, you're making some big demands," Saafir said, hoping to bait Wasam into admitting the role he'd played in recent events, enough that he could jail him without public backlash.

"I am not making these demands alone. I am making them as the leader of the Conservatives. We are hundreds of thousands strong. We have an international reach. Perhaps you need a display of my reach and power to see that I am serious. I am willing to do what is necessary to protect Qamsar."

Saafir didn't want Wasam instructing his followers to take action against the people of Qamsar or the Americans. Some were stupid enough to follow them without regard to their lives or others. "I know you are serious. You don't need to prove anything to me."

"Royals are all the same. You want your special treatments and your pampering. When it comes time for the real work, you're useless. Step down and let a real man take over."

Saafir had once held a great deal of sympathy for the man who had lost his leg in a military operation in which Saafir had taken part. But Wasam's thirst for revenge against those he believed were responsible was too great. He could only see his anger and his resentment and had lost the ability to have a balanced perspective.

"Our country needs us to band together," Saafir

said. He should disconnect the call. Only the slim ray of guilt and sympathy for Wasam kept him on the phone.

"Our country needs me to lead them out of the darkness and into the light. You're a fool to believe that a progressive direction is a good direction. When America owns every one of our streets, what will you do then? When they're making you dance like a puppet, who will help you? You're being their willing pawn and everyone will see the truth."

Saafir had heard these accusations before. His intel monitored Rabah Wasam and his website and various social networks to keep tabs on him. "You are letting your past cloud your judgment. This agreement will help Qamsar."

"My past? You mean the time I spent in prison being tortured nightly while you walked free?" Wasam yelled.

Wasam was losing control. His temper was on a hair trigger and it wasn't Saafir's intention to rile him. The consequences of Wasam unleashing his rage had a ripple effect. "We can meet and I can help you to understand how this agreement will help—"

Rabah Wasam disconnected the call. He was likely worried that Saafir was tracing it. Saafir had no intention of going after Wasam directly until he had more intel on the man and his movements. Saafir needed a way to defuse the conflict without massive bloodshed and a revolution inside Qamsar's borders.

Adham entered his open office door. "Captain, Sarah's here to see you. She's waiting in the hallway."

Sarah? After not seeing her for what seemed like an eternity, he hungered for her. The mention of her name ignited his senses and expectation plowed through him.

He'd been carrying a torch for her, hoping she would return. Speaking to Wasam had him on edge, and his stress level was too high. Talking to her and seeing her would make it better. It wouldn't change Wasam or the problems his country faced, but she eased him.

"You want to take over here and let me take a break with Sarah?" Saafir asked Adham, pointing to his side of the desk.

A half joke. In a different world that acknowledged all children as legitimate, Adham would be in his position. Though he and Adham had only spoken of it a few times, Saafir often pondered the leader that Adham would make. He had been a leader in the army and a true Qamsarian Warrior, one of the few with almost pure bloodlines. With his family ties, he was an obvious choice as the emir's lead guard, even if his position did not allow him to use his talents to the fullest.

Adham lifted his brow. "I have no interest in being the emir, even for an hour. A twist of fate I consider a gift that I am here and you are there. I don't need to ask, since I know the answer by your expression, but do you want to see her?"

He did. Desperately. He couldn't turn her away. His body and his heart beckoned to her. Even if she were here in some official capacity, Saafir wanted to talk to her.

Growing up, Saafir had known his wife would be handpicked for him by his parents. The woman he had been promised to when he was three years of age had died in a car accident a few years before they had planned to wed. Parveen was a stranger to Saafir, though he'd mourned for her family and their difficult loss. Arranging his marriage after Parveen's death hadn't been a priority for his parents though Saafir knew his marriage would be to another woman who had the same status and credentials. Never to someone like Sarah. His wonderful Sarah.

"Please tell her to come in," Saafir said.

Half a minute later, Sarah entered carrying a white box tied with red-and-white string. "I have dessert if you have tea."

"Tea can be ordered." Saafir pressed a button on his phone and requested more tea be sent to his suite. He couldn't take his eyes off her. She looked enticing in a purple dress with a low neckline and skirt that hugged her body.

Sarah sat across from him, the desk between them. She set the box on the top of the desk and untied it. When she opened the lid, the scent of sweet pastries filled the room.

"My favorites. How did you know?" Saafir asked.

Sarah smiled. "I'm your event coordinator. I'm paid to know what you like." She blushed. "What you like to eat, that is."

She knew what he liked in the bedroom, as well. She'd proven that. "Is this a parting gift or a peace offering?" he asked, trying to read her intentions.

"A little of both," she said. "I know this will end. I know it can't go anywhere. If I see you for personal reasons, we have to do it behind closed doors, in secret and accept it won't lead to a future. But I've been thinking about you. I'm not ready to say goodbye."

"Nothing has changed with my marriage plans," he said, needing to be clear. He didn't want to hurt Sarah.

"After my disastrous marriage, I'm in no hurry to rush into a serious relationship." She paused as if checking her words. "I realize you're the leader of a country. It's not something I can conceptualize, but I know you have responsibilities to others that may overshadow personal plans."

If he wasn't the emir, he would have made different choices over the last several months. "What are you suggesting?"

Sarah sighed. "I'm suggesting we do what feels right and that what we do stays between us." She nodded over her shoulder. "Although I think Adham knows more than he should."

Adham could be trusted to say nothing on the matter to the public.

A secret affair without expectations of a future was perfect for the moment and yet was sad, too. It highlighted how far out of reach Saafir's personal desires and wants were. Love came second to duty.

"Given what I saw in the news, I thought maybe you could use a friend," Sarah said. She circled the desk and leaned a hip on the edge of it. She crossed her ankles, one over the other, drawing his gaze to her legs. She was wearing shoes with straps that laced up her ankles in a crisscross pattern. He wanted to unwrap her feet, start at her toes and use his hands and mouth on every inch of her body.

He could smell the light, refreshing scent of her skin. The scent brought an immediate visceral reaction and reminder of the night they had spent together. Being alone with her, lacking sleep and his country's problems playing on his mind, Saafir wanted the relief of confiding in her. He wanted to tell her what had been going on, let loose the thoughts and decisions running wild in his head.

Saafir couldn't discuss the situation with Rabah Wasam, not when his PR team was working to spin the situation to maintain America's faith in the trade agreement and Qamsar's faith in him. "I have a lot on my mind."

She waited for him to continue.

"I tried calling you," he said.

"I tried calling you, too. You are a difficult man to reach."

He'd have to give out instructions that her messages were sent through with higher priority, or better, her calls forwarded to him immediately. "I'll tell my staff to make sure you can reach me," he said. "I'll tell them you could have a food-related emergency that needs to be addressed immediately."

Sarah pursed her lips. "Are you making fun of my job?"

"Not at all. Just trying to keep our cover," he said. If she wanted their liaison to remain a secret, he would honor her request.

"I'm here now. Tell me what's going on."

He had too much to say and it was hard to find a place to start. He spoke the first thing that came to mind. "You know my brother stepped down as emir. I'd been working on other things and then this big wave swallowed me up. I've been swimming, but I'm paddling against a tsunami. I feel like I need to keep going, but I'm not sure where exactly I'm trying to go."

It was the first time he had spoken the words to anyone and the dam of his restraint collapsed. He had been presenting a certain face to the world and he hadn't had the time to consider how it was wearing on him.

"Every time I get some distance and make progress, another wave hits me and drags me back."

"By all accounts, you're doing a great job," Sarah said.

"There's an entire political party devoted to forcing me out of power and some people are trying to kill me," Saafir said, thinking of the Conservative party and the extremists.

Sarah pressed her lips together. "That sounds bad when you phrase it that way, but no leader has a one-hundred-percent approval rating. Political analysts say you're doing the right things. World humanitarian organizations are on your side. Economists believe the decisions you are making will help Qamsar. I think you're doing a good job with the economy. You're making the decisions that will lead your country somewhere better."

Saafir didn't hear an agenda in her voice. He heard honesty. It sounded like she was aware of the situation. She must have been reading about him in the media. "How do you know so much about political analysts and economists?"

She blushed. "I looked you up on the internet. Not just your food preferences this time. This time I read the heavy stuff. The stuff that made me wish I had paid better attention in social studies to understand."

She took his tie between her hands and played with it. Heat flamed across his body. He could bend her shapely body over the desk and make love to her. Pull her into his lap on this chair. Carry her to his bedroom and stretch out beside her on the bed. The possibilities were endless.

His heart rate escalated. As close as she was, his

palms ached to reach out and touch her, to run his hand over her fair skin, to slide his hand around the back of her neck and draw her close to him. He gripped the chair handles harder to keep from grabbing her. He wanted her to make the first move. She had come to his hotel room, but he'd give her every opportunity to change her mind. Once she started something, he wouldn't stop.

"You're a good man and this is a tough situation. You're under pressure. No one can withstand it without some release," she said.

Saafir ran a hand over his face. Pressure was part of the job. "Since I took over for Mikhail, I haven't had a day off. I haven't taken a vacation. Qamsar needs me and I am honored to serve. But this wasn't the life I expected. Before I was emir, I started every day meditating. Now the day starts with someone telling me the problems that developed overnight that need to be addressed even before I've had breakfast."

Sarah nodded in understanding. She dropped his tie. "You're the leader of your country. If you don't like something, change it."

Saafir met her gaze and held it. "I am a servant to the people. I make decisions thinking first of their prosperity, their happiness and their needs."

"What about your needs? What keeps you sane?" she asked. Her hands moved to his shoulders and down his arms. Back up again.

Saafir stood and raked her with his gaze. His thoughts turned to her more often than they should. His country was in crisis and he was thinking about Sarah, her curvy body and the seductive way she moved. She didn't even know how sexy she was. The more he tried not to think about her, the more he found her in his thoughts. Their attraction was an inconvenience to her. To him, it was unexpected and downright impossible to ignore. "Having you in my private office is not helping me stay sane. Touching me is not making this easier. It's making me want to kiss you." He wanted to take her into his arms with the pent-up emotions that had been running hot in his blood from the moment he'd met her. He'd pull her against him, take off all their clothes and not let go until they were both sated. Once, twice, a dozen times—whatever it took.

Sarah's lips parted. Shock? Invitation? Sarah skimmed her hand down the side of his face. The caress set his lust wild.

"What's stopping you?" she asked.

Her question pushed his desire for her over the edge. He could no more keep his distance than he could stop breathing. He pulled her tight against him, and shifted his pelvis to press his arousal against the V of her legs. She had to know just how much he wanted her. Rocking against her, he read the excitement in her widened eyes and in the firm grip she had on his shoulders. Possessiveness roared inside him. He had to have this woman. She had to belong to him. "While you are mine, I will treat you like a princess. I will spoil you for every other man. You will think of me and the nights we spend together long after I'm gone. Is that what you want?"

She nodded, the corners of her mouth turning up. "As long as you know the same."

He loved her spunk. "I want you to say the words," he said. "Say my name and tell me what you want me to do to you."

"I want you, Saafir."

"To do what?" he asked, running his hand between them, pressing his fingers close to her core.

She said a phrase that was hot and dirty. He had never been this hard, his arousal straining against the zipper of his pants. He wanted to be free and he wanted to be inside her.

Bringing his lips to hers, he let them brush against hers for a long, slow moment. Then he deepened the kiss. This was his opportunity to have this woman and he would take it and enjoy it as the gift it was.

Sarah sat back on his desk and spread her legs. He pushed her tight dress up her thighs, tempted to rip it off. Her skin was soft and her hair like silk between his fingers. She smelled of cinnamon. The scent of her perfume would cling to his clothes for hours.

A knock on the door. "Room service." The tea he'd ordered.

"Leave it outside," he said.

He turned his full attention to Sarah. She was breathing hard, her chest rising and falling, her skin flushed. Burning with need, he kissed a trail from behind her ear to her collarbone and he ran his hands over her delicate skin. He skimmed a hand down the side of her breast.

She shivered and clasped the sides of his face so he was looking into her eyes. While she studied him, he waited for her to speak. She said nothing and pushed forward off the desk. He took a step back and bit off a groan as she turned and bent over his desk, spreading her feet and wiggling her hips. Clasping her hips in his hand, he mimicked exactly what he planned to do with her.

"How did you know I was thinking about this?" he asked.

She looked over her shoulder, her brown hair swinging to the side. "I guessed."

He lowered the zipper on the back of her dress, tugging the dress over her arms and dropping the dark fabric to the ground. She stepped out of it. She was wearing a pink lace thong.

Excitement tweaked at his body where her backside pressed against his hardness. A sharp knock at the door. Room service again?

"Later," he said, unable to take his eyes off that backside and the way the pink scrap of fabric disappeared.

"Captain."

Adham stepped into the room and averted his eyes to the ceiling. Saafir pushed Sarah behind him, blocking her near-naked body. Of all the times to be interrupted, this was not it. "This better be life or death."

"We need to leave," Adham said.

Saafir noted the alarm in Adham's voice. He wouldn't question Adham when time could be of the essence. "Sarah, let's go."

She was already pulling on her dress. "What's wrong? Is there another shooter?" Fear was taut in her voice. Saafir helped her zip up her dress, cursing their luck. Asking for time alone was a heavy request, but he had hoped to carve out at least half an hour for them.

"A journalist is in the lobby pressing the front desk for information about you. We have you both registered under assumed names, but she knows you're here. If she knows, others know," Adham said.

He handed Saafir a bulletproof vest, a holster and

gun. Adham handed a vest to Sarah. She slid it over her slim shoulders. She was in danger because of him and Saafir hated that. A man should provide safety for his woman, not bring peril to her doorstep.

"Why do I need to wear this?" Sarah said. Saafir adjusted the vest to fit her.

"It's a precaution," Saafir said.

"This seems like more than a precaution," Sarah said.

Saafir took her hand in his and kissed the back of it. "I will keep you safe. That is my vow to you."

They were in the hallway, moving away from the elevators and toward the stairwell within minutes. Saafir took Sarah's elbow, trying to convey she was safe. "We'll be okay. Adham is the best at what he does. This is just a precaution so there aren't any further incidents."

Sarah glanced at Adham, wariness in her eyes. The same distrust he had for her, she seemed to have for him.

They entered the metal-and-concrete stairwell. A few flights down, they heard voices. Saafir opened the door to the fourth floor and ushered Sarah inside to avoid whoever was on the stairs. Adham followed him. It could be guests of the hotel or it could be the reporters.

"Someone will see us," Sarah said.

"Hopefully not," Saafir said.

They didn't wait around to find out. They rushed down the hall to another set of stairs. Adham looked inside and they listened for noise. It was quiet. "Let's move," he said.

They took the stairs to the parking area under the hotel.

Saafir wasn't claustrophobic, but being underground with the lack of light, the low ceiling and the shadows made him tense and edgy. They could be cornered or shot at from between any of the hundreds of cars jammed in the area. His training in urban warfare had made him wary of places where attackers could hide.

"Keep your head down," Saafir said, tucking Sarah against him.

They followed Adham, staying low. When they reached a running, nondescript black sedan at the stairwell exit, Adham opened the door. Adham put Saafir between the concrete wall of the garage and himself. Saafir helped Sarah into the car. Once Adham was inside, they drove out of the parking garage and away from the hotel.

Sarah was shaking. Saafir clasped her hands. She drew them away from him.

"This keeps happening," she said.

"The men after me will not give up easily," Saafir said. "We are working to get control of the situation."

Sarah stared at him. "Working to get control? I'm not someone who needs the PR spin. Just tell me the truth."

She touched her shoulder where she'd been hurt. Saafir's chest ached. He had drawn her into this.

"I'll keep you safe. Let me get you a drink," Saafir said, gesturing to the small refrigerator in the car.

Sarah nodded. "Water, please."

Saafir took out a bottle of water, opened it and poured it into a glass. He handed the glass to Sarah.

Adham knocked and then rolled down the window

between the front seat and them. "We're clearing the reporter from the lobby and we're relocating every member of the committee who was staying in this hotel."

Sarah let her head fall against the car seat. "I should
start carrying my suitcase around with me like a
nomad."

Someone would collect their personal items from
their rooms and find a way to get them to him and
Sarah, but it was an inconvenience.

"I hate to see you this way. What can I do to make
you feel more comfortable?" Saafir asked.

Sarah interlaced their fingers. "You said you would
protect me. I want to believe that. But I know what
you're up against. You can't defend me or yourself
when you don't know exactly who is doing this or what
they are planning."

He tried not to take offense at her words, but imply-
ing he couldn't protect her didn't sit well with him. "I
oversee one of the best intelligence-gathering agencies
in the world. We know who is laying claim to these
attacks, and we're working to infiltrate his group to
find out more."

"Is it Rabah Wasam? The man leading the protest
in Qamsar?"

Saafir wouldn't lie to her. Making a public accusation against Wasam for the shooting would be akin to
a declaration of war, but he could trust Sarah with his
thoughts. "I believe so."

"Why does he hate you?"

"Captain," Adham said, warning in his voice.
Adham wouldn't want him to tell Sarah the story. It
had been kept out of the media, except in rumors and
whispers.

Saafir could tell his story and leave Adham out of it. "Wasam and I served in the urban assault unit in Qamsar. We were trained in urban warfare and intelligence gathering to combat terrorist infiltration. We received word that we were being sent on an important mission. Our company was split and half were being sent into combat. My father arranged for me to stay behind so that I wouldn't see action and be at risk."

"Wasam was sent into battle and blamed you?" Sarah asked.

Saafir shook his head. "I was furious with my father for benching me from an important mission and Wasam hated the nepotism that could save my life. We secretly switched places. When my father found out, he charged Wasam as a criminal and put him in prison."

Sarah eyes were wide. "He blames you for the prison time?"

"He does. It took me six months to convince my father the plot had been mine and that Wasam was innocent." Six months and threats as extreme as disowning his family. "When Wasam was freed, the damage was done." Though Wasam had declared himself Saafir's mortal enemy, Saafir still harbored guilt over what had been done to Wasam. "He'd been starved and beaten and lost the use of his leg."

Sarah gasped. "What did your father say?"

"About what?" Saafir asked. Once his father had doled out a punishment, he hadn't liked going back on his word, much less apologizing or trying to make reparations for his decisions. "I was lucky Wasam was freed."

"That's why you've revamped the country's prison system," Sarah said.

It was part of the reason. "I have a personal interest in prison reform. I lost a friend, made an enemy and learned a terrible lesson about the consequences of lying."

It was a lesson that haunted him to this day. Though Saafir had wanted to put the incident behind them, Wasam wasn't on the same page. He wouldn't stop until he'd had his vengeance and to Wasam, that meant Saafir dead.

Sarah wanted to return to her home, her home before it had been destroyed. She wanted her soft bed, her big bathtub and her comfortable couch. She wanted to walk around barefoot and shower in her bathroom. Managing meetings and organizing the caterers and conference room setups were proving more stressful when she could only rely on her phone and the data she had saved inside it. Though the security team assembled for the trade agreement committee had taken over arranging hotel accommodations, the constant changing of meeting locations made her job harder. The security team wanted to release the name of the site as close to the meeting time as possible to mitigate the possibility of a breach, but it meant Sarah was scrambling every day to keep up.

Sarah fought the frustration that made her feel like punching someone. She was tired, over-emotional and scared. She didn't have anyone to whom she could direct her anger, although Rabah Wasam was sounding like a good candidate.

The incident in Saafir's office had turned her on fiercely and then she'd been doused in fear. It was an unsettling place to be.

"Wasam played an equal role in what happened to him," Sarah said. She hated to hear adults blaming the consequences of their actions on others. It was how Alec had justified so many of his terrible decisions.

"He doesn't see it that way," Saafir said.

Saafir's expression was dark and serious. His brown eyes were rimmed with exhaustion and sadness. His thumb rubbed hers almost absently. She wished she had come to see him sooner.

"We can ask our American counterparts to suggest a place to stay," Saafir said.

"No," Adham said. "If there's a leak of information, it's not from us. Nibal is dead and there are no other plants."

Sarah felt an accusation in the words. Was Adham blaming her for the assassination attempt and the problems with security? Or Americans in general?

"No one took a shot at me until I was with Saafir," Sarah said, feeling her blood pressure rise. The threat had to be from someone in Qamsar who'd followed the emir to American soil.

"There are many who seek to harm the emir," Adham said. "Some are Qamsarian and some are foreign."

Sarah narrowed her eyes at him.

"I thought you didn't want to spend time with the emir outside your meetings," Adham said.

Had Saafir spoken to Adham about their relationship or was he perceptive? "I changed my mind." It was her prerogative and since Saafir wasn't complaining, Adham didn't need to be involved.

"I think it's worth noting that you come around and then we have a security problem," Adham said.

"Adham, that's enough. Sarah has nothing to do with the problems we've had. I have many enemies. It's too soon to know who is responsible for this," Saafir said. He sounded firm, but tired.

Adham gave her a long look, letting her know he wasn't directing his suspicions away from her.

"It could be an inside job," Sarah said, feeling her temper get the better of her.

Saafir didn't say anything, but she regretted the words when she saw the hurt in his eyes. His recent family history was filled with betrayals and hidden agendas. A veiled accusation aimed at Adham was a low blow.

"Saafir, I'm sorry. I didn't mean to accuse anyone."

Saafir slipped his arms around her shoulders bringing her against him. He kissed her temple. "I know you didn't mean any harm."

Sarah buried her face against him, feeling like she could shut out the rest of the world. Forget the media and Adham and Wasam. She was with Saafir, a man who made her feel alive and excited and safe. He was carrying around so much on his shoulders, she wished she could take some of the burden or help in some way.

Inspiration struck. "I know a place where I can spend the night," Sarah said.

All eyes turned to her.

"My former sister-in-law has a houseboat." No one would think to look for her there. She and Evelyn had remained friendly after her split from Alec, but Evelyn wasn't someone she associated with frequently.

"Does she have room for all of us?" Adham asked.

Sarah hadn't meant to suggest she, Saafir, Adham and the other two guards take over Evelyn's boat. "If you don't mind sleeping under the stars." Near the dock were a trailer park and a camping area.

"A night off the grid could help," Saafir said. "Whoever is tracking us will lose the trail."

"I don't want to put Evelyn in danger," Sarah said, thinking through her suggestion.

Adham stiffened. "I can give you my personal guarantee we will remain vigilant for the duration."

Adham could be prickly and surly at times, but Sarah saw glimpses of the warrior in him. If he promised to keep Evelyn safe, he would do it.

Sarah called Evelyn and Evelyn was happy to host them. Evelyn was a lot like Alec, and Sarah enjoyed most of those similarities. Unfortunately, one of those shared traits was Evelyn's propensity to drink. Though her drinking hadn't landed her in the trouble Alec's had, Sarah worried about Evelyn.

"Thank you," Saafir said.

"You're welcome. I'm just doing my job."

"This is more than your job," Saafir said. "This was an inspired idea."

Sarah blushed under his praise. He made her feel like she had solved a great mystery of the world. How did he manage to make her feel special for something so simple?

Evelyn's boat was docked on the Chesapeake Bay in a private community made of trailers and houseboats. It was quiet when they arrived. The sound of water lapping against the shore was melodic and comforting.

They parked and walked along the dock to Evelyn's boat.

"Well, well, aren't you a sight for sore eyes. Welcome," Evelyn said, greeting them from her boat. In her hand was a wine glass mostly filled. She took a swig of her drink and waved them aboard.

Sarah hugged Evelyn. "Thank you for letting us stay with you. We've run into some problems."

"You were vague on the phone, but I know trouble when I hear it. Please, come and I'll show you around. The grand tour takes less than two minutes."

Ten minutes later, Adham and one of the guards were asleep on Evelyn's guest bunk beds; the other guard was situated on the boat, facing the dock, not drawing attention to himself, but staying alert. Saafir, Evelyn and Sarah sat on the main deck in canvas-backed beach chairs. Evelyn had offered everyone a glass of wine and Saafir had declined.

"You picked someone who's about as different as can be from Alec," Evelyn said. She looked between Sarah and Saafir. "I'm not sticking my nose into someone else's love life, but I've seen the news, I know who you are."

"It's important that no one know we're here," Sarah said. Evelyn knew how to keep a secret, but when the wine started flowing, Evelyn could be loose-lipped.

"I don't want to invite trouble," Evelyn said. "I have enough troubles."

Sarah questioned her decision to bring Saafir and his guards here. But where else was she safe? Her social circle was small and whoever was looking for Saafir could easily connect him to Sarah and then to Molly, Krista or Owen. Because Evelyn didn't live in Washington, D.C., and because Sarah didn't see her as often, Sarah hoped the distance kept anyone from tracing them to Evelyn's place. Besides, they were staying for one night. How quickly could the men hunting them find them?

"I appreciate that you've opened your home to us," Saafir said to Evelyn.

"I owe Sarah after what she's done for Alec."

Sarah didn't want Evelyn to elaborate. She had told Saafir she had been married, but talking about Alec was a delicate subject. Those wounds were deep and hadn't quite healed.

"I visited him the other week," Evelyn said. "It was family day at the center and Alec's been there long enough to be allowed visitors. He was hoping you'd come."

Guilt stabbed at her and she wished Evelyn wouldn't talk about Alec, especially not now, not today. Sarah had cut Alec from her life forcefully and purposefully. "I told him I wouldn't." Everyone involved in the situation had agreed she needed to stay away. Why then the overwhelming sense of self-blame every time someone spoke of Alec?

"That's what I told him, too," Evelyn said. "But you know how bullheaded he can be. He surprised me by showing up here about a week ago."

A week ago? Had Alec left rehab? "Did he quit the program?" Sarah asked, worry heavy in her stomach.

"He had a momentary lapse in judgment. Owen had to pull some serious strings to have the program overlook his leaving and agree to keep him in and not turn him over to the police," Evelyn said.

Sarah couldn't hide her annoyance. Evelyn was describing classic Alec: impulsive and thrill-seeking with no regard for his safety, the consequences or how his actions hurt others. "I'm glad he's sticking with it." She glanced at Saafir. He was listening, but she couldn't get a read on his face. She hadn't wanted Saafir to know about her ex's substance abuse issues.

"He wants to see you," Evelyn said. "I told him he had to stay in rehab."

Evelyn and Alec were twins. They were close. While Sarah and Alec had been married, she and Evelyn had been good friends. After she had filed for divorce from Alec, Evelyn had supported her. But when Sarah had begun to move on with her life, tension had grown between the two women. It was as if Evelyn had wanted Sarah to use the divorce as a threat to help Alec get and stay clean, but she still wanted Sarah to stick around and patch things up down the road with him.

Sarah had known ending her marriage would mean losing the people who'd become her family, but she hadn't expected how much it would hurt to look at the people she cared about across the chasm of divorce, knowing she would never be as close with them.

"Alec knows I'm not part of his life, and until he gets clean, we can't be friends." She glanced at Saafir. She expected him to look either uncomfortable or to be looking away. It was how most people reacted when Sarah spoke of Alec and his problems.

Instead, he was watching her, curiosity written on his face.

Evelyn changed the subject to her life on the boat and her plans for the summer. The next couple of hours passed in easy conversation. When she finished her glass of wine, Evelyn said good-night, leaving Sarah and Saafir alone.

Saafir hadn't said much during the conversation. This far away from the city lights, the sky was filled with stars and Saafir was reclining in his chair, watching them.

"I feel like I need to explain about Alec," Sarah said. The smell of citronella wafted from the candle burning on the nearby table.

"No need," Saafir said. "You don't owe me an explanation for anything. You have a life and I have no right to pry into any part of it."

Didn't he have questions? Most people who knew about Alec couldn't grasp what they had gone through. They usually had blame for either Alec or her or wanted to know more about his addiction and their marriage. It bothered her that Saafir didn't want to know anything. It seemed to speak to his disinterest in her and it highlighted their affair was a brief one. It was what she had wanted, wasn't it? Could she ask Saafir to care knowing she wouldn't be in his life long? The request was ridiculous and Sarah didn't voice it.

If they had limits, she would learn them and play within them.

"I suppose I only have one question and it's really only relevant because it relates to me," Saafir said.

Sarah waited for the question. She sensed it would be loaded.

"Are you in love with him?" Saafir asked.

"No." It was her gut reaction. She'd thought about that question before she'd filed for divorce. Their romance had withered and most of their marriage had limped along with only their friendship holding it together. When her trust in Alec was broken time and again, that had been destroyed, as well. What remained was a sense of obligation and those words from her marriage vows, "in sickness and in health."

She couldn't allow herself to stay with a man who was killing her, but she'd owed it to him to do whatever she could for as long as she could. "I remember good times with him," she said. "From the first day I met him, Alec was someone who partied hard and drank. He was fun and exciting, and when I was with him, life was a good time. But after a while, it wasn't just drinking. It was pot. Then cocaine. Then being late for work every day. Then not going to his job at all. The DUIs. The arrests. Failed rehab. Relapses. Lies. Financial problems." From others in similar positions she had learned her story was common. The drugs of choice for the addict might be different, but the consequences were as severe.

"I am sorry you went through that." Saafir extended his hand to her and Sarah stood and let him take her in his arms and into his lap. She cuddled against him on the chair, feeling something therapeutic about his non-judgment.

Saafir kissed the top of her head. His arms were wrapped around her waist in a protective, comforting gesture.

When Saafir returned home, he would meet his wife-to-be. Wife-to-be was no doubt beautiful and rich and lacking excessive baggage. Even if Sarah and Saafir stayed in touch over email, their friendship would drift away. An email a day, then once a week, then monthly, then one or two around the holidays. When he was married, having any interaction with him might be inappropriate. Plus, Saafir was the leader of a nation. How much free time did he have? A few hours a week? Those would be spent with his wife and family, not talking to a woman he'd met and had a brief affair with in America.

A mother who'd been estranged from her family and then had died when Sarah was eighteen, a deadbeat father who had never wanted Sarah in his life and a family who she'd lost when she divorced Alec weren't the makings of a great family history.

Though she had been alone for a long time, Sarah wished she had someone stable to hold on to, someone to come home to and call her family.

Chapter 6

Sarah entered the office building carrying in one hand her large soft cooler filled with materials for breakfast and a jug of fresh-brewed coffee in the other. Though she wasn't late, the last-minute change of venue—again—had thrown her. She'd had to travel across town to the caterer's kitchen to pick up the food. Darting around the city was costing her time and adding confusion.

In addition to the trade agreement meetings, which were running longer due to delays, she was coordinating an outdoor wedding that night. She could handle the unexpected and unscheduled overlap of events, but the added stress the trade summit brought left her feeling frazzled. Looking at the sky, she hoped the weather held and the wedding guests weren't forced to stay under the tents she'd rented for the outdoor ceremony and reception. The gardens where the wedding was being held set the stage for a quiet, romantic night.

Sarah was moving quickly, having lost time finding this new meeting location. She tried to calculate how long it would take her to get to the sixth floor by the stairwell or if waiting for the elevator would be easier.

The building had a grand foyer that stretched the length of the offices that ran up along four sides, ten stories high. Medical offices, law offices, insurance groups, financial groups and dozens of businesses were contained here. The nondescript and busy location was the perfect place for the members of the trade agreement committee to blend.

Perhaps Wasam and the extremists would focus on their protest in Qamsar. Owen had mentioned the possibility of everyone returning to their homes by the end of the week if no other problems or threats arose. The security team assembled to handle the situation was considering it. Since he was getting attention in Qamsar, Wasam may have decided to change tactics.

Getting home couldn't happen soon enough. Sarah needed to clean her apartment and bring order back to her life. She felt like she was living someone else's life, a life with a royal boyfriend and a crazy think-on-her-feet job that changed minute to minute. Her detailed plans and preparations were rearranged daily.

Jeff, her guard for the day, was two paces behind her. He had been her shadow all morning and she had started to forget he was with her.

She jumped at a loud noise, the sound of a heavy book falling on the glossy ceramic tile and echoing off the walls.

Sarah turned to check on Jeff and was knocked over.

The jug of coffee fell to the ground, bursting open and splashing hot liquid on her legs. Before she recovered her balance, a hand went around her throat. She was dragged to her feet and something cold pressed to her temple. She dropped the cooler she was carrying.

A gun. Someone was holding a gun to her head. Movement went on around her as if no one else was seeing it.

"Everyone shut up and listen. Get on the ground or I will kill this woman and then open fire on anyone who moves. Do you understand?" An angry male voice Sarah didn't recognize, but with an accent similar to Saafir and Adam's.

She was being held too tight and she couldn't look at the man clutching her against him. He smelled like a gym, sweaty and hot. She pulled on his arm, digging her nails into his skin and trying to force him to release her.

He tightened his hold. "Stop moving or I'll kill you," he whispered into her ear.

It took a few moments for a hush to fall over the lobby. Movement slowed to a halt.

The man holding her yanked her in a three-hundred-sixty-degree turn. Jeff was on the ground, red blood leaking from under his body. A scream rose in her throat and fear tightened her voice. The noise came out strangled. The loud bang she'd heard had been gunfire aimed at Jeff. "Jeff! Please, someone help him!" She struggled to get free, but it was impossible.

No one moved toward Jeff to offer aid, and Sarah thrashed against the man confining her. "Please let me help him. He needs an ambulance." The pool of red was growing larger. Sarah had never seen someone losing so much blood and the sight terrified her. The longer he lay there, the worse it would be. Was it too late? Sarah wouldn't think about Jeff already being dead. Someone would help him.

The attacker tightened his arm around her. "Shut your filthy mouth. I will kill you and then kill everyone in this room." He was shouting, rage heavy in his voice and the words spreading across the silent lobby.

The response was more chaos as people ran for the exits. The man fired his gun three times in the air. Glass shattered and rained to the ground, the pieces rolling and bouncing. Silence fell again. The people remaining in the lobby didn't move.

"Please," Sarah said, trying to move his arm off of her and managing to get a look at his face. "What do you want?"

"Call your boyfriend," the man said.

Saafir. This was one of the men targeting Saafir. From the pictures she had seen of Rabah Wasam, this wasn't him. It was one of his followers. At least as a politician, Wasam had some public accountability for his actions. This man had none.

Sarah wouldn't call Saafir to this lobby to be gunned down. Should she deny Saafir was her boyfriend? Pretend he had the wrong woman? Her life wasn't the only one in danger. "He won't answer if I call. He's in meetings."

The man pressed the gun harder against her head. "You better hope he answers or you're about to have a very bad, final morning."

Saafir hadn't gotten enough sleep and drinking the strongly caffeinated coffee Evelyn had served had given him a headache. He usually didn't drink coffee, for that reason.

Little compromise had been reached on the trade agreement. Owen was doing his best to find middle ground, but Virginia Anderson, the rep from the oil company, was holding fast that Stateside Oil wanted complete control of the oil refinery in Qamsar. Virginia passed around colorful booklets of pie charts and bar graphs to show how the oil company would bring jobs to Qamsar and the United States, how they would provide education and job training, and how they were in the best position to invest in this endeavor.

Charts were useless. Statistics could be made up, skewed and presented in whatever light made one party appear stronger than another. Saafir had his bottom line and Virginia was campaigning for more than he was willing to give.

"Perhaps Qamsar should run their refinery. It's their environment and their laws," Henry said.

"Based on my numbers, I'm not seeing one side over the other gaining a huge advantage by running the refinery," Thomas Nelson said.

Frederick snorted. He knew where Saafir stood on matters and they were unlikely to give in to Stateside Oil.

Saafir didn't like where the negotiations were leading. Frederick was becoming prickly and increasingly irritated during discussions. Rescheduling meetings and living out of hotel rooms was grating on everyone. People missed their families and the comforts of their homes.

"Thomas, do you have the analysis of the costs to

staff and run the refinery operations in Qamsar?" Virginia asked.

Saafir kept his patience. They had been over the numbers. It was an expense both sides were willing to shoulder because the upside was huge. Virginia continued to twist the facts and figures to show how Stateside Oil would handle the operations in Qamsar better and more efficiently.

It didn't matter to Saafir if another company could run the refinery better. It was about bringing jobs and pride to Qamsar. That couldn't be done if he allowed another country to take over their oil fields.

Saafir's phone vibrated. He had changed the settings so that only Sarah's number would ring through during his meeting. "Excuse me," he said to the room, interrupting the conversation. Walking away would give him a minute to clear his head. Based on the circular nature of the conversation, he wasn't missing anything.

"Hey, you," he said into the phone, quickly stepping into the hallway and pulling the door closed behind him. The two security guards, one his and another hired by the Americans, were posted outside the door.

"Saafir?" Sarah asked.

The moment she spoke his name, he knew something was wrong.

"I'm here. What's happened?" Saafir asked.

His voice must have been louder than he thought because the meeting room went silent.

"I'm in the lobby. There's someone demanding to see you. He says if you don't come down in fifteen minutes, he'll kill me and open fire on everyone around me." A small sob escaped at the end of her words.

"Where's Jeff?" Saafir asked, thinking of her security detail.

A sharp intake of breath. "Hurt. Send help. Call the police. Don't come down here. No! Stop! Please!"

The clatter of the phone striking something hard and then the line went dead.

Panic engulfed him, but Saafir marshaled his emotional response. He threw open the door to the meeting room. He wanted to race into the lobby to be with Sarah and to find out what was happening, but he had to think like a leader, not a lover. Every face swerved in his direction. "Owen, please call the American police. Someone is holding Sarah and others hostage in the lobby and demanding to speak to me."

His next call was to Adham.

The police were scrambling to make sense of the scene, and Saafir was entirely frustrated with the response. Sarah was inside with a gun to her head. Mistakes and oversights would get her killed.

Saafir left the two guards to watch over the committee, knowing they could also be a target.

SWAT had been called, but all four local teams were working other emergencies. They promised to send available personnel as soon as possible. As soon as possible wasn't good enough for Saafir. He needed action now.

Saafir had ordered Adham to rest that morning, and he'd been happy to learn Adham had been sleeping when he'd called. Adham had seemed off to Saafir since the shooting, and while Saafir knew he wouldn't admit anything was wrong, Saafir was worried. Injured or not, Adham arrived in ten minutes looking every bit the soldier he'd been groomed to be.

Something in Adham's eyes concerned Saafir when he was in protect-and-defend mode, almost as if he could kill without thinking twice. Adham could have a deadly focus and a cold detachment. To date, it had saved Saafir's life on multiple occasions.

It was why Adham made a better solider. He could block any thread of empathy or compassion. He could think with a single intent: to kill. While qualified in his own right, if Saafir hadn't been the son of the emir, Adham would have been selected to run the urban assault unit over him. It was a fact that had put Adham initially at odds with Saafir, but in addition to their family relation they'd overcome it to form a solid friendship.

Adham and Saafir approached the policeman attempting to control the scene and introduced themselves.

"We're trying to split one of the SWAT teams and we're calling available resources to assist. Every wacko in the city has decided to start a problem today," the policeman told Saafir, wiping at the sweat that ran down his face. His badge read "Sinclair."

"Adham is the head of my security team. We've been combat-trained in urban environments and we have experience negotiating with terrorists. Adham has expertise in tactics and weaponry. We can help."

Sinclair seemed relieved to have someone to help him and who could provide information. Every moment that passed was another moment Sarah was in danger.

Saafir would press until he got what he wanted. "If the hostage taker has political motivations, he only needs Sarah until he's brought attention to his cause. That's why he asked for fifteen minutes. That's enough time to get the media and cameras here. He will kill Sarah and himself if he believes it will help him." The larger and more dramatic the show, the more media coverage he'd get.

Adham nodded his agreement. They had seen it too many times in their country. Desperate men sometimes chose violent means to meet their goals. Most of the time, those goals remained too far out of reach, driven by poor planning and emotional decisions rooted in anger.

The media was arriving, driving their vans close to the scene and pushing their way up to the police wood post blockade.

"What are you suggesting?" Sinclair asked, rubbing his forehead and appearing overwhelmed. He was flushed and not in control.

"Continue to evacuate the building. Let Adham and me near the scene to contain the hostage taker. Let me talk to this man and find out what he wants. Until your SWAT team can assess the situation and defuse it, Adham and I will delay him. You don't want an active shooter running around the building and finding a place to hole up."

The American police had jurisdiction and they wouldn't appreciate an outsider stepping in and taking charge. He had to make Sinclair see the benefits Adham and Saafir brought to addressing the problem.

Sinclair looked at his watch. "This is not my area of expertise. I've been assigned crowd control until SWAT arrives. I'll allow you inside to keep this woman alive.

When SWAT comes, you do exactly what they say, exactly how they say it, all right?"

Sinclair's inexperience was showing. It was a stroke of luck for Saafir and Adham. No skilled professional in hostage negotiations would have allowed him and Adham to interfere. "Agreed," Saafir said. He wanted to see Sarah and know she was okay. He checked his emotions, knowing if he was upset, his judgment would be skewed.

Adham and Saafir entered the building through a back stairwell.

Adham glanced at his watch. "It's been twelve minutes since you called me."

That left three minutes. The clock was working against them. "He wanted fifteen minutes, but he'll want the most media coverage possible. He's got a message and he wants to deliver it internationally. I'll bring that up when I speak to him. I'll distract him with the news coverage, you take him out," Saafir said.

Adham paused. "It's my job to keep you away from danger. You're walking directly into it."

"I'll be fine. I have my body armor."

"That won't help you if he shoots you in the head."

"I know how to handle myself," Saafir said.

Adham shook his head. "I can't let you get hurt."

"I won't. I'll be careful," Saafir said. "I have the best sniper in Qamsar watching my back."

Appearing reluctant, Adham handed him an earpiece. "You'll be able to hear me. I'll let you know when I'm in position."

"He'll expect marksmen," Saafir said.

"I'm sure he will," Adham said. "If I think he's planning to shoot you, he's done. I will take him out and never have a moment of unrest over it."

"Understood. You're my brother. I trust you to make the right decision."

They clasped hands. "Brothers," Adham agreed.

Though Adham and Saafir never mentioned their family ties in public at Adham's request, it was that connection that formed the basis of their trust. They had shared a father and not much else until they'd served together, but the bond was unseverable.

Adham looked around to see if anyone had overheard him.

The word "brother" conveyed what Saafir wanted Adham to know: *I trust you. We are stronger as a team. Take care.*

"Let's do this," Adham said.

Saafir took the stairs to the lobby. Talking down the hostage taker to get Sarah out alive was his primary concern. He couldn't live with himself if she were hurt. He should have insisted she quit or maybe he should have had her fired. If the money had been important, he could have hired her for another event.

But he'd known Sarah would not have stood for the interference in her life. She was a strong woman and Saafir wouldn't forget it.

In his peripheral thoughts, he was aware he was the leader of a nation and putting himself at risk. With Sarah in harm's way, he couldn't turn away and he couldn't delegate to someone else. He'd had military training and he trained with Adham on a regular basis to keep his skills sharp. It wasn't his first time negotiating with a hostage taker, but it was the first time he was negotiating for the release of a woman he cared about.

The shooter was agitated and twitchy. He had to be getting tired or running on adrenaline, which would drop and leave him exhausted. He could have had a picture in his mind of what would happen when he took a hostage. When it didn't play out how he expected, he would react badly. They weren't dealing with a mentally stable person. Mentally stable people didn't storm into a building, shoot someone, take a hostage and demand to speak to a visiting leader of a nation.

Adham had taken the stairs to the second floor to look for a perch to set up his equipment. He'd get into position, remain hidden and when the time was right, take one clean shot.

Saafir announced his approach to the hostage taker with the heavy thud of his shoes against the floor. Sneaking up on a man holding a gun was a mistake. "I'm here. Your demands are being met," he said. The bulletproof vest he was wearing rubbed against him. Though he'd never been shot in the chest while wearing it, he wasn't anxious to test it.

The hostage taker swung in his direction, holding Sarah in front of him. His goddess, Sarah. She had been through hardships and pain in her life, and even now she wasn't crying or begging. She appeared afraid, but her eyes gleamed with concentration. She was thinking of a way out. The slightest opening and she'd take it.

Jeff was lying motionless on the ground. Anger speared through Saafir, but he quelled it. He had to be calm and reasonable and give Adham a chance to get into position and get the right angle to make his shot.

When Sarah saw him, her eyes widened. She mouthed the word "no," warning him off. It was too late to change his course. He and Sarah were in this until the end.

"Sarah, are you hurt?" Saafir asked, holding up his hands.

Sarah shook her head. Saafir wanted the man to believe he had a way out. Given that he'd already shot Jeff, the die had been cast, but Saafir hoped to distract him.

"What is your name?" Saafir asked the hostage taker.

"You may call me Khoury," the man said, rage stamped on his face.

His name meant priest. Was that a message? Was this a religiously motivated attack? Saafir had believed this to be motivated by the protest in Qamsar led by the Conservatives and Rabah Wasam. He was open to the possibility he'd been wrong in making that assumption.

Saafir thought of his brother Mikhail and his problems with his former fiancée. Her culturally extremist beliefs had led to a terrible ending to her and Mikhail's engagement. Saafir didn't want to draw a parallel, but he was curious if this man had ties to the same group. "Khoury, tell me what you need to speak with me about." Saafir mentally urged his brother to move faster.

"You know what I want. I want the world to know about your dirty, underhanded tricks. I want the world to know about your plans to turn Qamsar into an American colony. We'll be a little America. You will rape the land of oil, sell it to the highest bidder and leave us with nothing." Khoury spat on the ground. He had started speaking in English and had switched to Arabic. Saafir recognized the accent as Qamsarian.

His accusations were ridiculous. Saafir was a proud citizen of Qamsar. He had no plans to turn Qamsar into America or forget the traditions and culture that made Qamsar unique and amazing. He only wished for greater prosperity and happiness for Qamsarians. Moving forward with economic and social progress wasn't akin to becoming "a little America." Saafir hid his emotion from his face. He was grateful for the practice he'd had feigning calm over the last several months. He needed it now.

Knowing Sarah was on the other end of that gun, a gun that might have delivered a bullet into Jeff, was making him desperate. Fear for her life had taken center stage.

"I understand how you'd feel this way. I'm not thrilled with how the negotiations have been," Saafir said. He had wanted the talks to go faster and be less tangled up in red tape. His dislike of the process was an honest admission. He needed to connect with Khoury and establish some ties to him.

He dared not look up to see if Adham was in place and call Khoury's attention to the area. Adham would alert him when he was ready.

"What will you do about it?" Khoury asked. He lowered the gun a few inches, but the muzzle was still pointed at Sarah.

"What do you want me to do about it?" Saafir asked.

Khoury paused, thought and then responded. "Tell the Americans you don't want their interference. Tell them you are from a great country that doesn't need their form of progress."

He hadn't asked Saafir to step down. If Khoury

was with the Conservatives, at least the message had changed somewhat.

"Captain, I can't get an angle on him without going through Sarah. Get him to walk toward you." Adham's voice in his earpiece.

Saafir shifted. He would back away and hope Khoury moved toward him as they talked.

"Why don't you let Sarah go and we'll talk about this? You don't need her. You have me." One step back. He waited for Khoury to follow.

Khoury laughed. "Will it kill you to see her dead? If I shoot your American lover and cover you in her blood would you beg me for death?"

Saafir didn't like the direction this was leading. Khoury was emotionally escalating and making dramatic threats. Khoury looked over his shoulder and stood straighter when he saw the gathering media and police outside the building.

Saafir took another step to the left and Khoury shifted. "Where are you going?" he asked.

"Not going anywhere. There's a lot of media following this story," Saafir said. He kept Khoury focused on his intention in taking a hostage.

"Now there's a pole in my line of sight. I'm moving to an alternate position," Adham said.

The expression on Sarah's face was killing him. He tried not to fixate on her and give away just how much she meant to him.

"Are there no Qamsarian women who are good enough for you? Why an American? Do you hate all things from your country?" Khoury asked.

Saafir looked for a response that was insulting toward neither Sarah nor Qamsarian women. "I am planning to marry a Qamsarian woman."

Sarah flinched slightly.

Khoury shook Sarah in his arms and she winced. Hot anger sliced through Saafir. "You don't need to do anything violent," Saafir said. He would kill Khoury with his bare hands if he hurt Sarah.

Khoury jerked his head in Jeff's direction. "I killed one American. What difference does it make if I kill others?"

Khoury turned and posed for the crowd gathering outside the building.

Saafir had to stall. Khoury's reaction to the crowd outside told Saafir he was enjoying the attention. However, Khoury had to know this couldn't end with Saafir walking away from the trade agreement with America or with Saafir changing how he ruled Qamsar. Walking into a hostage situation, it was understood that someone would die.

"No one needs to be hurt," Saafir said. "Why don't you put the gun down and we'll talk?"

"This is the police!" A shout from the American police outside the glass doors from what sounded like a bullhorn. The noise was grating and Khoury tensed.

Khoury tightened his grip around Sarah and Saafir stifled the urge to lunge for her. The police were interfering at the worst possible time. He was establishing a rapport with Khoury and keeping him calm and from putting a bullet in Sarah.

"We'd like to talk with you. We're calling the phone in the lobby. Please pick it up," the police negotiator said.

The phone rang in the lobby. Khoury didn't make

a move to answer it, though he twitched with every ring. When it finally stopped, Khoury relaxed slightly and Saafir was grateful. They didn't need to add to Khoury's jumpiness.

Then the phone rang again.

"Please answer the phone," the police negotiator said. The bullhorn let out a shrill feedback sound.

The police could enter the building through other means and Saafir guessed if a SWAT team had arrived, they were already inside and getting into position for a takedown. Perhaps the policeman calling out was a distraction.

"If you continue to ignore the phone, we will resort to other methods to get your attention," the negotiator said.

Khoury gestured to the large television in the lobby with scrolling news stories. "I'm there. My cause is there. The world will know why I needed to do this. Rabah will know I was a champion for our cause."

The television headline read "Muslim extremist holding hostages in D.C." That wasn't glowing support for Khoury's cause. It didn't mention it or his name. But Khoury had given away that Rabah Wasam was involved, however indirectly, with this incident. Had he called for his followers to take action? Had he planned this drama?

"That's a national news story," Saafir said, pretending to be impressed.

Khoury had shifted his attention to the television screen. The phone rang again.

"Why don't you let me answer the phone? The reporters might have questions for you," Saafir said.

Khoury looked out at the crowd and then back to Saafir. "Yes. Answer the phone."

Saafir walked to the phone, keeping Khoury in front of him and his eyes on Sarah. Saafir identified himself to the caller.

"We have limited visibility. Can you tell me how many hostages are inside?" the man asked.

"He is a Qamsarian nationalist," Saafir said, keeping his voice neutral. Sarah was the most at risk, but others remained in the lobby, hunkered down on the floor.

"A dozen?"

"Just about," Saafir said. By his count, they had about ten people in sight in the lobby.

"What are his demands?" the police asked.

"Let me ask him," Saafir said. "Khoury, the police and media are asking your demands." He'd given them a first name. It might help.

Khoury's mouth gaped open. "I want everyone to know that America is exploiting us."

"I'll tell them," Saafir said.

"Tell them that Qamsar will be an example of true values to the rest of the world," Khoury said.

Saafir repeated the message into the phone. Khoury had walked closer to him, dragging Sarah with him.

"I've got a clear line of sight," Adham said into his earpiece.

Saafir didn't move, not sure what angle Adham was shooting.

Sarah bucked and Khoury struggled to hold her.

Adham swore. "Tell her to stay still."

"Sarah, stay calm," Saafir said, terrified Adham would hit her if she moved.

Sarah scratched at Khoury's face and she twisted

to the ground. Khoury held his gun over her. "You'll pay for that, b—"

Khoury dropped to the ground.

"Done," Adham said.

Saafir rushed for Sarah and gathered her into his arms, pulling her away from Khoury. He was aware of police flooding the room, but he had Sarah safely in his arms and that was the best place for her to be.

In death, Khoury had succeeded in drawing international attention to the open opposition to the trade agreement by the Conservative party in Qamsar. Members of the media swarmed outside the building as police collected evidence at the scene for their reports and spoke to witnesses who had been in the lobby.

The media had snapped pictures of Saafir holding Sarah against him. Though it was the reaction of almost any two people in response to an emotional ordeal, some reporters were using it as evidence of the emir's affair with an American woman. Thinking about Sarah being identified and harassed filled Saafir with dread. Negative publicity about their relationship would impact the trade agreement and Sarah personally, possibly even professionally.

Sarah had given her account of the incident to the police and they were waiting in the building's security office, away from the eyes of the media.

"Thank you for coming to help me," Sarah said.

"You couldn't think I would have left you inside with him. I promised I would protect you. I will make good on that promise," Saafir said.

"Are you going to give up?" Sarah asked.

"Give up what?" Saafir asked. On them? Not while he had time.

"On the trade agreement. To deal with the problems at home," Sarah said. "To make sure this doesn't get worse and that more people don't get hurt."

He had never caved to the demands of bullies or terrorists. "Is that what you think I should do?"

Sarah shrugged. "I have no idea what you should do. Jeff is dead. The Conservatives are bent on getting you out of power."

"I can't back down. The trade agreement is good for our country," Saafir said.

"What about what is good for you? They'll assassinate you," Sarah said. "Khoury could have turned the gun on you today."

"What's good for Qamsar is what is good for me. If I let people like Khoury and Wasam dictate how the government should run, we'd have violence every day. To make a point, people would take hostages or shoot at each other. I refuse to let Qamsar be a country of politics through brutality."

"Jeff is dead and it's my fault," Sarah said, sadness clinging to every word.

"You are not responsible. No one blames you," Saafir said and handed her a handkerchief from his breast pocket.

Sarah dabbed at her eyes. "I blame myself. I was rushing around and I wasn't paying attention. Could I have said something to defuse the situation sooner?"

She was trying to make sense of it. Saafir couldn't provide rationalizations because it hadn't been a rational action. "Khoury knew he was putting his life and others at risk when he chose to take you hostage.

He couldn't have gotten out of the building without being apprehended or killed. He alone is responsible for Jeff's death."

Sarah shook her head. "I could have done something. Said something. Behaved differently."

"You did the best you could. You're alive. That's what's important," Saafir said.

Adham and the SWAT team involved in the shooting were in a debriefing. Three marksmen and Adham had fired shots at Khoury at near the same moment. The police would determine which bullet delivered the fatal shot.

Owen appeared in the doorway.

"Are you okay?" Owen asked, coming to Sarah and kneeling next to her.

Sarah's tears started anew. "I was scared. Helpless."

Owen hugged her and patted her back consolingly. Saafir felt a jolt of possessiveness. Owen was a married man and her former brother-in-law, and Sarah had a close connection to both Owen and Evelyn. Owen had been in her life longer than Saafir had. He shouldn't feel threatened by the other man. Her affection toward Owen had nothing to do with her feelings for him.

"I have some disturbing news," Owen said, taking Sarah's hands.

Sarah went stock-still. "About this? Or Alec?"

Owen appeared surprised and glanced at Saafir, a question on his face. Did he think Sarah wouldn't have told Saafir about Alec?

Though Sarah had told Saafir she wanted nothing to do with her ex-husband, her concerns about him were pervasive. Saafir wondered if her ongoing relationship with Owen and Evelyn was how she kept Alec in her life or if she secretly wanted Alec to get better and then have a happy reunion with him.

Owen and Evelyn could want that for their brother, too.

His jealousy was misplaced, especially considering Saafir's family was in the process of arranging his marriage to another woman. He had no right to make a claim on Sarah's heart.

"News about this situation," Owen said. "Thomas Nelson is dead. A self-inflicted gunshot wound to the head."

Sarah clapped her hands over her mouth.

"Thomas was sending information to the Conservative extremists about our location and our meetings."

The trade summit's economics expert had been a spy.

"Why would he do that?" Sarah asked.

"He had some serious gambling debts and the Conservatives were paying them," Owen said. "He heard that someone died today. He returned home, wrote a suicide note and shot himself. He couldn't handle the guilt." Owen paused. "He called me before he shot himself. He asked me to come over and review some ideas he had. He wanted me to find him."

"Oh, Owen," Sarah said, and hugged him.

"Maybe some things will return to normal now," Owen said.

Saafir didn't agree. The Conservatives would not be quick to give up. They may have lost their mole when Nelson died, but they wouldn't back away.

Owen stroked a hand down Sarah's hair and Saafir ignored the gesture. Owen was being a friend.

"The police want to look into everyone involved

with the trade agreement committee again and search for ties to the extremists," Owen said.

Saafir rubbed his temples. First Nibal and now Thomas Nelson. Both the Americans and Qamsarians had had traitors working against them.

The security office door opened again and Adham entered. He stumbled to Saafir. Saafir's alarm went on full alert. "What's wrong?" Saafir asked in Arabic.

For the Qamsarian Warrior to show any physical sign of injury was rare.

Adham opened his jacket and Saafir swore in Arabic. His brother's earlier gunshot wound, the one Adham had assured him was healing and under a doctor's care, was seeping enough to stain his shirt red and yellow.

"Before you get angry, I had an appointment today. I knew something was wrong," Adham said. Sweat beaded his forehead and his color was pale, his skin waxy.

Sarah gasped when she saw Adham. "Adham! What happened?"

Adham said nothing. To admit to Saafir he was injured would be a deep embarrassment to him. To admit it to a woman would be impossible.

"He's fine. I'll take care of this," Saafir said, leading his brother away.

Saafir called for his security team to assemble. He selected the two guards with the best skills. "Take Adham to the hospital. Do not under any circumstances allow him to leave. He is to remain until I hear from his doctors that he is better. I want to be appraised of his status at every change."

He turned to his brother. "Adham, this is a command." He wouldn't allow his brother's devotion to his protection override his need for medical care.

"Yes, your excellency," they said as they took Adham under his arms and led him away.

Chapter 7

"Why didn't Adham say anything sooner about being injured?" Sarah asked.

They were waiting in the building's security office for the FBI to arrive. A quick call to Saafir's FBI agent brother-in-law and they'd learned the agent assigned to their case, Lucia Huntington, though green around the edges, was thorough, smart and savvy.

"He's a Qamsarian Warrior. It is a mark against his honor to admit he is hurt."

"No, it isn't. It's common sense. He's no good to anyone dead."

Saafir had received a call from the hospital. Adham had a severe infection resulting from improper care of the gunshot wound he'd received earlier in the week. He had pushed himself too hard and he was paying the consequences.

Saafir rubbed his jaw. "Adham is too stubborn to die."

Sarah heard the resolve and worry in Saafir's voice and reached for his hand. "I know you care for each other. He'll get better. He's in good, healing hands now." She hadn't meant to be harsh with her words. The day had been overwhelming and showed no signs of slowing down.

Saafir swallowed hard. "Adham means a lot to me."

"I know he does. It's obvious how much you care about him."

"Is it?" Saafir asked, inclining his head.

"It is to me," she said. "He's so protective of you, and you trust him more than the others."

Saafir gathered her against him in that easy way he had. "Adham is important to me. As are you. I will be criticized for walking into that lobby. I wasn't thinking about my country. I was thinking about my lover in a madman's hands and I had to stop him."

Sarah rested her head against his shoulder. "Thank you for that. Thank you for what you did." It wasn't the first time she had spoken those words, but Saafir had risked his life for her and she would never forget that. "When you walked into that lobby, I was terrified. Khoury had been mumbling about you and the trade agreement. He was an unstable man. Something was wrong with him. You could have died. I could have died. Anything could have happened in those few minutes to end both our lives."

Saafir rubbed her arm in a slow, soothing stroke. "I wouldn't have let that happen. I am not supposed to have anything to do with you, and yet, in that moment, you were all that mattered to me. Getting to you, seeing you and talking to you took precedence over everything else." He sounded anguished, like he was wrestling with the decision he'd already made. "Your life is precious to me," he added.

Her heart ached for him. Ached for what he was going through and ached that it seemed his life was not his. He was concerned about the inevitable criticism from the media and the Conservatives. The more she learned about his life, the more Sarah realized Saafir the man had dreams and hopes a far cry from the dreams and hopes of Saafir the emir. He belonged to his country and the decisions he made were with Qamsar in mind.

Sarah could have told him she would stand by him through the fallout, but she didn't know if that would help or make him feel worse. Every time they had discussed their relationship, they had been clear that it had an end. But in her heart, they were no longer a throw-away, lust-driven, thrill-seeking adventure in bed. She returned to him again and again. That meant something a great deal more than a single night of passion.

Sarah's phone rang. She had almost forgotten about her handbag that the police had returned to her. Digging through it, she answered, not recognizing the number. It could be her clients who were having their wedding that night.

She answered it, injecting some energy into her voice.

"Hey, Sarah."

It wasn't her clients. It was Alec.

The familiarity in his voice and the laid-back, devil-may-care tone had always made her feel at ease. Today, it jarred her. How was he calling? If he had left rehab again, she would be furious with him and she certainly wouldn't cover for him, a favorite favor of Alec's.

It took Sarah a moment to find her emotional footing. "You can't call me," Sarah said. She and Alec had agreed it was healthier for them to remain unavailable and not speak to each other.

"I had to call. I've been worried. Do you know what they're saying about you in the news?" Alec said. "I saw something about a hostage and a shooting."

Sarah groaned thinking of her picture being splashed across the news.

"I'm fine," Sarah said. She didn't want to know. If they were posting her picture and mentioning her name, it would impact her business.

"They're saying you're some king's lover," Alec said.

Sarah flinched at the idea of her private life being displayed for the world to see. Were they actually using the word *lover?* "It's a misunderstanding."

Saafir glanced over at her with a curious expression on his face. Sarah forced a smile to let him know she was fine. Could he hear what Alec was saying? Shifting in her seat, she put some space between them and lowered the volume on her phone.

"Are you planning to marry a king?" Alec asked.

Speaking to Alec was a poignant reminder of how difficult a marriage was and Sarah had no plans to repeat that mistake with anyone. "That's ridiculous. I'm not marrying anyone."

"The pictures aren't so ridiculous," Alec said, hurt thick in his voice.

Sarah didn't know what pictures he had seen or

what exactly he was referring to, but she had to end the conversation.

"People do crazy things with photo editing. I have to go. I'm in the middle of a situation."

"Is he there now?" Alec asked, jealousy ringing in his voice.

"Goodbye, Alec," Sarah said. When she spoke his name, Saafir's gaze swerved to look at her.

"Sarah, wait. I have to see you," Alec said.

She didn't want to ask, but she had to. "Where are you?" If he said anywhere other than the rehab program, Sarah would lose it.

"I've been transferred to a house with a built-in work program," Alec said.

A halfway house, the next step for Alec post-rehab. It was a solid place for a transition. Was he ready for it? If he had been pushed too hard too fast, he would relapse. If he was presented with the same people and problems from his past, old habits would resurface. Sarah found herself simultaneously battling worry for Alec and her promise to herself to remain uninvolved.

Sarah turned away from Saafir and lowered her voice. "I'm happy to hear you're progressing. But the circumstances haven't changed. Unless your counselors have changed their minds, I am not good for you."

"Are you open to talking to them again?" he asked.

She wasn't. She couldn't get dragged into the emotional maze that was Alec's life. "We've settled this matter."

"I've changed."

She'd heard that before and his words fell on deaf ears. "So have I."

"I'll come to you."

"No." Mustering her courage she hung up the phone. She had talked for too long as it was. The phone rang again, but Sarah didn't answer. She couldn't talk to Alec. If he had been discharged from the rehab center and was staying in a halfway house, her involvement could cause a regression.

"Are you okay?" Saafir asked.

Alec's call was small compared to what she had gone through that morning. She didn't pretend Saafir was unaware of who had called. "It's hard when he calls. I feel like I need to do something. Or say something. But I've been down every possible road and guess what?" She threw her hands in the air. "I can't fix him. I can't do anything to make him better. I can't make him stay off drugs." A sob caught in her throat as several memories collided at once. Alec, passed out in their old apartment. Jeff, dead on the floor of the lobby. Khoury, standing over her aiming a gun at her. She had been certain her life was over. "My failures don't stop there. I also can't keep crazies from shooting at you. I can't repair my home and my belongings that have been smashed to pieces. Jeff and Thomas Nelson and Khoury are dead. Adham is in the hospital." She was screaming and her control had slipped beyond the point of reining it in.

"Sarah, you've been through an ordeal." Saafir's gentle, soft tone made her feel more out of control.

"Yes, I have. Several ordeals. And in almost every case, I've failed." She buried her face in her hands. Even as tears fell, she was angry at herself for breaking down. All her life, she'd had herself to depend on. She was strong and fearless and let problems roll off her shoulders. She'd never had a father or mother she could count on. She didn't have someone waiting at home for her to share her problems and her day with.

"What about you?" she asked, studying Saafir's calm expression. "You've stayed in control. You don't get upset. You don't lose it." She needed to feel like someone else was shaken by the events like she was.

"Of course I get upset," he said quietly.

"You don't look upset," she said. Couldn't he lose his temper and yell? Smash something? Throw something?

"I've been trained not to outwardly react to problems."

"Even when someone you care about is injured?"

Something flashed through his eyes and Sarah knew she'd hit on a sore point. She shouldn't have mentioned Adham, but she wanted Saafir to respond.

"Are you speaking of you or Adham?" Saafir asked.

She threw up her hands. "Adham. I don't expect you to care about me. Why should you? You're engaged."

He winced. "I care that you are injured. I already explained that I almost lost my mind thinking of you with a gun aimed at you. I've explained about Alaina. You seem so upset about her, but I don't know why. I don't even know her."

It was the first time he had spoken her name. Alaina. A beautiful-sounding name for a no-doubt beautiful woman. Sarah was tapped into her emotions enough to know she was spoiling for a fight, needing to pour off some of the excess anger and hurt and fear boiling inside her. That the person on the receiving end of her emotions was a sheik wasn't important. He was the closest friend at the moment.

"I care about you, Sarah. Of course I do. I have from the beginning."

His words took the edge off some of her anger. "I don't know what we're doing." Having a brief affair? Using each other for sex?

"I thought I made it clear."

He'd made nothing clear. Every time they were together, lust ruled her. Being in the same room with him meant she lost the will and desire to say no. To acknowledge that she was falling for him, really falling for him, scared her. "I don't feel clear."

Saafir looked away and then returned his gaze to her. "When you were in danger, nothing would have stood between you and me. I would have killed that man for touching you and for hurting you. I can't imagine what you are going through and I think the fact that you haven't completely shut down proves how strong you are. My resilient and strong goddess."

Saafir moved so fast she almost didn't have time to respond. He pulled her across his lap, clasping her against him. "What we're doing is making the most of every moment while we can. Does that answer your question?"

Though the action felt rooted in a protective emotion, Sarah felt desire overrule every other emotion. "You're making me forget the question."

Saafir touched the side of her face. "You are so beautiful. Let's run away together. Let's pack up and leave."

Sarah closed her eyes. An island vacation. A spa. A private yacht. All things likely at the emir's disposal. "If we leave, when we return, we'll have the same problems waiting for us."

"That doesn't matter. What matters is you. You've

been through a lot. I've seen men, strong men, under pressure who snap."

"I won't snap. Besides, I have a wedding tonight."

Saafir lifted his brow. "A wedding?" He had a face and a body that could make her forget about her work, her life and her friends. But what would she do when he returned to Qamsar? Pick up the pieces of the life she'd dropped in order to spend time with him? She had to keep together the little she had left.

"A job I took months ago," she said.

"You need a break," Saafir said.

"Speak for yourself," Sarah said.

"What will happen when you finally deal with what's happened to you?" Saafir asked.

Sarah stared at him. Her answer wasn't a deep one. If he wanted introspection and philosophy on life and the human psyche, she was in no mood to go there. If she looked too deeply into how she felt, she wasn't sure she could handle it. "I don't have time for a breakdown. I have a business to run and clients to keep happy."

"I am one of those clients." He gave the conversation a light overtone and that quickly, some of the knots of dark emotion unwound inside her.

"Do you have a complaint about my event-planning abilities?"

He let out a deep laugh. "No complaints about your event planning for the trade agreement. I do have a complaint about your private event planning. What will it take to get a night alone with you?"

"If I recall correctly, you already had that," Sarah said.

Saafir laughed again. "I'm a spoiled man and I like getting what I want."

"Are you saying if I don't acquiesce to your demands, you'll pursue me relentlessly?"

Hearing voices in the hallway that could signal the FBI's arrival, Sarah slid off his lap onto her chair.

Saafir groaned. "You didn't have to move. I was enjoying that."

"In America, commoners aren't supposed to act like this in formal situations," Sarah said.

Saafir gave her a sideways look. "In Qamsar, royals aren't, either."

For a fleeting moment, Sarah thought of his fiancée. She forced those thoughts away and locked them up tight. Their past relationships and their futures had no place in this moment.

"Then we'll find a place where we can be informal together. The wedding will be over by 2:00 a.m. I can meet you after."

Saafir pressed a kiss to her mouth that promised passion and pleasure. Sarah was surprised when he released her. "If you think after today I'd let you out of my sight, you are sorely mistaken. I am coming with you to the wedding. Don't Americans take dates to weddings?"

Discomfort dulled her excitement over the prospect of a late-night rendezvous with Saafir. "I don't bring dates to the events I plan. You'll steal focus."

"No one will know I'm there," he said.

"After the news day we've had, they'll know."

"I'm coming with you. As we've discussed, I like getting what I want and I always get what I need. This is something I need."

A woman in a crisp white shirt entered the room and introduced herself as Special Agent Lucia Huntington.

She looked between Saafir and Sarah. "Are you ready to get started? I have a lot of questions."

Seeing Sarah in her element turned Saafir on the same way it always did. Sarah was smart and passionate about her work. Even with the curious looks she was getting from the other staff hired for the wedding, Sarah ignored them and focused on her tasks.

Saafir wanted to keep Sarah close. He was worried about her and her safety. If she lost her cool, he wanted to be her soft place to land. If someone came after her again, he would protect her. Since her small breakdown earlier in the day which he had somehow handled, Sarah had held it together.

They'd stopped at her friend Molly's place, and Sarah had changed into a borrowed green gown. It fit her well, accenting the curves of her body he loved so much. While he watched her work, Saafir made some calls to have a private shopper acquire some items for Sarah. Since her home and clothes had been destroyed and they had been living in hotels, he hoped it would buoy her spirits to have some new things.

Saafir took a seat on the far side of the large white tent that had been set up for the event. He was curious to know more about an American wedding. In his country, marriages were large, multi-day celebrations involving hundreds, possibly thousands of people. He counted about fifty chairs at this event. His guards were keeping themselves hidden well, though Saafir knew they'd be watching him and Sarah.

As guests began to arrive, the dark gave him the perfect hiding place. Citronella tiki torches burned and netting draped around the tent kept out mosquitoes that would be drawn to the lights.

Sarah joined him several minutes later. "This is the part I enjoy the most. If I've done my job well and everyone does what they're supposed to do, this wedding will be beautiful."

With the guests' eyes on the bride, Saafir held Sarah's hand during the ceremony. Her eyes misted as the couple exchanged vows. Saafir thought of Alaina Faris, waiting for him in Qamsar. His arranged marriage was being negotiated. He wouldn't have a great love affair with Alaina. The passion and attraction he had to Sarah was once in a lifetime.

Thinking of marrying another woman while he had feelings for Sarah felt like a betrayal to both women. Though Mikhail had been sending infrequent messages about their negotiations with Alaina's father, she didn't seem real to Saafir. She was a name on a piece of paper. Duty demanded he marry her.

Yet he couldn't stop thinking of being with Sarah. She had so many qualities he wanted in a partner. Devoted, loyal, generous of spirit and kind. Qualities that would have served her well as the emir's wife.

"What are you brooding about?" Sarah asked.

"I'm not brooding. I'm thinking."

Sarah squeezed his hand and released it, then stood and walked in the direction of a woman in a tuxedo shirt who was signaling to her.

Sarah's posture tensed and he recognized the signs of a problem. He strode to join them. No unnecessary stress on Sarah tonight.

"What's wrong?" he asked.

"Can he do it?" the other woman asked, gesturing at Saafir.

"Do what?" Saafir asked.

"He can't. He's a friend," Sarah said firmly.

"A friend who can help you."

Sarah looked at Saafir and winced. "We're short one server and one bartender. Two of the staff decided not to show up and the caterer doesn't have anyone else who can be here in time for the cocktail hour. We need someone in ten minutes."

"I can be a waiter," Saafir said. Though he'd never been a waiter, he'd dined in enough restaurants to understand the gist of it. He could mimic the other servers.

Sarah mumbled something under her breath about a royal screw-up. Saafir pulled her to the side and motioned to the other woman to give them a minute.

"I'm here to help you, Sarah. Let me pass out a few plates. No one will recognize me."

"I suppose I could tend bar," she said. "Once dinner is served, the waitstaff goes home and the caterer can have someone take over the bar for me."

In short order, Saafir alerted his guards to the situation and changed into a shirt similar to one the other woman had been wearing. Sarah was at the bar, pouring drinks for the guests and laughing. It was her job to make sure the people around her had fun, but Saafir knew it was an act. Her pitch was too high, too strained, and her movements were jerky and tight.

"You look so familiar. Have we met?" a woman asked as he circulated with a tray of hors d'oeuvres.

"I don't think so," Saafir said. He smiled and extended the tray to her. He didn't want to steal focus from the bride and groom. Although to him, Sarah was the show-stealer. She was enchanting and she drew Saafir's attention again and again.

When his tray was empty and Sarah had someone take over for her at the bar, he met Sarah behind the kitchen.

"Thank you, Saafir. You covered for me and I needed that," Sarah said. "With everything going on with my other job, it's that much more important this one go well. Did anyone recognize you?"

"I don't think so. A few people said I looked familiar," he said.

Sarah threw her arms around his neck. "Can you imagine if someone knew they had been served by the emir of Qamsar?"

Saafir laughed and slipped his arms around her waist. "I was happy to help you." She relaxed against him. "When can we leave?" he asked. He wanted to have her alone, give her a massage or talk or watch a movie or do whatever would help her relax.

"I need to stick around until everyone's gone, including the clean-up crew, but we can take a walk around the grounds. This is a botanical garden and the path through it winds for over a quarter of a mile." Many of the wedding guests had already left and the party was dying down. She took his hand and led him to a path illuminated along the ground by small white lights. Saafir motioned to his guards to give him space. They wouldn't stay away, but they wouldn't follow on his heels.

Though he was surrounded by nature's beauty, nothing held a candle to Sarah. He couldn't take his eyes off her.

Music from the wedding floated through the air. It was a soft, romantic melody. "Dance with me," he said.

Sarah paused, smiled shyly and stepped into his arms. "Gladly."

As they danced on the path, Saafir reveled in holding her against him, the easy way she moved with him and the light, fresh scent of her hair.

"Where did you learn to dance?" she asked.

"My brother and I were required to take Western dance lessons. We sometimes entertained European dignitaries and the skill was useful." He was glad he'd had the lessons. When he didn't have to think too hard about the steps, he could concentrate on the woman in his arms.

Sarah's hands moved from his lower back to his hips. Her body brushed against the evidence of how turned on he was by her.

"It was a bad week," she said.

"Yes, it was," he said. He sensed she was ready to talk and on the verge of opening up to him. He waited, moving with her. Tonight was about her. He was hers to command.

"How many more people will be hurt before this stops?" she asked. The words sounded strangled as they left her mouth.

"I hope no one else is hurt. My team is looking into how we can stop Rabah Wasam."

"Have you heard from Adham?" Sarah asked. She had stopped moving and was biting her lip nervously.

"Adham sent me a text about an hour ago that your friend, Molly, is looking after him."

"Molly?" Sarah asked. "She didn't say anything when I stopped by to borrow this dress."

"They've been texting over the last several days," Saafir said.

Sarah appeared to think about that for a few moments. "Adham couldn't ask for a better woman to take care of him. Molly is sweet and warm, and she'll do anything for the people she cares about."

"That's something you have in common," Saafir said. "You've been there for me, for your ex-husband and for Owen. None of us deserve you and you ask little in return. Is there something I can do for you?" He would keep trying things and keep asking until he found the key to unlock her happiness.

"I do have a request," she said.

"Anything," he said. If it was in his power, he would find a way to get it. And if it was out of reach, he'd just work that much harder.

"Please, just hold me for a little while."

"That's easy. Holding you is what I most want to do." He put his arms around Sarah. Her body felt small and fragile against his and he never wanted to let go.

Sarah inhaled the scent of Saafir's shirt, spicy and male, and heat pooled between her legs. The energy to shore up her defenses against him was gone. Pretending she could stay away from him was a sham.

Sarah wanted this man as desperately as she had the first time she'd met him, when she had laid eyes on him in the darkened bar, when he had been a gorgeous man who she wanted to sleep with. She'd had no intention of getting to know him and she'd planned to have a one-night fling with him.

Now he was the man who'd been by her side

throughout some of the most dangerous and intense days of her life.

"Are your guards watching us?" she asked.

"They are close, yes, but they will give us privacy if you need to talk," he said. "You can tell me anything and it will stay between the two of us."

A confidante. A lover. He'd offered those roles to her. She could offer the same. His words cemented her decision to tell Owen nothing should she learn anything about the trade agreement. If Owen was angry with her about it in the future, then she'd face his wrath. "I don't know what's wrong with me. All I can think about is you and being with you. I'm very aware that you'll return to Qamsar and I may never see you again." The deeper she fell for him, the more likely she'd be hurt when he left.

"How do you feel about that?"

Sarah sensed he was waiting for her to say something critical or maybe waiting for her to have another breakdown. "I feel like every moment is important. I feel like I want to fold myself into your arms and show you how I feel for you."

She touched him in a way that left no question what she had in mind.

Saafir's eyes darkened. "You've been through an ordeal today. I don't want to take advantage of you."

"You're not taking advantage. I need this. I need you."

"I don't want to hurt you, goddess," he said.

She knew the events of the day would catch up to her at the worst possible time. Jeff, Thomas, Khoury and Alec's faces flashed through her mind. She couldn't handle heavy, difficult topics right now. "Before this happened, I was worried about my career. It was all I had left in my life. When I ended things with Alec, I lost passion and love and companionship and fun. But then I found you and I realized I missed those things. I miss being with a man. I miss being in his arms and being held." Saafir couldn't offer her forever and she wouldn't ask it of him. "This is still a one-night affair," she said. "It's just one more night. Don't hold back. Don't act like I'm glass that can be broken. Don't let what happened today ruin what we have."

Saafir anchored her to him. He ran his hand down her dress, lifting it at the end. His fingers stroked her bare thigh. The touch was just shy of rough and a shiver of desire piped through her. Hard and hot and fast was what she needed.

"Yes. More," she said, encouraging him. Saafir could be gentle and calm, but she had seen the wild, erotically charged side of him. She wanted passion and excitement tonight.

He lightly slapped her bottom and deep, carnal sensations swept over her. He led her to stand beside a wooden bench away from the pathway lights. Long branches extended over the bench, giving the illusion of semi-privacy.

Saafir bent to the ground and kissed her ankle, her calf and her knee. "My goddess. So strong and passionate." He was kneeling at her feet and a surge of power rolled through her. This man, this strong, sexy, intelligent, powerful man wanted her as much as she wanted him.

He lifted her foot, setting it on the bench. He kissed higher to where her dress met her thighs and then higher still. When he pressed a kiss to the apex of her thighs, she moved her hips responsively. She should stop him. But passion was sharp and consuming. She could no more stop this than she could slow it down.

This was exactly what she needed. Her problems seemed to drift away on a cloud of desire.

Saafir kissed to her outer leg and moved his lips to her hand. Kissing each fingertip, he pressed her hand to the back of the bench. "Hold here," he said. "Hold tight."

Sarah gripped the back of the bench, her thighs parted in a way that made her feel exposed and undeniably turned on. She wasn't sure what she wanted him to do, but she wanted him to do it fast. Anything to release the pent-up lust winding inside her, tighter and tighter.

Saafir moved behind her. She heard a zipper and the crinkle of foil. He pulled aside her thong and then he was rubbing against her center. She was wet and ready for him. She arched her back, beckoning to him to take what she was offering and give her what she needed.

He entered her slowly, drawing the moment out. It was difficult to move in her current position, but she flicked her hips, taking him deeper. He let out a groan and it touched something inside her, throwing lighter fluid on the desire, scorching her.

His lips came to her ear. "I'm going to take you hard."

Buried inside her, he stilled for a moment, reaching around to touch her, and moved his fingers in a small circle. His arm went across her chest, both controlling her motions and providing friction against her aching breasts.

He worked his hips, almost lifting her off the ground

with the power of his thrusts. Sarah gripped the bench, her nails grasping for traction. Saafir seemed to know what she needed. As he had from those first moments, he understood her.

He increased his speed and his power and Sarah was helpless to do anything except feel and ride the torrent of sensations. When it came to Saafir, she had no control.

She'd tried to keep her distance from him. She had wanted to pretend that first night together had been enough to satisfy her. But whenever she was near Saafir, whenever she thought of him, longing rebuilt and she craved him again. He made her feel special and needed and part of something bigger than herself.

She breathed his name on a sigh. His fingers moved across the tight bundle of nerves at her center and she shattered as an explosive orgasm rocked her. Saafir jerked into her and she felt his release as he joined her in incredible completion.

Saafir tugged her dress down and used a handkerchief to clean up. He pulled her into his lap and they sat on the wooden bench, exchanging kisses and soft caresses.

It was a long time before Sarah remembered where she was and what she was doing. "This could be the most fun I've had at an event I coordinated. Lucky that no one's come looking for me."

He ran his nose along her jaw. "I'm sure everything is fine. You're good at what you do."

Even so, she had professional standards. Despite having sex with Saafir—outside—she was working. "I should get back," she said. "Do you think everyone will know what we were doing?"

He rubbed his finger across her lips. "A little beard burn may give you away." He helped her to her feet and extended his elbow. "I'll escort you."

The night was perfect. Cool without being cold, the stars and moon casting light and the soft sounds of the wedding band's music drifting from the party.

"Why can't it be like this all the time?" Sarah asked, leaning her head on Saafir's shoulder.

"We'll enjoy it for now," Saafir said. "The rest of the world waits for us."

Sarah heard shouting and alarm zipped through her. She and Saafir exchanged a look and their stroll turned into a run.

Chapter 8

Sarah and Saafir arrived at the white wedding tent. The bride and groom were standing on the far side of the dance floor, the groom's arm around his bride, matching looks of shock on their faces.

Sarah scanned for the source of the problem. When her eyes landed on her ex-husband, humiliation and anger tumbled through her. Not tonight. Not while she was working. Not after a day that had been absolutely, horrifyingly scary. She was using every weapon in her arsenal to hold it together. She couldn't deal with more.

Alec had intruded on the party, and in typical Alec-style, he was creating a scene, talking loudly and greeting the people around him with effusive hellos as if they were old friends. He had to be under the influence. Her heart clenched at the realization. A few days out of rehab and Alec had relapsed.

She rushed forward, hoping she could steer Alec away from the party. She was responsible for this wedding and its success or failure rested with her. "Alec, what are you doing here?" She kept her voice quiet.

Though Saafir wasn't directly behind her, she sensed he was close. He was letting her handle this and Sarah was grateful. If Alec saw Saafir and got jealous, the situation would escalate further.

"I wanted to talk to you," Alec said. His speech was slurred and his pupils dilated.

Sarah could feel the accusing stares of the people around her. "Please, let's take a walk and talk."

"Now you want to be reasonable? Am I embarrassing you? When I called you earlier, you said you didn't want to talk to me," Alec said. He swore. "I want to talk to you so here I am."

He was putting her professional reputation in jeopardy. "This is not the time and place to create a scene."

For a moment, she thought he would let her lead him away. Alec looked around and Sarah's heart fell when his expression morphed from surprise to anger. He'd spotted Saafir.

"You're here with the emir of Qamsar?" Alec asked. His posture changed. He puffed out his chest and stood straighter.

Interested murmurs floated around her and Sarah wished she could disappear. Saafir stepped forward and though he didn't touch her, the message was clear. He was with Sarah and he was standing by her.

"You're sleeping with my wife!" Alec shouted. "Who do you think you are, some leader of some two-bit country in the middle of nowhere? Get off my land and go home! Leave my wife alone."

"Alec, stop this," Sarah said. Rationalizing with him wouldn't help. She needed him to be quiet and leave.

"I go to the hospital and when I come out my wife is sleeping with another man."

A skewed take on the events. Alec had a way of making her sound perfectly awful. "We'll talk about this."

Sarah pulled Alec out of the tent, beyond the netting. Saafir's guards appeared. She didn't want them to hurt Alec. "Alec, you don't want to get involved with security."

Alec shook her off and charged at Saafir, swinging at him. Saafir ducked the blows and he didn't retaliate. But the action was enough to bring Saafir's guards closing in. They took Alec under his arms and dragged him away.

Alec didn't stop screaming. He was on a full-blown, cursing, yelling tirade. Some of it was about her, some about Saafir and some Sarah didn't understand.

A police cruiser pulled up and two officers got out of the car. When Alec saw them, he stopped screaming.

Saafir stepped forward to speak to the officers. Feeling like she needed to explain to her clients, Sarah returned to the tent and to the bride and groom. The wedding was silent and no one was moving. Donald, the groom, looked furious, and Calista, the bride, refused to make eye contact.

"I'm sorry. My ex-husband is sick," Sarah said.

Calista met her gaze with tears in her eyes. "You've ruined my wedding!"

Sarah's stomach twisted. "Nothing could ruin this beautiful day. Everything has been perfect."

"Except that we hired you," Calista said.

Sarah swallowed hard, refusing to break down into tears.

"Leave. Just leave. We don't want you here," Donald said.

The band began playing, the singer encouraging people to dance. As the dance floor filled with the handful of remaining guests, Sarah backed away. She wouldn't argue with the bride and cause her more problems. Guilt consumed her and she was sure this blow to her reputation would cost her.

Sarah waited by Saafir's car in the parking lot. Though the police were speaking to witnesses and had taken her statement, thankfully they were being inconspicuous. Most of the guests were dancing again and laughter floated out in the night air.

Sarah shivered, a chill carrying on the breeze. She couldn't catch a break. She couldn't do anything right. She made terrible mistakes and then she paid for them.

Saafir joined her, dropping his jacket around her shoulders. It smelled of him, and the scent and his presence comforted her.

"Another amazing event by Sarah Parker," she said, feeling sick and disgusted with her life.

"You couldn't have known Alec would show up," Saafir said.

How had Alec known where she was tonight? The wedding wasn't a secret, but Sarah didn't post event details on her website. "The bride and groom blame me. What do you think they will remember about their wedding? What will they tell people? Someone probably took a picture and the incident is on social media by now with the caption, 'another terrible event by Sarah Parker.'"

Saafir rubbed his hand across his jaw where some stubble was growing. "Maybe it won't be that bad. Take it from someone who gets slammed in the media on a daily basis. For this, we can do damage control."

Sarah leaned against him. "How? Aren't you worried about your own damage control? Someone probably took your picture, too."

"My guards and the police are checking cell phones in the name of security and discretion. My guards will delete pictures and not ask questions. Where is the couple spending the night?"

"The Red and Blue hotel," she said. She had made the reservation herself. The Red and Blue was an upscale hotel known for its luxury and service. The nightly rate was over five hundred dollars for a basic room.

"I'll call ahead and we'll ask the hotel to put champagne and chocolates and roses in their room. They'll forget about the incident with your ex-husband."

If she hadn't been running on fumes, she might have thought of the gesture herself. While Saafir went to make the call, Sarah returned to her duties, staying out of the couple's eyesight.

Sarah awoke to the smell of coffee. When Saafir had called to make arrangements for the bride and groom the night before, he had also booked a room for them at the Red and Blue.

She had been exhausted, and after drinking a glass of wine, Sarah had fallen asleep in the large mahogany bed next to Saafir wearing a cotton T-shirt that belonged to the emir. He had been working on his computer, but it had felt good to have him close.

She was alone in the bed. Rolling over, she saw the alarm clock read 10:00 a.m. Sleeping this late was unusual for her. In the quiet of the morning, events from the previous day came screaming back to her. Saafir's voice was low and firm, drifting in from the other room. Getting out of bed, she peeked out the bedroom door.

He was sitting at the small desk near the window, his computer open in front of him and his phone pressed to his ear. He looked every bit the royal in his crisp suit with the sunlight shining on his dark hair.

She stepped into the room. He looked at her and a smile lit his face. Speaking a few words in Arabic, he ended his call and set down the phone.

Crossing the room, she sat on his lap. "Good morning."

"How are you feeling?" His arms slipped around her waist.

"In need of coffee," she said.

He reached around her and poured some dark brew from the silver carafe on his right into a white mug.

She took a sip and felt like she was coming up for air. "Thank you for this. And for last night," she said, kissing him.

"I apologize for not waking you when I got up. I thought you could use the sleep. I have a few conference calls this morning."

A knock on the door interrupted her before she could respond.

"Your excellency, you need to answer your phone," Frederick said. He barely glanced at Sarah. The intensity and worry on his face jolted her. Sarah glanced at the phone. It was lighting up with an incoming call.

Though Saafir's attention had been focused and absolute on her, he must have heard the immediacy in Frederick's voice. Saafir lifted his phone and answered it.

Sarah stood and gestured toward the door, unsure if she should leave. Her legs were bare, although Frederick was ignoring her.

Saafir shook his head, indicating she could stay. "How many?" he asked into the phone.

Something had happened. A family emergency? Saafir's brother, the former emir of Qamsar, had stepped down under a cloud of suspicion. The problems his terrorist fiancée had caused lingered around the royal family. Had something else occurred?

"Have you deployed the national guard?" Saafir asked.

National guard? A military problem?

Several more instructions and then Saafir set down his phone. He crossed the room and turned on the television, tuning in to a twenty-four-hour news broadcast. His face was serious and his eyes shadowed with worry. Sarah couldn't tear her eyes away from him and she wanted to go to him, but she was unsure of her role. Something big was going on and as the emir's lover, should she tuck herself out of the way? Lend an ear to listen?

The image on the television screen startled her. The story taking over the broadcast was about newly ignited oil field fires in Qamsar. Dangerous chemicals were leaking into the air and threatening the lives of everyone living in the area.

"Why?" Sarah asked. "How?"

Frederick was speaking to Saafir in Arabic, whether

to exclude her or because it was more natural to him, she didn't know. Sarah stayed quiet, feeling like an intruder.

The look on Saafir's face was both terrifying and sad, a combination of anger and misery. He spoke in English. "Not everyone wants this trade agreement. I have tried to show the people of my country that a trade agreement will help us on many levels. Those who do not want the agreement are trying to make a point. They'd rather burn the resource than see it in American hands."

He sat on the couch and stared at the television. Sarah sat next to him and put her arm around his shoulder. "I'm so sorry, Saafir."

Saafir balled his fists and then clasped his hands together. "This destruction is unnecessary. The resource, the environment and the people of Qamsar deserve better."

"You need to stamp down on this hard, Saafir," Frederick said, slamming his fist into his open hand. "Rabah Wasam is out of control. Put him in the jail near the oil fields. Let him breathe the damage he's caused." Frederick's face was red with anger. "Your primary concern should be making sure that Rabah Wasam and his cowardly followers see that they made a grave error and don't get the idea to start more fires," Frederick said. "What will we tell the Americans? If the oil fields are unusable, kiss the trade agreement goodbye. Say goodbye to progress. Forget new schools and services and infrastructure."

Frederick's words were mirrored on Saafir's face, and Sarah wondered what she could do to help. Saafir hadn't said much, but she could see the information churning through his mind.

Frederick glanced at her as if noticing her for the first time. He said something in another language and Sarah knew it was a curse.

"She needs to go. She is an American. They cannot be part of this. This could impact the trade agreement," Frederick said.

Saafir shook his head. "She is an American, but she may stay. I trust her."

His trust meant a great deal to her, and Owen's request that she inform on Saafir ran through her mind. She would explain to Owen that she would tell him nothing about Saafir, but how would Saafir feel if he learned she'd struck a deal with Owen in the first place?

"We're losing hundreds of thousands of dollars a day," Frederick said, punching his fist against the table for emphasis.

Saafir was aware that every hour the oil fires raged, a valuable resource was being destroyed. "What would you have me do?" He'd authorized the deployment of the national guard to protect the oil fields and prevent more from being set on fire. Emergency response teams were setting up in the area.

"You need to return home. Show your face for a few days. Let the country see that you're in control and you don't fear the extremists. Let America see you won't stick around and wait endlessly for them to come to more agreeable terms."

Saafir had delayed his return because the trade agreement meetings had been critical and he had hoped they'd come to a successful conclusion soon. With the events of the last twenty-four hours, the meetings had been postponed. While some emails were being sent to move forward with negotiations, Saafir wasn't needed. Since they weren't meeting in person, Sarah's services were on hold, as well.

But when Saafir returned to Qamsar, he would meet Alaina. Once he did, his relationship with Sarah had to end. He would commit himself to Alaina and anything less than his all was an embarrassment to himself and Alaina and unfair to Sarah.

"Set it up. I'll leave as soon as possible," Saafir said, feeling like he was lowering the boom on his relationship with Sarah. He glanced at her to see her reaction, but she appeared calm.

Frederick smiled, happy he had convinced Saafir.

"Stamp down hard on Wasam," Frederick said.

The slight sympathy Saafir had carried over Wasam's situation had been obliterated by these latest strikes against him and Qamsar. Saafir had respect for a man who wanted to improve the country, even if his way differed from his own. He had no respect for a man who used his influence to destroy.

Sarah had been attacked twice. Adham was wounded. Wasam's mission had hurt the people closest to Saafir and had hurt the country. Saafir had to take swift, severe action.

"We need to find him," Saafir said. "He'll have gone underground. Don't let him hide. Round up his followers and find out who was involved in this. If we hear even a whisper of plans of another attack, root out the source and destroy it."

"Saafir?"

He turned. Sarah was standing in the doorway to the

bedroom. While Frederick had been speaking, she had slipped away. She'd changed into clothes. She appeared timid, as if unsure if she should have said anything.

"Yes?" he asked. His adrenaline was racing and his anger had boiled over. He was sorry she had heard him declare war on the extremists, but something had to be done.

"I feel strange saying anything." She glanced at Frederick. "But I wondered about the people affected by the fires."

Frederick narrowed his eyes. "The emergency response teams have been deployed."

Sarah took a step toward Saafir. "I am not the leader of a country. I don't know how this works. But I know you. You care about people. You're angry right now, but your anger will pass and you'll have wasted your resources on revenge and finding Wasam when it would be better to spend the time helping those Qamsarians who need you."

Her words struck him hard. Saafir wasn't a man out for blood. He never had been. He checked his thinking, weighing what Frederick had suggested versus what Sarah was saying.

Sarah was right. Priority one had to be helping the Qamsarians who had lost their homes or whose neighborhoods were now too unsafe to inhabit. Saafir cleared his mind of the angry haze that colored his thinking.

He turned to Frederick. "Keep civilians away from the fires. Everyone who could be in danger needs to be evacuated. I don't care if it's thousands of people. Move them. Open schools, mosques, government buildings and any place where you can lay a cot." Saafir ran a hand over his face. "Grant access to the country's emergency fund for those affected. Move the prisoners from the local jail to somewhere safer."

Sarah smiled at him so brightly he felt like a hero. He had only done what was right. "Thank you, Sarah," he said. She centered him. Grounded him. Reminded him of who he was and what he stood for. "I need to return to Qamsar."

Her body tensed. "I understand."

He was duty-bound. "I have no other choice."

She looked at her hands and then raised her gaze to meet his. "I understand. We knew this was coming. In some ways, I feel like we've been together forever. In others, we've had only a moment. We can say goodbye and part as friends."

In the short time he had known Sarah, she had taken a place front and center in his heart. He wasn't ready to walk away from her. They'd known they didn't have a future together. Why did it feel impossible to leave her? "I want you to come with me," he said. The words were out of his mouth before he could stop them.

Her eyes snapped to meet his. "You want me to come to your country with you?"

"Yes," he said. He wanted her at his side. He wanted to talk to her, to hear her opinions and sleep beside her at night.

She shifted, appearing uncertain. "What about your fiancée? And your family? Won't they have something to say about this?"

"No! She can't come with you! Do you know the scandal you'll start? What about Alaina Faris? We need a union with her father and the Conservatives now more than ever. This is political and social suicide," Frederick said.

"My purpose of returning home is political. My family and my social life have nothing to do with my trip."

"You cannot be the leader of Qamsar and have a social life of your own. The two are integrally joined," Frederick said.

Sarah folded her arms across her chest. "I don't want to get you in trouble and make more problems." A long pause.

"I need you, Sarah. I need you to stay with me and help me through this."

Her eyes shone with unshed tears. "Yes, I will come with you."

"This is a total disaster!" Frederick said.

Whether he was talking about the oil fires or Sarah, he was right. But Saafir was determined to face whatever came at him with Sarah at his side.

Saafir had concerns about taking Sarah to Qamsar, but if he couldn't keep her safe in his country, he couldn't keep her safe anywhere. It was selfish to bring her, but he needed her as his sounding board. His cabinet acted as his official political advisors, but Sarah's advice appealed to the fair, honest side of him.

Just as his mother had filled the role of confidante and lover to his father, Sarah had taken that role for him. Saafir had never had someone in his personal life like her and now that he did, he realized what he'd been missing.

His schedule while in Qamsar was booked from sunup to sundown. Saafir would have liked to take

Sarah to one of his private homes and spend time with her, but it would have to wait.

Frederick handed Saafir his agenda. "You should not have brought her." He spoke in Arabic. He'd said the same words a dozen times since they'd left the States.

"I did what I needed to do," Saafir said. How could he make Frederick see that Sarah was important to him?

Frederick would never get on board with having Sarah in Qamsar. He wanted Saafir to devote himself to Alaina and their plan to unite the political parties.

Sarah appeared excited and nervous. She was staying close to Saafir and his bodyguards, but she wasn't touching him. He loved her respect for his position and their culture and yet he yearned for the warmth and connection of her hand in his.

They took an armored car to his family's home in west Qamsar. It was the closest property they owned to the oil fires. Even at this distance and though the air was declared safe, Saafir could smell the burning oil. The scent angered him. It was the smell of his country's most lucrative resource being destroyed.

Ms. Bourabbi, his mother's personal shopper, met them at the home. She had brought a large trunk of clothes for Sarah. She would need to dress in more conservative attire if she wanted to blend in in Qamsar. Clothes aside, Saafir didn't believe Sarah would ever blend in. She was more beautiful, more enticing, and her smile more radiant than any other woman's in Qamsar or in the United States.

Saafir looked for the words to explain the clothes without insulting Sarah. "It would be easier for you if you changed into more culturally customary clothes."

Sarah looked down at her clothes. "I picked something conservative. Do I look terrible?"

Saafir reassured her. "Of course not. You look beautiful. So beautiful that you'll stand out. Ms. Bourabbi will help you find something you like."

"That seems wise," Sarah said, letting Ms. Bourabbi lead her into another room.

Saafir turned his attention to Frederick and his secretary of health and human services. "I have forty minutes until I'm speaking at the disaster relief center. Update me on our progress."

Frederick looked at the tablet he was holding. "We've evacuated everyone in direct range of the oil fires. The winds are changing directions, and we've had reports of acid rain across the region. We're looking for more spaces to accommodate families and pets. Our lead engineer is telling me they have a plan in place and they've slowed the spread of the fire."

"Tell me more about the displaced people," Saafir said.

Frederick and the secretary grimaced. "We've opened mosques, government buildings and schools. Most are overcrowded. We've arranged for regular meal deliveries once a day, but water and basic hygiene facilities are at a premium."

"We've helped put people in touch with family members in other parts of the country, but it takes time to transport people across the region. We're battling meeting basic needs and providing services," his secretary said.

"Open the royal compound. Move people there. Contact every hotel in the region. Negotiate deals with them. Get a timeframe from the lead engineer when people can return to their homes," Saafir said.

"I don't think moving people into your home is wise," Frederick said. "Rabah Wasam has followers everywhere. If they get into your home, no telling what they might do."

Saafir wasn't an overly trusting man. He knew what a well-placed informant could find out. He didn't have anything to hide. "What are you afraid will happen? They'll report on what I'm doing? I'll stay here or at our country home with my mother. As long as my family is safe, that's priority one. Should I be the only Qamsarian not inconvenienced? How can I ask others to open their homes if I will not do the same?"

"Your excellency, I must again plead my case. Go after Rabah Wasam. Find him. Lock him away. Don't let your history with him color this situation. We've already heard rumors that he's fled the country. He deserves no pity," Frederick said.

Saafir had contemplated his response to Rabah Wasam on the long plane flight. He had spoken with Sarah about it at length. "The people of Qamsar come first. Finding Wasam is a high priority, but it comes second. It is not pity I feel for him. It is contempt."

Sarah opened the door and joined them in the hall. Saafir had never seen her look more stunning. She wore an emerald-green gown that set off her deep brown eyes. It was ornate and stylish and for an instant, he was transported to a moment where he was looking at Sarah as his bride.

Except she could never be.

His tongue felt too big for his mouth as he struggled to say something to her that was appropriate in front of others but also conveyed how seeing her dressed this way struck him.

"Do I look too awkward?" she said.

"Not at all. You've taken my breath away," he said.

His breath and another piece of his heart.

Saafir's national, televised address to his countrymen was important. They were looking for their leader to provide reassurance and explain the incidents of late without alarming them. He had to convey confidence in stopping the oil fires, in preventing more fires from being started and in the trade agreement negotiations with the Americans. The media had run the stories of the trouble he'd experienced in America and Adham's presence, or lack thereof, was noted. Adham remained in a hospital in America recovering.

With the weight of the country on his shoulders, Saafir strode to the podium. The media snapped to attention and cameras flashed. He was not taking questions until the end and the atmosphere in the room was heavy with curiosity and desperation. People wanted answers from their leader. They needed to know they and their families were safe.

"My fellow Qamsarians," Saafir said, his heart rate escalating. As many times as he had spoken in public, the importance of it was never lost on him.

"Our country has again suffered at the hands of terrorists. Men and women who would rather see their selfish ends met than the welfare and good of the Qamsarian people addressed. Our recent history proves that we won't bow under pressure. We will not let the extreme actions of a few angry extremists divert us from our goals. To move Qamsar forward, to see our families prosper and to show the world we are a capable, strong and important member of the international community, we must stand together."

Saafir took a deep breath. Sarah was standing to his right, off the elevated platform, but her complete confidence in him and her strength made him feel like she was at his side. She had her hands clasped together and he wished she were standing closer, as his mother had often stood at his father's side. A wave of emotion choked him and Saafir put thoughts of his family and Sarah aside. A display of emotion could be misinterpreted.

"I'm here to communicate our plans to cope with the disasters that have befallen our nation. I am opening my family's homes to those who have been displaced. Those who have been forced from their homes are being welcomed into mine. I have asked hotels and camping grounds and motels to open their doors to everyone who needs a place to stay. If you have an extra room, a trailer, a motorhome, a houseboat or a tent, I urge you to call the center for disaster relief and let them know of your willingness to provide shelter and food to those who need it. If you don't have room to spare, maybe you have extra clothes, blankets, pillows, towels or food to share.

"I've heard from grocers and restaurants who want to help. I've heard from bus companies who are willing to pick up those affected and deliver them to safety. I have deployed the national emergency response team. Employers are making temporary working arrangements. Everyone is working together to get our country back on track. We will not allow this act of malice to take us off the path of success."

He noticed a few misted eyes and hoped his message was finding a spot in the hearts of Qamsarians.

He provided more details for how to help and then he opened the floor for questions.

"Can you tell us what your administration is doing to find those who started the fire and prevent them from doing something more drastic?" A question from a reporter near the front.

Saafir knew who had started the fire and he knew whom he needed to watch. He would not openly accuse Rabah Wasam and declare war on the Conservatives, not now when he wanted the focus to be on helping. "Qamsar's intelligence community and military tactics teams are monitoring the situation. We have boots on the ground and ears to the wall on this. Any further provocation will be met with an immediate and relentless response."

"Why not strike back now?" Another question from a reporter.

"We will not lash out at those we believe responsible until we have evidence to prove it. More than that, I want all available resources directed at helping those in need. An assault takes time and money better spent elsewhere." Not that he hadn't assembled a team to search for Wasam and infiltrate his political party. If they tried other tactics, Saafir would know before they had a chance to attack.

"If you're worried about the country, why did you bring an American here? An outsider doesn't belong in your home." The question and comment came from a reporter in the fourth row.

Out of the corner of his eye, Saafir saw Sarah

stiffen. Saafir had brought Sarah and that opened him to criticism and thinly veiled insults.

"I have traveled here with a friend I made in America. She has been working with the trade agreement committee and she's here to consult on some other matters."

"Those other matters being your wedding?" a reporter asked.

The media had put together that Sarah was an event planner and Saafir could have lied and pretended she was in Qamsar to plan his wedding to Alaina. He wouldn't insult her with the lie. "Despite what the tabloids may have reported, I am not engaged and therefore I do not have plans for a wedding," he said. "Are there other questions about our plan for handling the oil field fires?"

"Alaina's father wants to meet with you. He saw the press conference and he knows you're in the city. Give the man thirty minutes of your time," Frederick said. "He'll be your family soon." He took a sip of his coffee and a bite of his biscotti.

They'd stopped at a local restaurant for something to eat.

Something in Frederick's voice reeked of censure. Frederick didn't approve of Sarah and the sooner he and Sarah had the distance of thousands of miles between them, the better, in Frederick's point of view.

Saafir couldn't think of a reason why he couldn't meet with Alaina's father, except that he wanted to return to his home after a long day and be alone with Sarah. The reminder of his impending engagement highlighted how little time he had remaining with her.

Meeting with Mohammad Faris would show the Conservatives he was not punishing the entire party for Wasam's actions and Saafir could use the meeting to learn what the rest of the party was thinking.

Sarah was stirring her bowl of soup and staring into it.

"Everything okay?" he asked. She was being unusually quiet.

"Feeling a little lost. I don't speak the language."

Some of the conversation was in Arabic and he didn't know how much Sarah was following. He considered lying to Sarah about whom he planned to meet, and then thought better of it. "Mohammad Faris wants to meet with me."

Sarah looked up from her bowl, dropping the spoon into it. "Now?"

He nodded. "Mr. Faris wishes to discuss the current political environment."

"And your engagement to his daughter," Sarah said, looking out the window, a vacant expression in her eyes. While their table was in a private corner of the restaurant, they were still being watched. How could Saafir communicate better with her without stirring up controversy?

He had no doubt his engagement would come up in the conversation with Alaina's father. Mr. Faris would have read the media reports detailing his relationship with Sarah and want answers. "I am sure he will ask me about his daughter."

Sarah cringed. "I assume I am not wanted for this meeting?"

"It's a political meeting," he said. He felt awful for

putting Sarah in this place. "It was selfish for me to invite you here. But I needed you. I need you."

"We're fooling ourselves," she whispered. "This can never work." Sarah stood. She looked at one of Saafir's guards. "I'm ready to leave."

The hurt on her face was plain. "Please take Sarah to our country home," Saafir said. "I will be along shortly."

"Shortly" turned into two hours. Mohammad Faris, a high-ranking member of the Conservative party, had questions he wanted answered about Saafir's plans for the country, his response to the oil fires and the trade agreement.

Saafir was as honest as he could be with his answers. Faris seemed to respect that.

"There is talk in the party about publicly distancing ourselves from Wasam and his extreme rhetoric. Many of the party believe he is taking his stance too far," Faris said.

"The royal family appreciates support in condemning terrorism and extremists." If Faris and other prominent members of the party openly discussed their viewpoints with the media, it would alienate Wasam and his followers and he would lose power.

Only after hashing through the topic of their strategy for Wasam in great detail did Faris turn the conversation to his daughter.

"Mikhail has been working hard to make sure your marriage to my daughter proceeds unencumbered. Do I need to be concerned that you'll back out of the arrangement? Jilting my daughter would be embarrassing for our family and create more tension between our party and the royal family."

Saafir hated lying to Mr. Faris, hated lying to Sarah and hated what he had to say next. He didn't have a choice. "There is no reason why Alaina and I will not be married." Though Sarah was the woman who took first place in his heart, he could not put his needs and desires before those of his countrymen.

Chapter 9

"Our oil fields, the most economically significant resources at our disposal, are being destroyed while our leader is gallivanting in America with an American consort. Where are his loyalties?"

Saafir pressed Mute on the television, shutting Rabah Wasam's words from reaching his ears. Wasam was speaking live from somewhere outside Qamsar. His decision to flee the country was telling to Saafir.

Saafir had been in meetings with his disaster relief chief and the lead of the engineering team he'd brought in to stop the oil fires. His priority was stopping the fires from spreading to protect human lives and the environment.

His phone rang. Only the highest priority calls were being sent through. Saafir answered.

"I heard you met with Alaina's father," Mikhail said.

It was good hearing his brother's voice. "Yes, I did," Saafir said.

"Will you see Alaina while you're in Qamsar?" Mikhail asked.

"My time is booked."

"Of course," Mikhail said. His voice hitched.

"What aren't you telling me?" Saafir asked. Mikhail had been in his shoes. He knew better than anyone that this job was a balancing act that required careful prioritization.

"There are murmurs among the Progressives that you're not taking a strong enough stance against Wasam."

He could count on Mikhail to be honest. "My plan is to keep this country running, even if I have to do so with my last breath. You know Wasam's problems with me are personal and he's using every possible angle to attack me."

"How will you counter?" Mikhail asked.

"I have a team looking into Wasam's activities."

"Be careful, Saafir. People are not always what they seem. Be careful who you trust and what intelligence you believe," Mikhail said.

Saafir's curiosity rose. "If you know something, say it plain. I don't have time for verbal games."

Mikhail sighed. "I don't know how you'll react to this and I considered not telling you, but I heard a rumor that Sarah Parker is working for the Americans and is using you to manipulate the trade agreement. She's a plant, Saafir."

Saafir bit his tongue over an adamant denial. After his brother's experiences with his former fiancée, Saafir understood why Mikhail would be quick to believe a conspiracy. "She is not a plant. She wouldn't betray me."

A long pause. "If she does?" Mikhail asked.

"She won't," Saafir said. Mikhail hadn't seen his fiancée's deception. Saafir knew Sarah's heart and intentions were pure. While she had initially approached him in the bar, she had not pursued him aggressively. She had been ready to walk away from their relationship. Her actions were not those of a mole.

"I'll let you know if I hear anything else. I have to go," Mikhail said.

They said their goodbyes. The distrust from Mikhail was understandable, but Sarah had never asked him about the trade agreement, at least not about the terms or his thoughts.

As if knowing he was thinking about her, Sarah entered his private office. Her cheeks were flushed and she was carrying a stack of magazines in her arms. "I went with two of your guards to the souk." She set the magazines in front of him.

On the cover of the top magazine in the stack was a picture of Sarah on the left and Alaina on the right. "No one will tell me what this says. What does it say about me?"

Something uncharitable that implied she was a whore bent on breaking up his marriage to Alaina. "You can't worry about what every tabloid is saying about you."

"Then it says something bad." She moved aside the top magazine and spread them out across his desk. "Are they all bad? Does everyone think I'm a home-wrecker?"

"Home-wrecker?" he asked, unfamiliar with the phrase. His English was good, but not perfect.

"It means a woman who causes problems in a marriage and destroys families."

He picked up one of the magazines. "This one is calling you an American princess."

He flipped it open and found the article. Her pictures danced across the pages. They'd included a few of him and Sarah together, all taken in America.

"What does it say?" she asked. She muttered something about needing to learn Arabic.

Saafir tossed the magazine onto his desk. "Please don't torment yourself with these things. I could gather a dozen political magazines that have bad things to say about me."

Sarah rubbed her forehead. "About your politics. Not about your personal life."

"To many, they are one and the same." In Qamsar, the royal family was fodder for the tabloids, especially when a member was of marriageable age and single. Saafir had learned to ignore the stories about him. Usually, their perspectives were skewed, their sources some distant acquaintance of the royal family with little information and the articles borderline libelous.

"An entire country of people hates me," she said.

Saafir gathered Sarah against him. "It's not a country of people. There are a few reporters digging around for information about you. Normally, you'd have a PR person who would make a statement, but since we are denying any official relationship, it is best to ignore this trash."

"Tell me what the article says and then I will ignore it."

He kissed the tip of her nose. "No. Ignore it. I have to get to a meeting. Can we have dinner after?"

She turned away. "You haven't said anything about your meeting with Alaina's father."

"It went well." Telling her the details was akin to twisting the knife.

Sarah pulled away from him and crossed the room to the window. She stared out of it. "It's harder being here than I imagined. I want to be here for you, but I had no idea about the pressure."

He almost said, "Being the emir's wife is hard." But for the hundredth time, he reminded himself she was not and could not be his wife.

The emir's country home was opulent and relaxing, almost like visiting a vacation spot. Being there away from the prying eyes of the media took the edge off some of her anxiety. Sarah wanted to answer the media's questions to stop the rumors, but if she told the truth, that could be spun into a lurid tale. She would stay quiet and do her best to ignore the attention.

Saafir was in another meeting with his advisors, preparing for a new speech he was giving. Sarah changed channels on the television, reading the translated closed captioning on the news. She was interested in following what was happening with the oil field fires. The reporter on screen was standing close enough to the oil fires to see smoke in the distance.

An explosion rattled the camera and the reporter ducked as if under fire. As shouting commenced, the screen went black and the news switched scenes to the network's studio. Sarah's heart rate escalated. What was happening? The closed captioning wasn't keeping pace with the images on screen.

"We've received reports of an explosion near the oil fires. We're trying to get in touch with our contact at the scene to find more details."

Sarah knocked on the heavy brown door to Saafir's office. Saafir might have a meeting going on, but he needed to know about this.

Frederick opened the door and glared at her. Saafir waved her inside. He had his phone in his hand and the other members of his cabinet watched her.

"Saafir, the news is reporting—"

"Land mines." He swore under his breath. "There are land mines buried in the oil fields."

Sarah rushed to him and slipped her arms around his shoulders. This national catastrophe was complicating and it was wearing on Saafir. He seemed to have aged years in the last several days. Stress was exhausting him.

"You need to pull the engineers fighting the fires out of there," she said.

"And leave the oil fields burning unchecked?" Frederick asked.

Saafir's advisors looked between her and Frederick, appearing unsure if they should jump into the conversation.

Sarah's temper flared. Saafir was doing everything he could to protect everyone else and was being pulled in a hundred directions.

"Saafir doesn't want any more injuries. We'll pull the people from the fields until we can get experts in land mines to secure the area," Sarah said.

Frederick scoffed. "Experts in land mines? Who are

you to suggest that? You haven't served any time in the military. Do you know where you can find these so-called experts?"

The disdain in his voice infuriated her. "The world has an expert for everything," she said. Somewhere in the world, someone was fascinated by fire, explosions and bombs. Saafir could find them and bring them in to help.

"Stop. Both of you," Saafir said sharply. "We are on the same team. I won't have open and hostile dissent among my advisors."

"She is not one your advisors," Frederick said.

"She is my guest and her opinions matter to me," Saafir said.

Her heart leapt free of some of the confusion that clung to her. When she was with Saafir, even in a country where she was an outsider and everything felt topsy-turvy, he centered her and made her feel important.

"Sarah's right. We have to protect the team fighting the fire and make sure whoever is in the field is trained to search for and handle land mines," Saafir said, rubbing his forehead. "Please, leave us alone."

Sarah retreated to the door. If Saafir wanted to be alone with Frederick and his cabinet to talk state secrets, that was fine with her.

"I mean Sarah. I need to be alone with Sarah."

Hiding her surprise, Sarah took a seat next to Saafir. Frederick and the rest of Saafir's cabinet left the room, a mixture of shock, annoyance and amusement on their faces.

"How can I help?" Sarah asked.

Saafir pulled her from her chair into his lap.

He jammed a hand through his hair. "My sister is

married to an American FBI agent. He's the man I contacted to find out who'd be handling the situation with Khoury. My brother-in-law has some powerful connections. He called me a couple days ago and offered to lend a hand. I was hesitant to involve the Americans in this cleanup since I don't want to be indebted to them and be forced to make concessions during the trade negotiations."

Sarah stroked her hand down the side of his hair. Even lacking sleep, he was still polished and gorgeous. "I am sure if your brother-in-law offered to help, it was a personal offer. Call him and talk to him. Get your sister involved if you have to. Be honest with him about what you need and what you're willing to do to get it."

Saafir was already dialing his phone. "Harris, it's Saafir. I need a favor."

Saafir had held off calling his brother-in-law, Harris Truman, because he wanted Qamsar to handle their problems without international interference. But the danger had escalated to the point that he had to alter his thinking to protect his people.

Sarah was not military and she had no background in dealing with explosives. She had no experience in handling national disasters. But she was logical and Saafir needed someone who had no skin in the game. She didn't have an agenda, only solutions that were simple enough to work.

Harris had answered after one ring. Saafir explained he was looking for some resources and Harris paused a few moments before offering help. "I have a friend who runs a consulting company that handles difficult problems," Harris said. He spoke the words "difficult problems" with emphasis.

"Tell me about this friend and his company."

"He wouldn't appreciate me telling you about him, but I can tell you his company is top-shelf. He hires the best in the world and he gets jobs done. He has former special ops and ex-military on his payroll. His contacts include spies, secret agents and computer hackers. What are you after specifically?"

Saafir didn't dance around about what he needed. He could trust Harris not to run to the media about the problems Qamsar was experiencing. "I need an expert in disabling land mines."

Harris made a sound of disgust. "Only cowards set landmines. A memo hit my desk about turbulence in the area. Laila is practically twisting my arm to let her fly back to Qamsar to help."

"Keep my sister in the States." Laila was safer far away from the mess in Qamsar. Harris wouldn't let any harm come to Laila.

"She'll be pleased to know I'm sending experts from Connor's team. She's met Connor and she trusts him."

His sister's stamp of approval meant a great deal to him. "I need them here fast," Saafir said.

"That's how Connor's team works. Fast. Precise. Quietly."

It was what Saafir needed to handle the land mines. But what else would the extremists have planned?

Saafir's security team took Sarah to the local shopping district. She was surrounded by high-end boutiques and she could not afford to purchase one thing inside them. Couture clothing and gold and platinum jewelry weren't in her budget.

Since his meeting with Alaina's father, unspoken tension had been heavy between her and Saafir and she'd needed to get out of the house. They'd had little time alone and when Saafir came to bed at night, he collapsed with exhaustion. She had nudged him and kissed him, but he had only pulled her close to sleep.

Sarah's phone rang and she answered, hoping it was Saafir calling to say his meetings were done for the day and he'd meet her for a late dinner. They needed to talk. She felt him slipping away and she wanted clarity.

It wasn't Saafir. It was Owen.

"Alec has gone missing," Owen said.

Sarah waited. She didn't want to get involved in yet another of Alec's disastrous decisions. "I'm sorry to hear that." After the stunt he'd pulled at the last wedding she'd planned, she hadn't forgiven him. "I posted his bail and he ran. Any ideas where he is?" Owen asked.

"You know I'm not in the country right now. I haven't seen him," Sarah said. She was relieved to have the excuse of the distance for why she couldn't help find him. She didn't want him found. Let Alec run away and start his life over. Every other do-over option had been exercised and hadn't worked. Alec had been lucky time and again, but it was very likely the next step would be jail.

"Has Saafir told you anything about the trade agreement?" Owen asked.

She had promised Owen she would back-channel information for him, but only because she never thought she'd have any information. "He's been busy with other things. He hasn't mentioned the trade agreement." She wasn't planning to tell him even if he had.

Owen paused. "Will he walk away from the deal because of the problems with the oil fields?"

Sarah had no way to know that. "Putting out the oil fires is a priority." Saafir's guards weren't looking at her, but they spoke English and she knew they were listening to her conversation.

Owen swore. "He hasn't been responding to emails. Is he coming back to the negotiations' table? I can't get a straight answer from Frederick."

"I don't know."

"When are you coming home?" Owen asked.

"I don't know that, either."

"Is this an open-ended invitation to stay with him?"

She and Saafir hadn't talked about it. Sarah had assumed they'd be in Qamsar for a few days to address the problems with the oil fields and then they'd return to America to finish negotiations for the trade agreement. She would step back into her role as event coordinator when they resumed meetings. Saafir hadn't clued her in on his plans or his thinking. "It's not something we've discussed. He has a life here and I have a life in America. I'm just visiting."

The words stuck in her mouth. Every word she spoke to Owen was the truth, but it burned to admit.

A woman approached. "Excuse me, are you the emir's lover?"

The question caught her by surprise. She was wearing traditional Qamsarian clothing and had been trying to blend. How should she answer the question? The woman was young and Sarah didn't sense malice in the question, just curiosity.

Saafir's guards moved closer. They were watching the exchange, but they hadn't gotten involved. Couldn't they whisk her away? Saafir had told her to ignore the media. Should she also ignore anyone angling for information?

"You have me confused with someone else," Sarah said. "I'll call you back," she said into the phone to Owen.

The woman moved closer. "It is you. I recognize you from your picture on the internet. Tell me what the emir is like. He is so dreamy."

The woman called to her friends. Sarah found herself in the middle of a pack of women who were launching questions at her in a mix of Arabic and English. Is the emir a good boyfriend? Does he give you expensive gifts? What about Alaina Faris? Are you upset he is marrying someone else?

Sarah backed away. "I need to go."

She turned and fled and the guards prevented the women from following her. Sarah didn't stop walking until she was inside the car. Overheated and shaken, Sarah called Molly.

"Adham told me you went with Saafir to Qamsar," Molly said.

"I did. I'm here now shopping in stores where I can't afford anything while Saafir is in meetings." Sarah told her friend what had happened in the shopping district.

"I'll kill Evelyn. This is her fault," Molly said.

Evelyn? What did Alec's sister have to do with this? "What did Evelyn do?"

Molly groaned. "You haven't seen the news? Someone connected you to Evelyn and she told a reporter that you spent the night with Saafir on her boat."

Not a lie. Why would Evelyn not keep her secret? "That happened. She said she would stay quiet about the incident. We were looking for a safe place to stay."

"You don't have to explain anything to me. You're an adult. You can do what you want. But Sarah? You know better about Evelyn. All you need to get a secret out of her is a ten-dollar bottle of rum."

Sarah hated hearing Evelyn cast in a bad light. Though they had been through a lot, she felt protective of Evelyn, whom she considered family. "What can I do about what everyone is saying about me?"

"What do you mean? You know what you need to do. When Alec made a scene in your neighborhood and embarrassed you in front of your neighbors, did you hide inside? Nope. You walked around, smiling like you had the world on a string."

"This is different. This isn't a neighborhood. This is a country of people. A hostile country of people. As far as I can tell, at least half of the people here hate me."

Molly let go a curse she rarely spoke. "You've done nothing wrong. Head high. Get back to those stores and you shop like you've got an orchard of money trees growing in your yard."

"I can't afford to do that," Sarah said.

"Charge it to Saafir."

An idea formed. She wouldn't pretend she had money to burn, but she could maybe do something to help. "You gave me a good idea. I'll text you later."

"Sarah? Don't let them see you sweat."

Sarah said goodbye to her friend and then texted Saafir for permission to spend some money. He didn't question why or what she planned to buy. She received an unequivocal "yes" from him.

* * *

Saafir arrived in his compound at eleven that night. He expected to find a sleeping Sarah in his bed. She wasn't in his bedroom and she wasn't in the guest bedroom.

He called her, worried. His guards would have alerted him if there had been a problem.

Relief passed over him when Sarah answered.

"Hey." Sarah sounded out of breath. Was she at the gym?

"Where are you? Are you okay?" Saafir asked. The last he had heard, she had asked him for permission to charge to his family accounts. He'd been pleased she had asked. Shopping might make her feel better.

"I'm fine. I was shopping, but that went awry, so I'm at the emergency response center. I'm helping get things organized. Saafir, I'm helping and I'm good at this."

Pride and happiness burst across his chest at the enthusiasm and spirit in her voice. It was the most upbeat she'd sounded since arriving in Qamsar. "You don't have to do that."

"I'm good at organizing events and they're shorthanded. Volunteers have been coming from various places around the world, so it's been easy to blend. No one knows of my connection to you."

Saafir heard something between her words. Her connection to him was upsetting. The magazines, the clothes and the media questions bothered her more than he'd thought. He'd grown up with people prying into his life and it no longer upset him. But it was new to Sarah. Saafir should have anticipated it and taken steps to make her feel more comfortable.

"You are amazing, do you know that?" he asked.

Sarah laughed. "I'm doing what I can. Are your meetings finished for the day?"

"Yes. I was hoping we could have dinner." He was aching to see her. He was determined to at least have a conversation with her before falling asleep.

"Let me finish what I'm working on, and I'll be home. I mean, to your place."

He knew what she'd meant, but calling it their home didn't feel as strange as he would have thought. After saying their goodbyes, he looked around his sparse bedroom.

When he had taken over this part of the compound from Mikhail, he had done some redecorating, primarily getting rid of the ornate items that Mikhail loved. Saafir preferred his inner sanctum to be clutter-free. It helped him to clear his mind at the end of the day.

He took a shower and asked for a dinner to be delivered. Sarah arrived about an hour later. Though her hair was tied in a messy knot on top of her head and she wasn't wearing jewelry, she captivated him. His entire body responded to the sight of her. The last several nights, they hadn't made love and he was suddenly starving for her.

"How did you decide to spend the day at the emergency response center?" he asked. Some of the tension that had built between them seemed to thin.

Sarah shrugged. "I needed something to do. When your boyfriend runs a country, that leaves a girl with a lot of free time."

"You didn't miss me?" Saafir asked, reaching for her. He couldn't be in the same room with her for another minute without touching her.

She brought her hand to her mouth and pretended to think about it. "I suppose I did. A little. Maybe you need to remind me what I was missing."

Unfolding the shawl from around her shoulders, he let it drop to the floor. When every article of clothing was on the floor, Saafir pulled her to the rug with him. Her giggles turned to moans in record time and Saafir showed her how much he appreciated and had missed her.

Sarah woke to the smell of Saafir—clean and spicy. He was fresh from a shower and was knotting his tie around his neck in the mirror. She watched for several long moments before he noticed she was awake.

"How did you sleep?" he asked.

Sarah stretched out on the cool sheets. "Great. Where are you off to this morning?"

"I have a meeting with my defense secretary. He has news about Rabah Wasam's movements."

Sarah shivered. She wanted Rabah Wasam caught, but she knew a man with power and influence and a mob of followers could evade the law. "Please be careful. He won't react well to you coming after him." Wasam's means had been violent and aggressive. Would he up the ante when Saafir went on the offensive?

"I will be safe," he said and kissed her forehead. "Order breakfast and relax. We'll plan to have lunch together."

Sarah showered and then called for breakfast to be brought to the room. When it arrived, she pushed the cart onto the balcony. Lifting the sterling silver lids from the platters, she found a pink box tied with a white ribbon, stamped with the word LUX. It was one of the boutiques where she had window-shopped the day before.

Saafir had gotten her a gift! She was so excited her hands were shaking when she took the box in her hands. The ribbon was soft and perfectly tied onto the crisp white box. It was too heavy to be jewelry and too small to be clothes, but perhaps something sentimental, a thoughtful trinket to remind her of her time in Qamsar.

Pulling open the ribbon, she lifted the lid carefully. Plucking aside the delicate pink tissue paper, Sarah screamed and dropped the box. She stepped away, feeling sick and disgusted.

Two guards rushed into the room. She pointed at the box. An explanation wasn't necessary.

The box was filled with severed snake heads and syringes spattered with blood.

"I want every surveillance tape reviewed. I want security measures tightened," Saafir said, still clasping Sarah to him. He had been pulled from his meeting to address the breach. Since Saafir had been in a conference with his defense secretary, he'd brought him along to assess the situation and lend his expertise.

Someone had gotten close enough to deliver Sarah a threat. The perpetrator had been inside Saafir's private wing and could have done worse than leave a disgusting gift. Sarah's food could have been poisoned.

Sarah hadn't said much. While his team promised to find out where the LUX box had come from and who had put it on her food cart, Saafir turned his full attention to Sarah.

"Tell me how you're feeling," Saafir said.

"It was a warning, wasn't it? I'm the snake and the syringes must be something with my ex. Your countrymen know who I am and they don't like it. They want me to leave."

An elaborate explanation. "It isn't personal."

"Of course it's not personal."

Saafir turned to the sound of his mother's voice. Sarah was still pressed against his side and if his mother took offense to the display of intimacy, she said nothing. Saafir couldn't let her go. The threat was still too raw.

"Over the years, I've received death threats. I've received nasty letters and emails. Anonymity means people will be more vicious, more self-righteous and ruder than if they had to talk to you in person," Iba said.

Sarah looked between Saafir and his mother. Saafir introduced them.

"It's nice to meet you, but this is not how I planned it," Sarah said.

His mother reached out and took Sarah's hand. Saafir released Sarah.

"If it were up to Saafir, I wouldn't meet you at all. Saafir has always been very private about his personal life."

"You know I can't openly date Sarah," Saafir said.

His mother shot him an incredulous look. "You haven't done a good job keeping it a secret. I've been on the phone with Alaina's mother every day reassuring her that my son is committed to moving forward with the engagement. That's hard for me to do when the media wants the world to know about you and Sarah."

Saafir's mother surprised him with her frank honesty. Though she could be gentle and sensitive to others' needs, his mother didn't pretend to be unaware of what her sons were doing. She didn't feign stupidity because she was an intelligent woman and stupidity didn't suit her. "Was the box a gift from Rabah Wasam?"

"I suspect it was," Saafir said.

Iba patted Sarah's shoulder. "I will spend the day with Sarah. You handle your meetings."

Being with his mother may not be Sarah's idea of how to spend her time in Qamsar. It was a step in their relationship they'd never planned to take. "Let me speak to Sarah for a moment."

Saafir led Sarah into the sitting room attached to his bedroom. "If you have other plans for the day, my mom will understand. I will tell her you are busy."

Sarah touched the side of his face. "Thank you for being concerned about me. But I'm fine. I'll go with your mom. It will be nice to spend time with her."

"Will it make it harder for you?" Saafir asked.

Sarah sighed. "No. I've known all along where this couldn't lead."

Saafir knew the same. A nonexistent future. No chance of a life together. It wasn't in the stars.

"How long have you been in love with my son?" Iba asked as soon as they were alone.

Sarah smoothed her dress and looked out across the balcony, giving herself a few moments to think. It was an awkward question, given the culture and tradition of Qamsar and because it was obvious she had spent the night with Saafir since she had been in his private bedroom. "Saafir and I are not in love."

Their relationship was unconventional in Saafir's

country and explaining it in intimate details wasn't necessary.

"There's something about the way you look at him and he looks at you that makes me wonder," Iba said.

Passion? Desire? Uncertainty? "Our relationship has progressed quickly." From the moment they'd met, everything had been on an accelerated timeline. They wouldn't have much time together and that knowledge hanging over their heads had spurred them to take chances, like traveling together to his country.

"My son is obligated to marry a Qamsarian woman."

Why did everyone need to tell her that? They either thought she was dense or Saafir was lying to her. Neither was true. "I know," Sarah said, trying to sound casual.

"My son never wanted to be the emir. He never worked it into his life plan. I think he is disappointed to have the role."

Disappointed? Saafir seemed proud and honored. "He's mentioned he feels honored to serve his countrymen."

Iba sighed. "That sounds like Saafir. He took up the responsibilities of the position, but he isn't like my older son."

"Saafir is a good man," Sarah said.

"He has a soft heart and I don't want him to get hurt." Iba gave her a pointed look.

Saafir get hurt? He was the one who would have an amazing life with a gorgeous woman waiting for him. What did Sarah have waiting for her?

"My daughter Laila married an American. At first, I wasn't sure if he was the right man for her. They have so many differences. But they are happy. I see how my son-in-law treats her and I could not have asked for a better man for my daughter."

Iba had spoken plainly earlier in the day. Now, Sarah felt like Iba was feeling her out. "I am wrong for Saafir. He knows it. I know it."

Iba inclined her head. "Wrong in what way?"

Listing their incompatibilities was easy. "We're from different cultures. We're from different worlds. We want different things. I've been married before."

"And yet you are together," Iba said.

"It's what works now."

"What do you want most from a relationship with a man?" Iba asked.

"A family," Sarah said. The automatic response was telling. She wanted something Saafir could never give her. Something she had hoped would come with her first marriage, and for a time, it had.

"My son would like a family," Iba said. "He has never indicated otherwise."

Sarah looked away. She thought Iba would appreciate knowing an American woman wasn't fouling up her son's plans for his future, but she seemed to be trying to talk Sarah into believing she and Saafir were compatible. "I would never be accepted here. Look at what the news is saying about me."

Iba nodded. "Vicious remarks that sting. I've been there myself. After I had my daughter, I gained so much weight that I had to buy all new clothes. The tabloids wrote of my husband having an affair with any younger, thinner woman who came within ten feet of him. It hurt."

Sarah hadn't known that about Saafir's parents. "How did you handle it?"

"I learned that the truth of our love was between my husband and me. No one could know what went on between us, and I wouldn't let lies fester between us and cause unhappiness. I was confident in our love and when I reminded myself of that, I forgot the hateful words."

But Iba was Qamsarian. She had been the emir's wife. She undoubtedly had the credentials and the social status and the breeding to be perfect for the emir. "Once Saafir marries a Qamsarian, I'll be forgotten." The short attention span of the media would turn to other more interesting matters, like the emir's fiancée.

Iba clucked her tongue. "Then you don't know my son well. He doesn't forget people he cares for."

Chapter 10

Two days later, Saafir and Sarah boarded the emir's private plane en route to America. Stateside Oil had been in negotiations with Frederick and they were willing to cede the issues most important to Saafir to see the trade agreement through.

The men that Harris had sent to Qamsar had been working to find and disable the land mines. As yet, they had located and destroyed four, saving countless lives.

When Saafir's plane touched down in America, they took an armored car from the airport. Frederick was riding in the back with them, casting occasional disapproving looks at them as he read on his tablet.

Saafir ignored the looks.

He and Sarah had their issues. Saafir was worried about her. She had been quiet and distant the last two days. Had she hated being in Qamsar? She hadn't said much about her day with his mother.

He'd been working on a plan to make her feel better. "I feel responsible for what happened to your apartment after we met. I wanted to buy you a new place to live, far away from the city, surrounded by an iron gate with a security service and a guard monitoring the premises. But I knew you wouldn't have accepted such a gift."

"You're right about that," Sarah said, nodding her head.

"I think you'll like what I decided to do instead," he said.

Sarah tensed. "You didn't have to do anything. I have it under control."

Had he made a mistake in assuming she would want his help? He had money and resources at his disposal and he wanted to use them to help her. "With the changes to the trade agreement meetings and our trip to Qamsar, I've kept your plate full. I am grateful for everything you've done and I hope this is a sign of that gratitude."

"What did you do?" she asked.

"You'll see," Saafir said.

They pulled up to her apartment building. The car waited at the curb and Saafir led Sarah up the stairs to her apartment. He opened her front door, disabled the alarm and turned on the lights.

He watched her face for a reaction. He may have overstepped his bounds. She might feel that he'd invaded her personal space.

She turned, confusion on her face. "You cleaned my apartment. You fixed my things." She bit her lower lip. "I had the insurance money. I would have taken care of this."

"I wanted to help you."

Sarah stabbed a hand through her hair. "This was nice of you."

Her words sounded garbled. "But?"

"But it's a lot to take in. Being in Qamsar was overwhelming. Being near you is intense. Your money and your power and your family..."

She wandered into the room and Saafir waited, still unsure if she was upset or just astounded at how different her place looked.

Her apartment! Saafir had had it cleaned and her furniture repaired. Sarah picked up a photo frame on her kitchen counter of her, Molly and Krista. The picture had been repaired and the frame pieced back together.

Sarah was swamped with emotion. It was a nice gesture, but it felt like an exorbitant gift and one she couldn't repay.

"It's my fault your home was destroyed and I couldn't live with that," Saafir said from the doorway.

Sarah walked through her place, taking it in, opening drawers and cabinets. Things were out of place, but she was home. "Does this mean we can sleep here tonight?" She was tired of living in hotels. She wanted to be in her home.

Saafir glanced over his shoulder at his guards and then nodded. "Yes. They'll keep watch."

Suddenly self-conscious about her place and an emir staying in it, Sarah amended her statement. "If you

are more comfortable in a hotel, we can stay somewhere else."

Saafir looked around and Sarah followed his gaze.
Was he seeing the cracks in the ceiling or the dinginess
of the paint? Was he feeling cramped? His bedroom in
Qamsar was the size of her entire living space in D.C.

"I like this place. It looks like you," he said. "Bold,
creative and warm. We'll stay here."

"Then let me give you the grand tour," she said. She
took his hand and walked backward to her bedroom. It
was the one place where she felt on equal footing with
him, the one place where they connected.

Sarah refused to look too deeply into that thought.
If she did, she knew she wouldn't like what came of it.

A phone ringing in the middle of the night never
delivered good news.

Saafir's hand went to the bedside table for his phone.
"Hello."

"Your excellency, we have bad news." One of Saafir's guards.

Saafir had learned to wake completely at a moment's
notice. "Tell me."

Sarah was sleeping at his side and she stirred. He
set his hand on her to calm her.

Was it Adham? His mother? His sister?

"Frederick has been taken," Jafar said.

Anger and worry coursed through him. "Tell me
everything you know," Saafir said.

After Jafar gave him the information, Saafir shook
Sarah. "Sarah, I need you."

Sarah opened her eyes. "What's the matter? What
time is it?"

"Frederick has been taken. He's missing."

Sarah sat up. "How do you know?"

"Jafar called. The guard assigned to watch Frederick was drugged. Someone took Frederick from his hotel room. A night houseman found the guard in the hallway."

"Do they know where he was taken? Do they know who took him?" Sarah asked.

"Witnesses described a car in front of the hotel and the police are looking into it. The hotel had some security footage and it's being reviewed for clues."

Sarah put her arms around him. "Saafir, I am so sorry. I know how much Frederick means to you."

"Frederick has no military training. He was raised in Ireland and his parents are wealthy businesspeople. He spent his entire life in school." He wouldn't fare well under torture or questioning.

"You need to reach out to Wasam," Sarah said. "If he's not directly behind this, he knows who is."

"Why would Wasam help me?"

"Because he doesn't want to hurt Frederick. He wants to get to you," Sarah said.

"Why Frederick?" A cold wash of fear passed through him. "What if this is an attack on multiple fronts? What if Frederick wasn't the only person taken?" He dialed Jafar. "Find my sister, my brother, Adham and my mother. Get in touch with every member of my family and my cabinet and the trade agreement. Find out if anyone else is missing. I want to know if everyone is safe."

Saafir disconnected the call and rang his mother. She answered on the first ring.

"My son, are you okay?" Iba asked.

"I'm fine. Frederick has been kidnapped. I needed to know you are safe."

"I am safe. Your guards haven't left me for a minute. I can't get a cup of tea without someone shadowing my movements."

Guilt assailed him. "I'm sorry, but it has to be this way. You need to be kept safe."

"Saafir, things are escalating. It was never this bad with your father."

Guilt turned to shame. Saafir couldn't fill his father's shoes. It was his job to keep the peace in his country and he was doing a poor job. He had politicians at each other's throats and their followers taking actions and lashing out. "I'm sorry. I never thought I would be in this position." The words sounded weak and it made Saafir loathe them.

Saafir heard the click of his mother's worry beads tapping together. She kept a set on her bedside table, and in times of trouble, she would hold them while she meditated and considered her options.

"You could ask Mikhail for his opinion," Iba said. "Our family needs to be strong now. We need to rally together and support each other."

"I might do that. He spent more time being groomed for this position. I will think on it. I want to call Laila and make sure she is safe."

"Harris wouldn't let anything happen to her," his mother said.

His brother-in-law was a strong and capable man. Saafir trusted him with Laila's life. He wouldn't have approved the marriage otherwise. But he still needed to hear Laila's voice.

A few minutes later, Saafir was speaking to his sister. She sounded wide-awake despite the hour.

"What are you doing up so late?" he asked.

"Harris and I are working on something."

Worried he would have to hear about her sex life, he groaned. "I'll pretend you're doing home repairs."

Laila laughed. "Close. I don't want to burden you with the details—"

"If this is about your sex life, please don't continue."

"You can't see me, but I'm rolling my eyes. We're assisting on a project for a friend's consulting firm."

"The same consulting firm that you sent to lend Qamsar a hand with the land mines?" Saafir asked, not liking the idea of his sister being involved in dangerous jobs.

"The very same. Turns out security consultants are in red-hot demand and the company has more work than they can handle. We're talking about taking permanent positions with the company."

His delicate sister working for a security consulting company? Saafir didn't approve. He didn't see how Harris would agree to it, either. Talking to his headstrong sister about it now was futile. When Laila wanted something, she got it. He made a mental note to bring it up with her later. Or maybe he was better off not knowing the details. "I'm calling to be sure you're okay. We've had some more trouble in D.C."

"More trouble? Do you want Harris and me to fly to D.C. to help?" Laila asked.

He wanted his family as far from him and Wasam as possible. "Stay where you are. I'm not interested in lining up more targets for Rabah Wasam. I want you and Harris to be on alert."

"I'm the emir of Qamsar's sister. We are always on alert."

After he had talked to his sister for a few more minutes, his phone beeped that he had an incoming call. "Laila, I need to go. Another call."

"Take care of yourself," Laila said.

Saafir answered the call. It was Jafar again.

"We've gotten in touch with everyone from the committee except the rep from Stateside Oil. Virginia Anderson isn't answering her phone and the guard assigned to watch her has been unreachable."

"Keep trying to find her," Saafir said, a heavy feeling of dread in his stomach. He needed to talk to Adham. Adham might not be physically able to defend and protect him, but his mind was sharp and trained on tactics and countermeasures.

If Saafir didn't stop Wasam, it would end in more deaths, maybe even Sarah's or his own.

"What's their angle in taking Frederick?" Saafir asked. "To force my hand? Wasam believes I left him to rot in that prison. Why would he think I would do anything to save Frederick?"

Adham shifted in his hospital bed. He looked much better, his coloring strong and his eyes clear and alert. Saafir hated to burden him with problems, but he trusted Adham and his opinions.

"He knows you. He might believe you weren't willing to risk anything to save him, but he knows Frederick is important to you."

Molly linked her fingers through Adham's. He didn't pull away and Saafir was surprised by both Molly's actions and Adham's inaction to the gesture.

"With the oil fields on fire, we're in no position to do anything with our oil," Adham said. "Why not step away from the trade agreement and let him believe he's won?"

"He won't stop at the trade agreement. He's selling the trade agreement to his followers as the reason I need to be removed, but Wasam wants the throne."

Sarah squeezed his arm, a reminder of her unceasing support. "You need to stay strong. Don't give him an inch. You know that saying. We should strike back."

Fighting words from his usually diplomatic Sarah told him how involved she had become in Qamsar's problems. In his problems. In his life. "The leaders in the Conservative party have been publicly denouncing Wasam. He must know he's losing power and he's growing more desperate. How do you suggest we counter his actions?" Saafir asked.

"He loves to play to the media. When I was in Qamsar, every time I turned around he was yapping to the media about his problems and spouting his criticisms. Why don't you use the media against him? You've stayed quiet and you've spoken to the press through official channels. You've maintained decorum and professionalism. Forget that. Give the media a good story. Distract him. Let him work to put out fires as quickly as you've had to."

"If we change tactics, it will keep him guessing. That will buy us time," Saafir said.

"Time for us to find Frederick," Adham said.

"You are still on medical leave," Saafir said, not willing to let his brother risk his health again.

Adham cracked his knuckles. "My doctors say the infection is better. It will be another day or two and

I'll be out of here and watching your back. Where I belong. You're my family. I hate knowing you're out in the world without my protection."

Sarah's eyes misted. "That's such a nice thing to say, Adham. You think of each other as family." Saafir didn't know how to respond to that. His blood relation to Adham was one of the best-kept secrets of his father's life.

"What? What did I say?" Sarah asked, looking between them.

"Nothing," Adham said.

"You both looked away," Molly said.

Adham waited and shrugged at Saafir. "You can tell them."

"Tell us what?" Sarah asked.

"Adham and I are half brothers," Saafir said. "So when I call him my brother, he is."

Sarah looked between them. "How? Iba had another husband? Or a lover?" Disbelief highlighted every word.

Adham shook his head. "We have the same father. I'm older than Saafir, Mikhail and Laila."

"My father met Adham's mother when they were young. Too young. When she became pregnant, my grandparents would not approve a marriage because Adham's mother wasn't to their liking."

"She wasn't rich or cultured enough," Adham said, sounding bitter.

"Like me with Saafir," Sarah said.

Molly frowned sympathetically.

The parallels in the stories were unmistakable. "My countrymen may not believe that you could be an acceptable wife, but I do not believe they are correct in that matter," Saafir said, squeezing Sarah's hand.

Sarah looked at him, the expression in her eyes difficult to interpret.

"My father financially supported Adham and his mother, but didn't visit them. It wasn't until Adham and I served in the military that we realized the connection."

Saafir had often wondered if his father's avoidance of Adham and his mother had to do with unresolved feelings. From what Adham had told him, their father had been deeply in love with Adham's mother.

"I see the resemblance now. You're lucky you have each other. You're lucky to have family supporting you," Sarah said.

Molly stroked the side of Adham's face. "The doctor doesn't want you getting worked up. You need to rest and heal. I can see your heart rate jumping around on the monitor."

Adham turned his head and Saafir expected him to tell Molly to be quiet. It was the sharp reaction he had seen from Adham most times he was with a woman and she commanded him. Instead, he kissed the inside of her wrist.

"What will you do about Sarah?" Molly asked. "I don't want her caught in the middle of this."

The media and Wasam's political party were holding up Sarah as a representation of what Saafir was doing wrong: allowing American influences into their purely Qamsarian world. "If you're asking me to walk away from her, I won't." Not until he had to, until he had no other choice.

Adham glanced at Molly and then back to him. "No

one is asking that of you now, but we know you have to marry Alaina Faris. I have a solution to solve your problem."

Sarah leaned forward, listening more intently. "Tell me."

"Arranged marriages have been part of our culture for hundreds of years. But throughout history, love has gotten in the way more than once. What does a man do when the woman he wants to marry is not an option? He marries the woman he must and he keeps the woman he wants close," Adham said.

While Saafir found the idea distasteful and would never have considered it before meeting Sarah, he could see some potential in it.

"Like a mistress?" Molly asked, giving Adham a disgusted look.

"But without the sneaking around. Most Qamsarians are tolerant of men having more than one woman in his life," Adham said. "Some men even have more than one wife."

Saafir and Adham had spoken at length about why his father had not chosen that route with Adham's mother. It was, in part, Saafir's father's wish to set an example for his children of devotion and, in part, because Iba would never have stood for it.

Saafir was familiar with the practice. If the only way to be with Sarah was to divide his time between Alaina and Sarah, was he willing to do that? Would Sarah accept that? Sarah had become important to him and losing her would be difficult.

"No," Sarah said, as if reading his mind. "I will not be someone's mistress. I will not spend weekends and holidays alone while you're with your wife and your children. I will not have a child with you and tell him he doesn't have a father because his father is spending time with his real family. I am not sure why you would think I would consider this, but forget it."

Saafir heard anger and bitterness in her voice. He should never have considered it, even for a moment, even if it was the only way for them to be together. He knew that path was fraught with hurt.

"Sarah, did you tell him about your dad?" Molly asked, touching her friend's hands. "Maybe if you explained, he would understand."

"You didn't tell him?" Sarah asked Adham.

Adham shook his head.

Sarah folded her arms over her chest and took a deep breath. "My father was married to someone else when my mom got pregnant with me. He was never part of my life. He never wanted to be. I was the child he didn't want, and my mom lived her life waiting for him to come back to her. He broke her heart and I don't think she ever got over it."

Saafir was desperate enough to keep Sarah in his life at whatever cost to him, but he wouldn't risk hurting her or reopening deep, painful scars. "You deserve better than just a share of my attention. You deserve everything you want to make you happy."

Sarah hated herself for even thinking about it. Her father hadn't been part of her life because he'd had another family. She had been the rejected one who didn't have a dad at her birthday parties, who hated Father's Day and who had been jealous every time she saw a girl in her neighborhood riding a bike or playing catch with her dad.

Sarah couldn't do that to herself, much less to any future children she may have. The fact that it was acceptable to be someone's mistress in Saafir's culture didn't mean she'd personally find it okay.

Saafir's phone vibrated. He answered and spoke quickly to the caller. "Virginia was taken, too." The news slammed down on the room. Frederick being kidnapped was bad enough, but the more people taken, the greater Rabah Wasam's reach and the harder it would be to stop him.

"Are they sure?" Sarah asked.

"Her bodyguard was found drugged in an alley. He told the police she was taken."

What was Wasam planning? If he couldn't force Saafir to stop work on the trade agreement, would he try to kill everyone involved with it?

"No one has called in with a ransom request or with demands," Saafir said.

"Wasam is waiting for you to make the next move," Adham said. "I like Sarah's idea of using the press."

It was the first time Sarah could remember Adham agreeing with her. Perhaps her revelation of how much common ground they shared in regards to their sordid family histories had helped form that bridge.

Adham straightened in his bed. "Let Wasam know that you're willing to negotiate for the release of Frederick and Virginia. Once the lines of communication are open, we can find out where he is holding his hostages."

"We?" Saafir asked. "You are staying where you are."

Adam held up his hands. "I might not be field-ready, but there's nothing wrong with my brain or my hands.

Let me get looped into this and handle logistics over the phone."

Saafir stared at Adham for a long moment. Sarah knew he was considering it. "I will allow you to advise me over the phone. Keep me involved in every big decision. I don't want to add to the body count. Wasam isn't afraid to kill to get what he wants."

"Do you want the good news or the bad news?" Owen asked, taking a sip of his coffee. He made a face, likely finding the diner's brew as unpleasant as Sarah had.

They'd chosen the diner because it was close to the police precinct, it was open at this late hour and they needed to refuel after being questioned by the police for more than four hours. Everyone involved in the trade agreement was being interviewed in the hope that someone had information to lead the authorities to Virginia and Frederick.

"I can't handle more bad news. Tell me the good news," Sarah said.

Saafir's guards were sitting in the booth behind them. Sarah could see them in the reflection of the diner's windows. Though the American police were handling the kidnapping, Saafir was running an investigation and had doubled her security detail. Everyone wanted Frederick and Virginia found unharmed.

"Alec is back in rehab, not jail," Owen said.

Sarah stared across the table at Owen. In light of the kidnapping, her and Alec's problems seemed unimportant. "I suppose that's good news." She didn't want to explain again that Alec wasn't her problem.

She didn't want to tell Owen that Alec didn't matter at the moment. It served no purpose.

Owen's face flamed red. His hands fisted on the table. "Don't you care about him anymore?"

Sarah was tired of having this conversation. "I am not paying for his rehab this time. I can't. I'm sorry, Owen. My stance on Alec hasn't changed."

Owen leaned back, his eyes cold and steady, his mouth drawn into a hard line. "Ready for the bad news?"

Sarah held up her hand. She dug for the strength to keep her cool and be strong and honest. "If it involves Alec, I don't want to hear it."

Owen said nothing as he stared across the table at her. "You've changed, and it's not a good change."

It was a slap in her face, an unnecessary insult. Sarah had been trying to hold it together and stay calm and do her job. Her anger bubbled over. "Because I'm unwilling to be someone's doormat? Because I am unwilling to listen to and believe someone's lies again and again and again? When will you understand that we cannot save Alec? He needs to save himself. Until he somehow understands that what he does hurts himself and the people around him and he wants to change, nothing will."

"He needs his family," Owen said.

Family. That word could ignite a thousand firestorms in her soul. She had never had a family and the closest she'd come was the friendships she'd formed. But she didn't have a soft place to land. She didn't have guaranteed holiday plans or people to eat with every day or a group who had known her all her life and understood her in a way that only came from lifelong relationships. "I wanted to be Alec's family, but I can't do that when it's tearing me apart."

Owen shook his head as if disgusted with her. "Maybe you don't have a family because you don't understand what family is. Family is sticking around for each other. Family means being there when it's too hard for other people. Family means forever and always, not because we have to, but because it's in our blood and it's who we are."

A punch to the gut would have hurt less. What could she say to defend herself? She couldn't argue with him. She didn't have firsthand experience with families and she had walked away from the situation with Alec. "Is that how you and Evelyn see it?"

"I can't speak for my sister, but it's how I see it."

Sarah stood from the table. She fumbled in her handbag for some bills and threw them on the table. Sitting in a greasy diner and being emotionally shredded wasn't on her agenda for the day. She walked out of the diner and onto the dark street. She was aware of the two guards following her at a distance.

She folded her arms around herself, feeling like she could be blown apart at the slightest wind.

Her cell phone rang and she answered it, feeling numb. It was Saafir.

"Where are you? You sound upset," he said.

"I'm near the police precinct," she said, wiping at her eyes.

"I'll come pick you up. I'm leaving there now."

"I want to be alone," she said.

Whenever it had mattered, she had only been able to count on herself. No one had come to her high school graduation. Her mom had had to work. It didn't matter.

Her side of the church during the wedding had been almost empty. It didn't matter. Surviving was what she had learned to do, to seal herself off from the world when she was most vulnerable. She could count on herself. She had never been able to look at another person and say, "yes, always, irrevocably, forever."

She disconnected her phone and kept walking. Tears blurred her vision and she swiped at them with the heel of her hand. The ache in her heart wouldn't let up. Denying it and pretending she didn't need a family was a survival mechanism. Having the word pressed against her had brought the desperate longing to the surface.

She heard a car pull up beside her and she turned to see Saafir climbing out of a black sedan.

He ran to her and took her arms. "What's the matter?"

She was tempted to break down into sobs, but a cold place inside her took over and she refused to let someone else see her raw, unguarded and weak. Saafir was part of the problem. While she had been falling in love with him, she had forgotten about her hopes for the future.

Her dreams included having a man who would be with her forever and give her a family. Maybe then she would know what that word meant. Owen's hurtful words echoed through her mind. The future had never been part of her plans with Saafir, but they should have been.

Why had she thought she could have an affair and have that lead to happiness?

"I love you," she said.

Saafir fell back a step, but didn't release her. "You're upset because you love me?"

How could she explain this? It was an epiphany she had only just realized herself. "I can't have a future with you. You know it. I know it. I don't know why we're playacting at this, pretending like we'll be fine when this ends."

Saafir tried to pull her against him, but she held up her hands. If she were wrapped in his arms, her resistance would fall away and she would fool herself into thinking she could do this. Being with him felt too good and so right, but he wasn't what she wanted. He was missing the key component that she needed to feel complete and safe enough to hand over her heart.

"We're not playacting. If what Adham said about being my mistress upset you, I'm sorry. I thought it was an option. Not a good one, but a way we could be together."

It wasn't about Adham's suggestion she become Saafir's mistress. It wasn't about Owen's words, either. It was about a fundamental truth she knew about herself that she had been denying. "I can't be with someone who will never really be with me. I can never be your number one. I need to be someone's number one." She wouldn't play second to someone's drug addiction or their wife or their job. She had to know she was important to someone.

Saafir could tell Sarah that she was the woman he wanted. He could tell her he loved her. But he couldn't offer what she was asking of him or give her what she needed. He was obligated to marry someone else. His country was depending on him.

If he told her he loved her, would it make it harder for her to walk away?

As it had been since becoming the emir, Saafir's personal desires played a distant second to the needs of his countrymen. He had to let Sarah go now or risk hurting her more. She was close to breaking down. He sensed a deep vulnerability and fear inside her. He wouldn't exploit it or risk hurting her further.

"You deserve more than to be someone's mistress. You deserve to be the center of someone's world."

"And that can't be you," Sarah said. Her voice was flat. It wasn't a question or spoken with malice. She was as resigned to their fate as he was.

"I never should have taken you with me to my hotel room knowing I couldn't give you more than a few nights," Saafir said. It was as close to an apology as he could muster. He wouldn't apologize for what they'd had as if they had been a mistake. Not when it was everything to him.

Sarah shrugged. "I started it, didn't I? When it got complicated, I should have walked away."

This was over. The realization shook him and left him cold. "I am not sure I can let you go," Saafir said. He wouldn't have been able to after one night. How would he now?

"You don't have a choice," she said.

He'd never had one. The moment Mikhail had stepped down as emir, Saafir's future had been decided and his fate sealed.

One of his guards got out of the car and joined him. "Your excellency, we've got trouble."

More trouble? He wanted to talk to Sarah and be certain she was okay. Looking at the devastation on her face, he knew she wasn't. A breakup should be quick and clean. He wasn't ready to let her go, but he knew discussing it wouldn't change anything, no matter how much he wanted it to.

"Tell me," Saafir said, his tone sharp and angry. The anger had everything to do with losing her and nothing to do with the woman herself.

His guard switched to Arabic. "We've been looking into leaks within the committee, trying to get a lead on Frederick's location. We found paperwork in Frederick's hotel room. He believed your lady friend was back-channeling information to America about your decisions on the trade summit."

"You're accusing Sarah of being a spy?" Saafir asked in Arabic.

At the mention of her name, Sarah looked at him.

Sarah wasn't a spy. She wasn't faking what she felt for him in order to get information. They'd found the mole on the committee, hadn't they?

Saafir asked her plain. He wouldn't be left wondering, even if it was wondering for a sliver of time. "I need to ask you something. Whatever you tell me, I will believe you."

Sarah waited.

"Are you a spy for America?"

Sarah opened her mouth and closed it several times. She started to speak and faltered.

Dread crept over him.

Sarah cleared her throat. "I am not a spy. Owen asked me to tell him if I knew anything."

"About me? About the trade agreement?" Saafir asked. Was this a misunderstanding?

"About both."

Saafir's heart hardened against the shock that battered him. She had betrayed him. He was worried about her and her heart and he had been blinded by the strength of his feelings for her. "You were using me to get information for the Americans. This is an act?" He stepped away from her and gestured between them.

Her mouth fell open. "No! I didn't know anything. I never told him anything."

"My guards tell me you and Owen met near here a short while ago. Are you involved in the kidnapping? Are you working for Wasam?"

Sarah brought her hand to her head. "What? Do you hear yourself? I am not a spy. I am not working for Wasam. Owen is my brother-in-law. That is all."

"But you agreed to give him information about the trade agreement that you learned from me?"

She lowered her head and her shoulders fell. "Yes."

Fury exploded inside him. One minute ago, he wouldn't have questioned her loyalties. Now, he didn't know what to believe. His brother had been betrayed by the woman he'd loved and now Saafir was in the same position. How had he let this happen? "I never want to see you again."

Sarah brought her hand to her mouth and a sob escaped.

"You can drop the act. The jig is up. But if I find out you had anything to do with Frederick or Virginia's disappearance, you will wish you had never spoken to me."

"You're letting her go?" his guard asked.

"What choice do I have?" Saafir asked. If this were Qamsar, he'd have authority to demand she be arrested for betraying him and Qamsar.

Sarah turned away and walked down the street. Saafir nodded at her guards to continue to follow her so she'd arrive home safely. Suddenly, she stopped and put her phone to her ear.

She turned around, her face pale beneath a street night.

"Saafir," she said. The word lacked any guilt or remorse, only strain and heartbreak. "It's Virginia."

Chapter 11

Sarah had been through an emotional hurricane in the last ten minutes and her mind had to be playing tricks on her. Her apartment phone number was showing on the display and it was Virginia's voice on the line.

Relief and confusion struck her at once. "Virginia? Are you okay? We've been trying to get in touch with you. Rabah Wasam—" She hurried back to Saafir and put the phone on speaker so he and his guards could hear the conversation. If she missed something important, it could cost Virginia her life.

"I hoped someone knew I was taken." The words escaped on a moan. "He has Frederick and me. We're in your apartment. He wants you and Saafir to come here."

Saafir leaned closer and the scent of him threatened to destroy her. It was now a scent she would associate with heartbreak.

"Why does he want us there?" Sarah asked.

"I don't know. Just come now. Please," Virginia said.

"Can he hear you right now?" Sarah asked, wondering how freely Virginia could speak.

"Yes," Virginia said. She hiccupped.

She wouldn't press Virginia for details while Wasam was listening. "We're on our way. We'll call the police."

"No police." A muffled conversation and then Virginia spoke again. "He says he has followers posted in this neighborhood watching for you. If he sees a police car, he'll shoot us both. You must come alone. If you bring the emir's guards, he'll kill us."

Wasam would trap her and Saafir along with the hostages. "Hang in there, Virginia. Try to stay calm. We're coming." The line was silent. "Virginia?" They'd lost the connection. "She's gone."

"Call her back," Saafir said. "Make sure the number wasn't spoofed. We're not walking into a trap if Frederick and Virginia aren't there."

Sarah dialed the number with shaking hands. Virginia didn't answer. A man did. She switched the call to speaker.

"To what do I owe this pleasure?" the man asked.

Saafir mouthed Wasam's name. A chill piped over her.

"Please let them go," Sarah said.

"Since you asked nicely, I won't laugh. But no," Wasam said.

What could she say? She looked to Saafir for help. He took the phone from her. "Wasam, this doesn't involve them. I will come alone to Sarah's apartment. You need to let Frederick and Virginia go."

"How delightful. The two lovers are together. I had

hoped that was the case. You will come. If you're not here in ten minutes, Frederick dies. Ten more minutes and Virginia is dead. How many more deaths do you want on your filthy hands?"

Wasam was trying to rattle them. It was working. Panic clawed at her.

Saafir appeared calm. "I will come alone."

"You are not in a position to negotiate with me," Wasam said. "Come now. I have an important job for you. Hurry up. Time's running out."

Saafir looked at the phone. "We need to go now if we're going to make it in time."

Fear made the neurons in her brain fire faster. A dozen thoughts raced through her mind. They had to call the authorities. This wasn't something they could handle alone. Then again, if Wasam wasn't bluffing and he had his followers posted in her neighborhood, he could make good on his threat and kill Virginia and Frederick. Or would he kill them anyway?

"We'll go to your apartment. It's not Frederick or Virginia he wants. It's me. The guards and my driver will contact the police and they'll find a way to help. At a minimum, we have to stall Wasam until help arrives," Saafir said. Saafir's driver stepped out of the car and joined the other men on the sidewalk. Saafir barked additional instructions at them in Arabic.

Sarah climbed into the passenger seat.

Before he pulled away from the curb, he looked at her. "If this is a trick and you are leading me into a trap—"

"It isn't," Sarah said. How could Saafir think so badly of her? She had agreed to help Owen under duress. It wasn't an excuse, but if she could go back in time, she would be more firm with Owen and tell him no from the start. She would hold her ground and not let guilt or obligation or her need for the job play a role in her decision.

"I know you don't trust me now, but I never asked you about the trade agreement," Sarah said.

"You agreed to betray me," he said. Ice frosted his words.

She wouldn't harp on the subject. Wasam was demanding they walk into a dangerous situation with no information except his word that he had Virginia and Frederick. He could have followers with guns with him. Virginia and Frederick could need medical attention.

"My guards will handle this delicately. They'll call Adham. Wasam is smart. If he says he planted people in your neighborhood, believe it. Have you ever held a gun?" Saafir asked.

"No," Sarah said.

"There's a gun underneath the seat. Get it," Saafir said.

She drew out a cool metal box. Saafir gave her the combination to open the lock. Her hands were trembling and she needed three tries to get it right. When she opened the lid, a gun stared back at her. She lifted it, feeling awkward and unsure. "It's heavy."

"Don't point it at anyone unless you are willing to kill them." He pointed to a spot on the gun. "This is the safety. If you feel threatened, take it off. If you have to protect yourself, shoot to kill. Pull the trigger and don't stop until you know you are safe."

Though she had broken his trust, he was arming her. "Thank you for looking out for me."

"I gave you my word and my word is my bond," Saafir said.

A lesser man would have brought her along and not cared about her well-being.

"You know my history with Wasam. He is an unstable man, but he is persistent. He will see this through until someone is dead. You don't have to come with me. I can talk him into taking me and letting Frederick and Virginia go."

"I won't let you go in alone," Sarah said. If Wasam saw they hadn't followed his instructions, would he lose it and shoot everyone?

"How does he plan to get out of this alive?" Sarah asked.

"I don't know, but he's a master of deceptions and trickery. He's not planning to die tonight," Saafir said.

Seven minutes later, they pulled in front of Sarah's townhouse. Wasam was in her home holding hostages and that knowledge filled her with terror and a sense of violation.

Wasam didn't play by any rules. He felt justified in hurting or killing to get what he wanted. She and Saafir would need to be careful not to make it worse by triggering an outburst from Wasam.

Saafir pointed to the gun. "Aim and shoot if you get the opportunity or you need to protect yourself. Don't get scared and shoot. The likelihood of you hitting a target at any distance is slim, and bullets flying mean someone will get hurt."

Saafir was wearing a gun under his suit jacket. He moved it to the back of his pants. "Once we are inside, I need you to get behind something, like your kitchen cabinets or your couch, anything that could shield you.

Nothing is completely bulletproof, but it might help. Once Wasam pulls a gun, you can be sure he plans to kill all four of us."

Sarah grabbed Saafir's forearm. "He could be planning to do that anyway."

Saafir looked at her hand and emotion smoldered in his eyes. Anger?

"He wants power. He needs me to hand that power over to him. He'll kill me as a last resort, but not until he's gotten me to admit that he's the rightful leader of Qamsar. Just as I have to unite the three political parties to be powerful, so does he."

If Saafir was angry, he was controlling it well. "Sarah, I know that you are afraid. You can do this. I saw you handle Khoury. You were brave. Find that courage again. I will be with you and I will back you up no matter what happens."

She and Saafir parked and took the stairs to her apartment. The door was unlocked and Sarah pushed it open. Saafir stepped in front of her.

"Come in, come in. So nice of you to join us," Wasam said. His accent was heavier than Saafir's, but he was speaking English.

Sarah's legs shook and her knees felt boneless. She was greeted with the smell of gasoline and the sight of Frederick and Virginia tied to chairs in the middle of the room. They were back-to-back and their mouths were taped. Adrenaline shot hard through her and she felt like her body had suddenly turned stiff.

Virginia shook her head at Sarah. A warning? Her eyes were red-rimmed, as if she had been crying. Frederick was slumped forward, his eyes closed. Was he dead?

Rabah Wasam pointed his gun at Saafir. The other two men with Wasam aimed their guns at the hostages and at Sarah. "This can go my way or this can end with seven deaths in this room."

"We're here," Saafir said. "You asked us to come and we did. As a show of good faith, at least let the women go. They aren't involved in this."

Wasam shook his head. "Nope. I have a use for everyone."

Sarah's eyes watered, the heavy scent of gasoline burning them.

Wasam smiled. "Do you like how I decorated your place? That pleasing fragrance is gasoline. I thought it was poetic justice. You want our oil and now I'll use it for my purposes. I doused everything in it. If anyone fires a gun, including the great emir who never misses, the entire room will ignite and send this place straight to hell."

Sarah watched Saafir. He was circling the room slowly. Wasam tracked him with his gun. "Careful, Saafir. I haven't forgotten the time we spent training together. The great, amazing Saafir, prince of the kingdom, could do no wrong. I know your moves. Don't try to unbalance me."

"Let them go and then we can talk," Saafir said. His voice was low and even.

Wasam let out a yap of sharp laughter. "You think it will be that easy? I have demands that need to be met first."

Saafir tensed. Sarah tried to read the situation. She sensed a delicate interplay between Wasam and Saafir, each sizing up the other. Though Wasam had more firepower and two followers who were likely trained in using their guns, Saafir didn't appear ready to surrender. He was advocating for the release of the hostages. He wanted to get everyone to safety.

"You all deserve to die," Wasam said. He pointed to Virginia and Frederick. "She works for the bloodthirsty company who wants to rule Qamsar and he is your little errand boy. I'd be doing Qamsar a favor by getting rid of them. We don't need people working against us, pretending they want to help and plotting the demise of our country."

"No one in this room is working against Qamsar," Saafir said.

Sarah disagreed on that point. Everything Wasam was doing was destructive and wouldn't end well for anyone.

Rabah Wasam had not always been an extremist who dealt in threats and murder. He had once been a good friend, a man Saafir had admired. He'd been a good soldier who trained hard and had been dedicated to serving his country.

The time he had spent in prison had broken him. A darkness had taken over his thoughts. Whether it was bitterness or revenge, Wasam was bent on seeing someone pay for what had happened to him. Knowing Wasam many years before and knowing what had happened to him gave Saafir leverage over his psyche, but not enough for Saafir to be sure of the best direction to steer the conversation. Wasam could be unpredictable.

In public, he was polished and impassioned about his cause. In private, he seemed a sliver away from losing his sanity completely over a personal matter that had happened years before.

Wasam jammed a hand through his hair. "Your agenda will ruin everything that is good about Qamsar. You want progress? You want Qamsar to advance alongside its new partner, America the brave and stupid? Do you know what I saw today? I saw a woman on the street wearing almost nothing, bending over and offering sex to strangers who drove by in their cars. Is that what you want for Qamsarian women?"

Of course he didn't. Wasam was posturing as if putting on a show. "My hopes for Qamsar are for our people to prosper. Not through drugs or prostitution, but through good, honest hard work," Saafir said.

"Lies! You want to sell us out to American oil companies and live fat and happy off the proceeds, while the people in our country starve and give away the most precious natural resource we have."

Where was Wasam getting his ideas? Sarah had moved behind the couch, but she was exposed. Saafir wanted her to take cover somewhere else, maybe even get toward a window in case she needed an exit. "If I couldn't leave you in a prison to starve, what makes you think I would want anyone in our country to starve?" Saafir asked.

Wasam turned red and shook with anger. "How dare you address the past so casually? You did leave me to starve. You didn't care what happened to me. All that mattered to you was looking like the big, brave hero."

Saafir hadn't changed places with Wasam in battle to be a hero. He just hadn't wanted special treatment because he was the son of the emir. Being left behind had been no way to earn the respect of his team.

"Enough talking. I want you on video addressing our country. Tell them about your plans to sell us out to the highest bidder. Tell them you don't care about them, but you care about lining your personal coffers with gold. Tell them you've picked a new bride, an American."

If Wasam and his followers were busy with camera equipment and a digital feed, it would give him a chance to disable them. "If that's what it takes to get these people to safety, then we'll do that." He needed Sarah, Frederick and Virginia out of this room. A sound bite of Saafir admitting whatever Wasam wanted him to say would give Wasam leverage and pull more people to his cause. He'd lost footing when the Conservative party leaders had spoken out against him, and he was desperate to regain ground.

Wasam lowered his gun.

"I want a show of good faith. Let the women leave," Saafir said.

"Your whore stays. The other one can go," Wasam said.

One of Wasam's followers cut Virginia free. Her mouth was taped, but she ran for the door. Saafir hoped his guards had followed his instructions and had discreetly moved closer to the apartment without raising Wasam's follower's suspicions, if Wasam did indeed have men posted in the area. His guards should have also alerted the police to approach silently. If Saafir's guards could get to Virginia before Wasam's did, they could protect her and they could find out what was happening inside the apartment. Saafir didn't want anyone rushing inside with guns drawn, not with the chances for igniting a fire sky-high. Would Virginia alert the neighbors to flee for safety?

Wasam was arranging his laptop.

Saafir looked from Sarah to Frederick. Would she understand he wanted her to work to free Frederick? She still had her gun gripped in her hand. She narrowed her eyes slightly and nodded ever so subtly.

The gasoline smell in the air was strong and it burned his lungs. Saafir walked to the window and opened it. If the smell was bothering him, it had to be bothering Wasam and adding to his irritation.

"What are you doing?" Wasam asked.

"I need fresh air or I'll pass out," he said.

Wasam shook his head. "Pampered pansy."

Though Wasam was unstable and angry, the insult was one that had been thrown his way often when Saafir had served in the military. Because he was a member of the royal family, Saafir had been treated differently. It had bothered him more than it had bothered his comrades. He'd wanted to be one of the team.

He flicked the curtain out of the window, alerting his team to his location. Fresh air coming into the room made it easier to think.

"I wrote a script for you. Look into the camera and speak slowly. Read what is on the screen or I will shoot you," Wasam said.

Saafir sat in the chair Wasam indicated. His compliance was making Wasam and his followers more at ease. They had turned their attention to Saafir.

Wasam's followers were between Sarah and the door. Otherwise, Saafir would have wanted her to run for safety. Sarah was standing near Frederick, hopefully trying to rouse him or untie him.

Wasam planned to get what he wanted and then he'd kill Frederick, Saafir and Sarah. They weren't leaving here alive. Saafir waited until Wasam leaned forward to start the camera.

He then grabbed Wasam around the neck and slammed him hard against the kitchen countertop. Seizing his gun hand, Saafir hit his wrist against the countertop until the gun sprang free. Then he used Wasam as a shield.

Sarah had jumped onto one of the followers, wrapping her arms around his shoulders and kicking at him.

Wasam's remaining follower appeared confused.

The man Sarah had attacked flipped her over his shoulder. She landed on her back on the ground.

"Let her leave or I will break his neck," Saafir said, tightening his arm around Wasam's throat.

"Let her go," Wasam croaked.

"Run, Sarah!"

"I can't leave you here," Sarah said.

"Go, Sarah," Saafir said. He had much to say to her. If this was the last time they saw each other, he wanted to tell her he loved her. If he died, he wanted her to know. But if he confessed his love in front of Wasam, Wasam would know how treasured Sarah was and use her against Saafir. "Please, Sarah, go." Perhaps his actions would deliver the message his mouth could not.

Her eyes were filled with tears, but she ran.

"Untie Frederick," Saafir said as he circled Wasam's followers, dragging Wasam.

"No, no," Wasam said. "This does not end with you in power. No matter who has to die, it is worth the sacrifice to see you on your knees begging for forgiveness."

Saafir's senses went on heightened alert.

Wasam lifted a lighter from his pocket. "See you in hell."

He flicked the lighter and threw it into the room. Immediately, fire raced around the space, closing them in. The door was covered in flames. They'd have to run directly through it to get out of the room. Wasam's followers chose that route.

Saafir's options were slim. The fire was consuming the oxygen around him. He could jump from the second-story window and survive. Throwing Frederick down would kill him. Wasam went limp and Saafir released him.

Saafir needed to get to Frederick. Running through flames, Saafir lifted Frederick over his shoulder and carried him into the hallway.

He returned for Wasam.

From the doorway, visibility was terrible. He did not see anyone, but he couldn't leave someone inside to suffocate.

The intensity of the heat prevented him from going back inside to help Wasam. The flames were spreading fast and he had to get Frederick to safety. He lifted Frederick and carried him to the ground level.

Where was Sarah?

Saafir spotted Adham and ran to him. "Did you see Sarah come out?"

Adham shook his head.

"What about Wasam?"

"Are they still inside?" Adham asked.

"Sarah got out before the fire started." Had one of Wasam's followers grabbed her?

"The team called me in. Everyone is looking for Wasam."

"He set fire to Sarah's apartment while we were still inside. I don't think he made it out."

"Crazy lunatic," Adham said.

The police and fire departments had arrived on the scene. Saafir borrowed Adham's phone and tried to call Sarah. The call went to voice mail. Where was she?

They'd fought earlier in the night, and Saafir had said he didn't want to see her, but he needed to know she was okay.

"Is the building clear?" Saafir asked.

Adham nodded. "We evacuated everyone and are knocking on doors on this block."

"Saafir!" Sarah voiced from somewhere in the night.

Saafir looked around. Sarah was being dragged into a car across the street.

Adham pulled his keys, dangling them out to Saafir. "My rental is there. Go. I'll follow in the car."

A motorcycle. Only his brother would rent a bike to get around D.C. Saafir climbed onto Adham's motorcycle. It had been years since Saafir had ridden, but it came back to him easily. He couldn't lose sight of the car carrying Sarah or he might lose her forever.

The car drove erratically down the street. Saafir's thoughts were fixed on Sarah. She had to be safe. She had been through too much. How had Wasam's men captured her without Adham or his guards seeing?

Turning down an alley after the sedan, Saafir stayed close. Wasam's men would kill her if they hadn't already.

The sedan was weaving down the road, running stop signs and red lights. At the third intersection, Saafir heard the sirens before he saw the car. Acting on instinct, he slowed and veered his bike to the right. The sedan careened into the intersection, colliding with a police cruiser. A second cruiser slammed into the first, knocking the sedan across the road like a ball on a billiards table.

The dark sedan came to a stop against a streetlight. No movement from the car. Sarah was inside! Was she hurt? Saafir ran to the car and pulled on the door handles. The back door was unlockcd and Saafir nearly ripped the door off its hinges.

Sarah was inside, not moving. The other men in the car were bleeding, dazed or unconscious. Saafir reached for her, dragging her free of the vehicle.

Laying her on the sidewalk, Saafir saw one of the police officers jogging over to him, already calling an ambulance to the scene.

Not knowing what else to do, Saafir started CPR. She seemed so small and fragile in his arms. "Come on, Sarah, open your eyes."

He breathed into her mouth. "Come on, goddess. I have a lot to say to you. Starting with I'm sorry."

After what felt like an infinity, Sarah's eyes fluttered open.

"You came for me," she said.

"I told you I would protect you," Saafir said, gathering her against him.

Sarah nodded and closed her eyes. "Did you get Frederick out?"

"Everyone but Wasam made it out," Saafir said.

Sarah reached up and touched the side of his face. "You are a good man, Saafir."

He kissed her hand and stayed with her until the ambulance arrived on the scene.

"Are you riding with her?" the paramedic asked.

Sarah held up her hand. "No. No, I am riding alone. Goodbye, Saafir."

She had said goodbye to him in anger earlier in the night, but now he detected no malevolence in her voice, just resolve.

Chapter 12

"If you're planning to make pasta sauce by the gallon, at least buy some pasta so we can eat it," Molly said.

Sarah measured more oregano and dumped it into the pot. "I'll run to the store later." She needed to stay busy. Her business had dried up and she had lost the man she loved. She expected any day to see a headline announcing the engagement of the emir of Qamsar to the beautiful Alaina Faris. She dreaded the moment.

Molly laid a hand on her shoulder. "I was kidding. I'm worried about you."

"Nothing to worry about," Sarah said. She had gotten in over her head and she should have been more careful with her heart.

"Adham says Saafir has been in a bad mood since the fire at your place," Molly said.

It made her feel a little better knowing Saafir wasn't

unaffected by what had happened. Sarah stirred the sauce to keep it from burning to the bottom of her Dutch oven. "I never should have agreed to help Owen. I never planned to help him. Why couldn't I just have said no to him?"

"Because you think of him as family. Maybe Owen never should have asked you to do something two-faced."

"I am two-faced because I agreed to do it," Sarah said.

Molly wrapped her arms around Sarah. "You are not two-faced. You try too hard to please people. You need to worry about pleasing yourself more."

"I knew this would happen if I got involved with Saafir. From day one, I knew it had to end and it wouldn't end well. I don't know why I'm so upset over it."

"You're upset because you fell in love with him and now you have to watch him leave and return to his home and marry someone else. You know his fiancée is waiting for him on the other side of his plane flight."

His fiancée. The words sounded bitter and cold. "Maybe it's better knowing someone else is waiting for him. At least I won't be tempted to make a mockery of what we had by pretending a long-distance relationship would work when obviously we are from different worlds and we have different ideas about what a relationship is."

Sarah had gone over her decision a thousand times. She and Saafir had said goodbye to each other with so much anger, but after the fire, she had sensed he'd wanted to say more. Sarah couldn't have discussed more of the same. Her heart wouldn't have withstood it.

There was nothing either of them could say to change what was.

Molly sat on a bar stool and drummed her fingers against the countertop. "I heard from Adham that the trade agreement is close to being finalized. What will you say to Saafir at the ball?"

Sarah hadn't forgotten about the ball that would mark the successful completion of the trade agreement. She had a number of vendors on hold, since the date was floating. "I won't see him. I can organize everything from behind the scenes." It was what she had been doing and it was her plan to continue. She couldn't face Saafir. He had sent flowers to Molly's place the night after her apartment had burned to the ground. Sarah hadn't known how to respond to them. She'd said and done nothing.

"You'll see him. You're hands-on with your big events. You won't let Saafir think you're cowardly by hiding in the kitchen."

"It doesn't matter what Saafir thinks. I made the mistake of falling in love with him and now I have to undo it."

Molly let out a snort. "If only it were that simple." She leaned forward. "I know you're in the middle of a crisis, but I need to tell you something. Will you promise to keep it a secret?"

Sarah set down her spoon and turned her full attention to Molly. "Of course. You know you can trust me."

"I'm late," Molly whispered.

"For what?"

"Not for anything. Late late. My period is five days overdue."

Surprise flashed through her. "Adham? Are you pregnant with Adham's baby?"

"Maybe. I haven't told him and I'm too chicken to take a pregnancy test."

This was big news. "I'm calling Krista. I'll ask her to pick one up on the way over."

"I can't take it. It's probably the stress of what's been going on. I don't want to make a big deal about nothing."

Sarah wasn't listening. She'd already texted Krista to stop by the pharmacy on the way over.

"Never thought I'd see the day," Owen said, watching Saafir sign the finalized trade agreement.

Saafir handed the papers to Owen. "We made it happen."

The Americans had agreed to most concessions. The Loyalists and the Progressives were thrilled to learn about the agreement and its stipulations. Drilling, mining and refining the oil would stay in Qamsarian control. The Conservatives had been slow to comment on the deal. Factions within the party were scrambling to pick a new leader, though Mohammad Faris was mentioned often as the favored pick.

Owen put the signed trade agreement into an envelope, sealed it and handed it to the courier.

"I was sorry to hear about what happened with Wasam," Owen said. "I know he was against the trade agreement, but I never wanted anyone to get hurt."

"Wasam made some poor decisions," Saafir said. He would not dishonor Wasam, but he would not let others shoulder responsibility for his death. The body in the apartment had been charred and the remains returned to Qamsar and Wasam's family.

Owen was packing his file folders into his leather briefcase. "Sarah and I had an argument earlier that night and if anything had happened to her, I would have felt terrible."

Saafir had known Sarah was feeling badly that night. "An argument about what?" Saafir asked, hoping to gain some insight into Sarah's thoughts.

Owen sighed. "I was angry at her about what's happening with my brother and I lashed out. I had put her in the middle of that situation and I tried to put her in the middle of the trade agreement. I was wrong on both counts."

"In the middle of the trade agreement?" Saafir asked. He knew that Sarah was supposed to feed information to Owen. He wondered about Owen's take on the problem.

"I asked her to let me know your thoughts on it," Owen said. "I'm telling you this because she never told me anything. I think she agreed in the first place because I caught her in a weak moment and she was scared about losing the contract with the trade summit. Not one of my finer days, and I know she felt terrible about it."

The burn of Sarah's betrayal had faded. She'd been brave when they'd needed to rescue Frederick and Virginia from Wasam. She had visited his country and stood strong against the media. Wasam's persistence in scaring her away hadn't resulted in her leaving his side.

In the end, what had been their undoing was Saafir's cowardice to make a stand about his life and his personal relationships. He viewed the role of emir as a servant to his country, but that didn't mean his entire life had to be dictated by the position.

His phone rang and Frederick's number lit up the screen. He had never been so happy to see his old friend getting back into action. Saafir excused himself and answered the call.

"Enjoying your vacation?" Saafir asked.

Frederick harrumphed. "I suppose you think putting me up in a five-star hotel with attendants to see to my every need will keep me away." His tone was good-natured.

"I can only hope to have you back with me soon," Saafir said. "I've missed having you around. No one to hammer on me about the important stuff."

"Would one of those important things be Sarah's pregnancy?"

Saafir almost dropped the phone. "Excuse me?"

"I received a message from a friend at an American tabloid. They're planning to run a story that Sarah is pregnant and the baby is yours."

It was possible. Improbable, since he and Sarah had been careful. "That's the first I've heard of it."

"Maybe you should check in with Sarah," Frederick said. "If this is some fabricated nonsense, it will go away on its own. If there's truth to it, then we need to get ahead of it."

Saafir agreed with Frederick. He wasn't sure what to think about the rumor. Sarah would tell him if she was pregnant. After he'd sent her flowers, he had hoped to hear from her. Her silence was telling. Was she hiding a baby from him? Scared of his reaction?

He had already decided to ask for Sarah's forgiveness, but if there was a baby in the picture now, Sarah would have to allow him a role in her life. He wouldn't stand for his child to be fatherless and suffer the way Sarah had as a child.

"We need to talk."

Sarah whirled around at the sound of Saafir's voice. She lowered her phone, momentarily forgetting the disturbing article she'd been reading that was proclaiming her to be pregnant. A reporter had found out that Krista had bought a pregnancy test and connected her to Sarah and then to the emir.

Saafir looked good. Too good. Wearing a tuxedo for the ball at the embassy, he was a handsome treat for her eyes. She had forgotten how majestic he was, and seeing him brought to the surface how much she had missed him. She wasn't expecting her catering staff for another hour and the ball wasn't scheduled to start for another two. "You're early."

"And apparently, you're late."

The news article. He had seen it, too. Of course he had seen it. His PR team had probably alerted him the moment the incorrect story had hit the internet. "There's been a misunderstanding." She didn't want to tell him about Molly. It was Molly's private news and her story to share with Adham and anyone else when she was ready.

Saafir's eyes darkened and he closed the distance between them. "Were you going to tell me?"

Sarah stared at him. "Tell you about what? The nonexistent baby that the tabloids are reporting I'm having? It's not true, Saafir. If I was pregnant, believe me, you would know it." She would have called him, pride or not. She would have found a way to let him know.

"It's not true?" Saafir asked. Was that disappointment she heard in his voice?

In that moment, she wished it was true and hearing her heart make the plea deepened her sadness. "I'm not pregnant."

"I see." He sounded somewhat skeptical.

"What were you planning if I was?" Sarah asked. He couldn't force her to move to Qamsar. He couldn't demand custody of the baby.

"My response is the same whether you are or aren't pregnant."

Her heart beat faster as he closed the distance between them with three long strides. "I want—"

The door to the kitchen slammed opened and Alec stepped in. He stumbled to the stainless-steel counter and caught himself against it. "Isn't this pleasant. My wife is knocked up by a king. A day to celebrate, that's for sure. Come on, Sarah, break out the champagne. Oh, wait, a woman in your condition shouldn't be drinking." He made disapproving noises with his tongue.

Her anger was immediate. "What are you doing here? Owen said you were in a recovery facility."

Alec laughed. "Those don't work. They can't keep me locked inside. The only person who can save me is you, Sarah. I read that you were coordinating a big event here tonight, and I came to congratulate you on your new baby. I wish it were my baby, but what can I say? You never wanted to get knocked up by me."

Before Sarah had known Alec had a substance abuse problem, she had wanted to have a family with him. "Alec, you can't be here. You need to stay in the rehabilitation center or they won't let you remain in the program." Why was she trying to reason with him? When he was under the influence, he was irrational and impossible. She reached for her phone. First call was to the police and the second one was to Owen.

"Get it through your head, Sarah. I don't want to be in a program!" Alec screamed.

His yelling jarred her and she stopped dialing.

"I want my life back. I want my wife and my job and my friends. I don't want to sit around in a circle talking about my feelings and why I've become an addict."

It was the first time he had said those words. Every other time they'd spoken of his addiction, he'd told her he'd wanted to get better. He'd wanted to heal. He'd wanted to do better. "What's changed?" she asked.

Alec banged the counter and Saafir drew Sarah closer.

Alec narrowed his eyes at them. "Nothing has changed. I've never liked those places. Too much whining and boredom."

Saafir put himself between Alec and Sarah. "Sarah cares for you. I don't want to see anyone hurt."

"Mister Peaceful. That's not what I hear you really are. Do you read the news, Sarah? You know this guy was Qamsarian Special Forces? How many people has he killed? Thousands?"

Sarah stepped out from behind Saafir. This wasn't his fight. "You may never have killed anyone, Alec, but have you thought about how many lives you've destroyed by behaving how you are behaving right now?" Sarah asked.

"Drama, drama. I'm here to make things right," Alec said. He pulled out a gun and Sarah's chest tightened.

He would shoot Saafir.

"Don't take a step you can't undo," Sarah said. "Tell me what you want."

Alec shook his gun at them. "I already told you what I want. I want my life back."

"Alec, put the gun down." Owen stood in the doorway of the kitchen holding a gun of his own and pointing it at Alec. "You can go back to rehab and we can put this behind us. But if you pull that trigger, I can't help you. I can't fix a mistake that ends with you hurting or killing someone."

Alec pivoted, aiming his gun at Owen. "Look at you, big brother. Acting like you care what happens to me. You don't want me to tarnish your reputation. You just don't want anyone to know that you have a brother who's a mess. You want to keep me locked away in a medical facility so I don't embarrass you."

"That's not true, Alec. I got the call from the rehab center that you went missing. Your anklet tracked you here. That means the police are on their way. We care about you. We want you to get better. We don't want to see you hurt."

"I can't get better. I don't want to get better. I want everyone to leave me alone and let me do what I want to do. Why is that so bad? Why does it matter that I like to have a good time? Why is everyone so uptight?" Alec was screaming again.

Years of back and forth and Alec still didn't understand. He was still convinced his family didn't understand him. It was he who didn't understand how devastating his illness had been for everyone.

"Put your gun on the counter and we can go somewhere and talk," Owen said.

Alec banged his gun against the metal counter and

the noise echoed around the room. "No! Talking is done. Leave, Owen. You don't need to be part of this and I don't want to hurt you."

"Alec," Owen said, the warning strong in his voice. "Put the gun down."

"And let this guy take my wife?" Alec yelled.

"No one is taking anyone," Owen said. "You and Sarah are divorced."

"She didn't give me a choice," Alec said.

"You didn't give me a choice," Sarah said.

Alec took a step toward her. "I want to talk to Sarah. Give me a few minutes alone with Sarah."

Sarah didn't like the look in his eyes or the way he was handling his gun. He was too angry and too far gone. Police sirens sounded.

Owen pointed to the back door. "Hear that, Alec? This is over. Put down the gun and don't make this worse for yourself. If the police come in here and see you waving a gun at the emir, you'll be in a world of trouble."

Saafir's guards! Were they close by? They wouldn't fire at Alec, would they? Sarah didn't want Alec hurt. Not investing more in Alec was a far cry from wanting him wounded or dead. Sarah took a few steps toward him. "Alec, please give me the gun and we'll talk."

The police sirens seemed to be right outside. Alec looked at the door and then at Sarah. He lifted his gun and aimed it at Sarah. "You'll never give me what I want."

"Alec, no!"

The sound of gunfire exploded in the air. Sarah instinctively whirled away and ducked. Saafir was wrapped around her and it took her a second to register she wasn't hurt. She opened her eyes. Alec was slumped against the walk-in refrigerator.

Owen was shouting. "He shot me!"

"You shot me!" Alec yelled.

Sarah looked between Owen and Alec. Owen was moving toward Alec and clutching his arm. Sarah grabbed a cotton apron from the counter and pressed it over Owen's arm to staunch the bleeding. He winced.

Alec's eyes were closed, but he was breathing, his chest rising and falling. Saafir left through the back door, returning with his guards and the police.

His guards stepped in to administer first aid.

Saafir pulled Sarah against him. "Definitely not pregnant?" he asked.

Sarah shook her head. "Not pregnant."

"Ma'am? Can you answer some questions for us?" one of the paramedics asked. Sarah nodded and followed the medic outside.

Sarah stood over Owen as a paramedic was loading him into the ambulance. "When Alec left the rehab facility, I got the call he was on his way here. He's been more and more paranoid. He's making up stories and hallucinating. I couldn't let him hurt you."

"Thank you, Owen," Sarah said. "You saved my life."

Owen blushed. "What about the emir? I told him I pressured you into feeding me information, but that you didn't share secrets."

Sarah glanced over her shoulder at Saafir, who was speaking to police officers on the scene. He must have sensed her looking at him. He turned and one corner of his mouth lifted. She couldn't read the situation or interpret his feelings for her. Sarah had heard that his fiancée would be in attendance tonight.

"I think maybe I messed that up good," Sarah said. "He has his life in Qamsar, and I have my life here."

Owen closed his eyes. The paramedic poked and prodded him. "You gave up on Alec long after everyone else did. I know you have staying power."

"It's not staying power I need," Sarah said. "I'd need to be politically powerful or have a father who was."

Owen gave her a sideways look as the paramedic pushed the stretcher into the ambulance. "They called Chelsea. She's meeting me at the hospital."

Sarah was glad to hear some warmth in his voice when referring to his wife. "I'll call you or Chelsea tomorrow to see how you are," Sarah said and waved.

She sensed him behind her before she saw him.

"Sarah, please let me take you home," Saafir said, setting his hands on her shoulders.

Sarah faced him. "You can't leave. You need to be here for the ball. I've asked the staff to move the food and tables to the lobby. If and when the police are finished in the kitchen, we can use the ballroom."

"Forget the ball," Saafir said. "I'm worried about you."

"Your family is coming to see you. Everyone wants to congratulate you on your success. It will be a damper on the whole event if you're not here."

"I came here to talk to you, and I want to finish our conversation."

"I don't know that I have more to say." If he pressed her, she would admit that she would have liked being pregnant with his baby, even if it was a repeat of the situation her mother had been in decades before. If he pressed her even harder, she would admit the idea of being in his life, even in an off-to-the-side way, was tempting. She was trying to be strong and resist telling Saafir the truth.

Love and family wasn't in their future, but she wanted it in hers.

Saafir's guards remained close to him, ignoring his request to give him some space. Every available guard was on hand and his intelligence team had their ears to the wall. If the extremists were planning anything in retaliation for Wasam's death, Saafir would get in front of it.

The close call with Sarah's ex was enough to shake everyone on his security team. He wouldn't be getting much leeway the rest of the night and he wanted that leeway to talk to Sarah.

Tomorrow was too long to wait to say what he needed to say.

Guests had been arriving in a steady flow. Congressmen and congresswomen, the managers and owners of various oil industry companies and interested parties were attending the event to celebrate. Saafir shook hands and made small talk. Aware he was being watched and that rumors were spreading about what had transpired with Owen and his brother that night, Saafir was careful about every move he made. He tried not to look away from conversations too often as he searched the crowd for Sarah. He tried not to stare when she entered the room. He forced himself to remain at the event and not sweep Sarah away to a place where they could speak in private.

When his mother arrived, Saafir was struck by her

grace and beauty. She was escorted by Mikhail. Behind her, Alaina Faris entered on the arm of her father, Mohammad.

Saafir strode across the room to greet them as decorum demanded. As much as he enjoyed seeing his family, he was not anxious to meet Alaina or deal with her father.

"You look well, brother," Mikhail said.

"As do you," Saafir said.

"Have Laila and Harris arrived?" Mikhail asked.

Saafir's mother was already looking around the room, no doubt searching for her daughter so they might catch up.

"I heard from Harris they were on their way from their hotel," Saafir said.

Iba excused herself and moved in the direction of some politicians' wives she was friendly with.

Mikhail stepped to the side and gestured for Mohammad and his daughter to step forward.

Saafir extended his hand and Mohammad shook it.

"Your excellency, it's a pleasure to see you again. May I present my daughter, Alaina Faris."

Alaina stared at Saafir and said nothing. Her eyes were red and she looked exceedingly tired. Compassion strummed through him. Neither of them wanted this marriage. Not a thread of interest or eagerness entered her face.

"It's a pleasure to meet you, Alaina," Saafir said.

No response. Her father nudged her. She lowered her head and said something he didn't catch.

"Pardon?" Saafir asked.

When she lifted her head, her eyes were filled with tears. "Apologies, your excellency. I have heard you are a good and kind man. I had hoped that once we met, you would see that this is a mistake—"

"Alaina!" Her father's voice was quiet, but sharp. "We discussed this."

Alaina was still speaking, "—and that I am in love with someone else."

Saafir almost laughed. Nothing was funny about Alaina loving another man, but he, too, was in love with someone else. The circumstances were ridiculous. On first meeting, they had no instant attraction, no chemistry and they were both pining for someone else.

Mikhail took Saafir's arm. "May I speak to you for a moment?"

Alaina's eyes darted from Mikhail to Saafir and back to Mikhail. The beginnings of a smile turned up the corners of her mouth. She lowered her gaze to the floor.

Saafir excused himself and let Mikhail lead him away.

"I have something to tell you."

"You could have mentioned that she hated the idea of marrying me before letting me find out tonight," Saafir said.

Mikhail clasped his hands behind his back. "She doesn't hate the idea. She is in love with someone else and that makes it hard for her to accept the idea of marrying you."

Saafir lifted his brow. "It was never my intention to force anyone to do anything. I made my position clear. I want to marry someone for the benefit of our political position, but I will not force a woman to make a matrimonial commitment to me when she obviously doesn't want to."

Mikhail rocked back on his heels. "I knew you'd feel that way. How did you pick Alaina?"

"From a list Frederick provided." Saafir wouldn't pretend the selection had been romantic or based on his desire to marry Alaina.

"With Rabah Wasam dead, the Conservatives are in a scramble to pick a new leader. A lot of what he was doing was unknown to the entire party, and factions are breaking away. Alaina's father will likely be selected as the new leader of the Conservatives."

He knew all that. "Frederick updated me on that matter this morning." Despite his orders for Frederick to rest and heal, the man could not stay off his smartphone, tablet and television. He devoured the news like he was at a buffet.

"What about Sarah?" Mikhail asked.

It wasn't like his brother to pry into his personal life. Why did he want to know about her? "I need to speak with her about our relationship."

"Are you planning to keep her as your mistress?" Mikhail asked, narrowing his eyes, not approving of the idea.

"She would never stand for that," Saafir said. People were circling, looking to speak to him. He lowered his voice. "Cut to the chase, Mikhail. There are a lot of people here and I have much to do."

Mikhail took Saafir's shoulders. "I need a big favor. The biggest you've ever done for me."

"Will granting you a boon mean you will stop sulking around?"

"Yes. If you help me, my entire life will come back together."

Saafir waited for the request that would be a miracle healer for his brother.

"I'm in love."

"With Alaina," Saafir finished.

Mikhail appeared dumbstruck. "How did you know?"

"She was looking at you in a certain way. You've been spending time with her to help me. I put it together."

"I want to marry her," Mikhail said.

"How does she feel about it?" Saafir asked.

"She feels the same way," Mikhail said.

If Alaina married Mikhail and her father approved of the match, it would forge the ties that Saafir needed between the Loyalists, the royal family and the Conservatives. "I will speak to her father about it and make the arrangements."

Relief seemed to billow from Mikhail. "Thank you, Saafir. I've been worrying about telling you. I didn't know if you'd feel like I'd stolen her from you."

"Alaina was never mine to steal," Saafir said. "I'm in love with someone else, too."

Mikhail nodded swiftly. "I thought as much."

"But remember your promise to me. Stop sulking. Go spend time with Alaina and let's keep up appearances." Feeling free of his obligation to Alaina, Saafir went in search of Sarah.

Chapter 13

Sarah watched Saafir greeting Alaina Faris as she entered the lobby with her father. Alaina was even more beautiful than Sarah had imagined. Tall, thin and Qamsarian, qualities that Sarah did not and would never have.

Though it wasn't in her best interest to watch them, it was difficult to turn away. Perhaps seeing Saafir and Alaina together would give her closure. But every second felt as if knives were twisting in her heart. Finally, Sarah looked away. She didn't feel closure. She felt unabated sadness.

Saafir's sister, Laila, and his brother-in-law, Harris, had spoken to Sarah and thanked her for hosting the event. Did they know about her and Saafir's affair from the media, or Iba or maybe even Saafir?

Needing a place to be alone with her thoughts, Sarah

fled to the coatroom. She couldn't bear to see Saafir and Alaina talk and laugh together. They'd have their happily ever after. Not begrudging Saafir his happiness wasn't the same as smiling while having it shoved in her face.

Sarah sat on the small footstool in the coatroom. It wasn't the most elegant place to sit, among the few coats and shawls hanging in the walk-in closet. After the night she'd had, she needed to rest before her legs gave out from under her.

How had everything gone from bad to worse with Saafir? She had convinced herself she was better off alone. She'd had to let him go. Just like she'd had to let Alec go when she couldn't help him anymore and she couldn't let herself be pulled down into his spiral of destruction. Just like she'd had to let go of the idea of being part of her father's life.

Sarah let herself cry for a few minutes, and when the emotion was expunged, she stood and wiped under her eyes, hoping tracks of running mascara didn't give her away. She wished the tiny room had a mirror. She must look a wreck.

The door opened and Saafir appeared in the doorway. His frame filled it and Sarah was struck again by how handsome he was.

He was her client. At least, until this event was over. "Everything okay?" she asked. If he said one word about Alaina, she might kick him in the shin. Emir or not, she couldn't stand to hear about his new love.

"Everything is not okay." He pulled closed the door and locked it.

"What are you doing?" Sarah asked. She tried to go around him, but he took her shoulders.

"Getting you alone and talking to you. No interruptions allowed. I need you to listen to me."

Sarah removed his hands from her shoulders and took a step away. As their fingers brushed, heat smoked between them. "People are watching you. They'll know we're in here alone. Your wife is out there."

Saafir advanced on her and Sarah let him take her in his arms and hold her against his chest. It felt too good.

"I am not married. I do not have a wife. Alaina will be Mikhail's wife. It seems during the time that I was falling for you, she and my brother were falling for each other."

Sarah felt her jaw slacken. Saafir had fallen for her? Mikhail and Alaina were in love? "Are you upset?" What about his political plans and Qamsar's future?

"Why would I be upset? I am not in love with Alaina. Our marriage was always about politics. I'm in love with you, and I won't let you get away. I came here tonight to tell you that."

It was almost harder to know that he loved her when they had no future together. "Take it back, Saafir. Don't tell me you love me when you know we can't be together."

His mouth was drawn into a firm line. "We will be together. I won't settle for anything less."

How? She wasn't Qamsarian. She wouldn't be accepted by the people in Saafir's country.

"I've missed you. Owen told me how he cornered you into agreeing to spy for him," Saafir said.

"I didn't spy for anyone," Sarah said, lifting her chin.

"I know that now. What I don't know is if you'll forgive me for not trusting you and giving you a chance to explain."

"This isn't just about trust. What about your country? I will never be accepted in Qamsar as your girlfriend."

Saafir brought his hand to his jaw. "You're right. You wouldn't be. It's not proper for the emir to date an American. But if I marry you, they'll have no choice but to accept you."

He would do that for her? Put her before his country? Put her first in his life?

"I want another chance. I want to prove that I can be the man you need."

He made it sound easy. "I love you, Saafir, but how will we…" She didn't know how to finish the thought.

"We will together." Saafir delivered a kiss she felt across her entire body. Heat speared from his mouth and her worries melted away.

Together was a good way to think about the future.

"I won't accept being one of many wives," Sarah said.

"Is a condition of accepting my proposal that I disperse my harem?" he asked with a smile.

She swatted him. "No harem. No other women. Just me."

"Then the same applies to you. Just me."

Saafir and Sarah sealed the promise with a kiss.

A loud boom that sounded like gunfire had Sarah jolting. "What was that?"

The musicians had stopped playing and screams filled the air. Saafir pulled his comm device from his pocket and slipped it over his ear. He listened for several moments. "There are three men in black masks demanding to speak to me alone or they will start shooting people."

"You can't go out there. You'll be killed." Sarah grabbed his sleeve, desperate for him to stay where it was safe. His guards and the hired security would take care of the problem or they would contact the authorities.

"I have this under control. If I hide in here, they'll open fire on the crowd. They're saying for every minute that passes, they'll kill someone."

Now that he was in reach, she wouldn't let Saafir be taken away from her. "Think this through. There has to be another way."

Is this how Saafir would be forced to live his life? Wasam was dead, but the attacks kept coming.

"Adham is reporting at least five masked men, one at each entrance and three in the lobby."

Saafir took Sarah's face in his hands. "I am not a coward. I will not cower in here and worry about saving myself when other lives are at stake."

He had told her he loved her. She wanted a future with him. How could she stand here and watch him walk to his death?

"Do you know of a way to get to the kitchen from here without going through the lobby? I want to lure them away from the guests," Saafir said.

The strength in his voice made it clear he would do this, with or without her help. She might as well do everything she could to help and trust that Saafir knew what he was doing. "There's a service hallway that leads behind the ballroom, to the kitchen."

Saafir touched his earpiece. "Five seconds until they shoot someone." He closed his eyes. "Adham, tell them I'm in the kitchen."

With no time to spare, Sarah pressed a kiss to Saafir's

lips. He slipped from the coat closet. Saafir's guards came to attention and flanked him as they walked.

Sarah felt like her legs would buckle under her. She wouldn't stand around and wait for the extremists to kill Saafir. She would help how she could. He had said they would face the future together. Her plan took less than five seconds to form in her mind. She returned to the ballroom. The guests were sitting on the floor, belts, handbags and jackets tossed to the center of the room in a pile.

Seeing no sign of a shooter, she found Harris standing with Laila and Mohammad Faris. Harris was an FBI agent. He could get help. As quietly as she could, she explained the problem, that Saafir had gone to the kitchen to face the extremists.

Harris nodded. "The shooters went to meet him. They claim to have eyes on the room, which is why no one is moving. But you're making me wonder if that was a lie."

"What can we do?"

After exchanging nods with his wife, Harris faced Sarah. "We'll take a chance the shooters are lying about their numbers and try to save Saafir's life."

Sarah, Harris, Mikhail and Mohammad crept toward the kitchen and crouched behind the swinging door. Harris was leading them. He said he would act when the time was right. They needed to know how many men they were facing. Sarah peered through the gap between the door and the wall.

Her stomach dropped and her heart seized.

Saafir was talking to Rabah Wasam. He was alive! Wasam had a man on each side of him holding a gun on Saafir. Saafir's guards had to be close, perhaps at the other entrance to the kitchen.

"You didn't really think I would let myself burn to death, did you? I had a body planted to mislead you."

"You're a master planner," Saafir said.

Wasam was shouting and sweat beaded his forehead. He was looking erratically around the room, perhaps anticipating an attack from the royal guards.

"I'm the master of a lot of things and soon I will be master of Qamsar. You know what strikes me as the worst about this? No one will know you died screaming like a girl." He wiped at his forehead and then laughed. The pitch of his voice was eerily disturbing.

Sarah felt sick. What was he planning to do to Saafir? Exact revenge for some perceived mistreatment?

"You can kill me, but I won't beg. I won't scream," Saafir said.

Wasam laughed again, the gun in his right hand shaking. He was holding something in his left. What was it? "It doesn't matter how you behave. What everyone will know is what I tell them. My version of the story ends with you being a coward. You came to meet your American lover in a discreet place, and when I stumbled upon you, you attacked me. You didn't want Qamsar to know you had jilted Alaina."

Wasam didn't know that Alaina and Mikhail were in love. No one would believe that part of Wasam's story. "This won't end well for you, Wasam. The Conservatives are looking for a new leader. How will another problem reunite them and get them behind you?"

Harris, Mikhail and Mohammad had taken a step away from the door and were deep in almost silent discussion. Sarah couldn't tear her eyes away from Saafir.

"I have a plan," Wasam said. "Take off your earpiece and kick it over here."

Saafir did as Wasam asked.

"How does it feel to know you're doing to die alone?" Wasam asked.

"He's not alone," Sarah said, shoving open the door and bursting through. "You have to go through me first."

Fear registered on Saafir's face. Despite his outward calm when they had talked to Alec and again while facing Wasam alone, her presence in this room terrified him to the point that he could not hide it.

She stood in front of Saafir.

"You'll have to shoot me, too," Mikhail said, stepping in front of her. Mohammad and Harris moved to stand around Saafir, as well.

Saafir's guards entered through the back door, closing the circle around Saafir.

It was a more level playing field. Sarah reached for Saafir's hand.

Wasam laughed. "You think surrounding him and pointing your guns at me will stop the bomb from going off? That's right. I've always got a backup plan. My bomb is on a dead man's switch." He held up his hand where he was clasping a small black remote. "You kill me and I release this button, the whole building goes up in smoke. How many people will I take with me? A hundred? More? Is it worth it to you, Saafir?" Wasam was shaking hard with rage, his face red and sweat dripping down his temples.

His guards exchanged uncertain looks.

"As interesting as that sounds," Saafir said, "we won't let innocent people die."

What could they do? They didn't have time to evacuate. Though Iba and Laila had planned to lead people out of the lobby, Sarah didn't know how many had gotten out safely or if they'd been stopped by guards who Wasam had posted at the entrances.

"This time, you don't get to decide what happens," Wasam said.

"Last chance, Wasam. Disable the bomb," Saafir said.

Wasam laughed. "Ka-boom." He released the button.

Nothing happened. Silence.

Wasam pressed the button again. Same result.

Everyone around Sarah seemed to move at once. Saafir's guards, including Adham, surrounded Wasam and apprehended him and his followers.

"You can join the rest of your team outside with the American police," Adham said.

Saafir's arms went around her. "I told you I had this under control."

Sarah spun to face him. "How? How did you know the bomb wouldn't detonate?"

Saafir smiled. "After the incident with Alec, I had my team sweep the building. They found and dismantled the bomb. We suspected Wasam might still be alive and hoped he would show tonight and we could catch him and his followers."

"You should have told me what you were planning," Sarah said.

"No time. Information was coming in as events were unfolding and we were trying to stay one step ahead of Wasam's plans," Saafir said.

Sarah rested her head on Saafir's shoulder and

slipped her arms around his waist. She was glad it was over and she could start her life with him.

"Let's get out of here. As lovely as this party has been, tonight, I want to spend alone with my bride," Saafir said.

Sarah shook her head. "I'm not your bride. We're not married."

"We're not married yet. But you're an event coordinator, and I figure you can put something together in a week or two. Then we can get started with a family of our own."

"A week or two?" Sarah asked.

"With unlimited resources and your talent, should be easy," Saafir said.

"I'm not a princess. People won't like this."

"I don't care what people think. But you're right. You're not a princess. You're more. You're the queen of my heart, and nothing, not Qamsar, not duty, not my position comes before you."

* * * * *

Available September 2, 2014

#1815 COURSE OF ACTION: THE RESCUE
by Lindsay McKenna and Merline Lovelace
Two high-risk rescue missions have these military men facing the dangers of the Amazon to protect the women they love.

#1816 UNDERCOVER IN COPPER LAKE
by Marilyn Pappano
Sean Holigan, an ex-con and DEA informant, is forced to play both sides to try to save his sister's life, but he never planned on falling for his nieces' foster mom, the sweet-as-sin Sophy.

#1817 ONE SECRET NIGHT
Ivy Avengers
by Jennifer Morey
While on a mission to take down a killer, private investigator Raith shares a steamy night with the infamous Autumn Ivy, whose fame could lead danger straight to them.

#1818 WHEN NO ONE IS WATCHING
by Natalie Charles
Criminal profiler Mia Perez has no memory of the attack that nearly killed her, but when she teams up with Lieutenant Gray Bartlett to find a serial killer, the investigation uncovers deadly secrets from her forgotten past.

YOU CAN FIND MORE INFORMATION ON UPCOMING HARLEQUIN® TITLES,
FREE EXCERPTS AND MORE AT WWW.HARLEQUIN.COM.

HRSCNM0814

REQUEST YOUR FREE BOOKS!
2 FREE NOVELS PLUS 2 FREE GIFTS!

(H) HARLEQUIN®

ROMANTIC suspense

Sparked by danger, fueled by passion

YES! Please send me 2 FREE Harlequin® Romantic Suspense novels and my 2 FREE gifts (gifts are worth about $10). After receiving them, if I don't wish to receive any more books, I can return the shipping statement marked "cancel." If I don't cancel, I will receive 4 brand-new novels every month and be billed just $4.74 per book in the U.S. or $5.24 per book in Canada. That's a savings of at least 14% off the cover price! It's quite a bargain! Shipping and handling is just 50¢ per book in the U.S. and 75¢ per book in Canada.* I understand that accepting the 2 free books and gifts places me under no obligation to buy anything. I can always return a shipment and cancel at any time. Even if I never buy another book, the two free books and gifts are mine to keep forever.

240/340 HDN F45N

Name	(PLEASE PRINT)	
Address		Apt. #
City	State/Prov.	Zip/Postal Code

Signature (if under 18, a parent or guardian must sign)

Mail to the **Harlequin® Reader Service:**

IN U.S.A.: P.O. Box 1867, Buffalo, NY 14240-1867
IN CANADA: P.O. Box 609, Fort Erie, Ontario L2A 5X3

Want to try two free books from another line?
Call 1-800-873-8635 or visit www.ReaderService.com.

* Terms and prices subject to change without notice. Prices do not include applicable taxes. Sales tax applicable in N.Y. Canadian residents will be charged applicable taxes. Offer not valid in Quebec. This offer is limited to one order per household. Not valid for current subscribers to Harlequin Romantic Suspense books. All orders subject to credit approval. Credit or debit balances in a customer's account(s) may be offset by any other outstanding balance owed by or to the customer. Please allow 4 to 6 weeks for delivery. Offer available while quantities last.

Your Privacy—The Harlequin® Reader Service is committed to protecting your privacy. Our Privacy Policy is available online at www.ReaderService.com or upon request from the Harlequin Reader Service.

We make a portion of our mailing list available to reputable third parties that offer products we believe may interest you. If you prefer that we not exchange your name with third parties, or if you wish to clarify or modify your communication preferences, please visit us at www.ReaderService.com/consumerschoice or write to us at Harlequin Reader Service Preference Service, P.O. Box 9062, Buffalo, NY 14269. Include your complete name and address.

HRS13R

Glancing at her, he saw that she had gone even more ashen. She kept touching her neck. Damn. He turned, kneeling down. Taking her hand away, he rasped, "Let me." She nodded, allowing him to examine the larynx area of her throat. When he pressed a little too much, she winced. But she didn't pull away. Aly trusted him. He dropped his hands to his knees, studying her.

"You've got some cartilage damage to your larynx. It has to be hurting you."

Aly nodded, feeling stricken. "I'm slowing us down. I'm having trouble breathing because that area's swollen."

"You're doing damn good, Aly. Stop cutting yourself down."

She frowned. "Are they still coming?"

"They will. Being in the stream for an hour will buy us some good time." He glanced down at her soaked leather boots. "How are your feet holding up?"

"Okay."

He cupped her uninjured cheek, smiling into her eyes. "Who taught you never to speak up for yourself, Angel?"

Josh closed his eyes. Aly was a trouper, and she did have heart. A huge, giving heart with no thought or regard for herself or her own suffering. He leaned down, pressing a kiss to her brow, and whispered, "We're going to get out of this," he rasped, tucking some strands behind her ear.

He watched Aly's eyes slowly open, saw the tiredness in them coupled with desire. Josh had no idea what the hell was going on between them except that it was. Now he had a personal reason to get Aly to safety. Because, general's daughter be damned, he wanted to know this courageous woman a lot better.

Don't miss
COURSE OF ACTION: THE RESCUE
by Lindsay McKenna and Merline Lovelace,
coming September 2014 from
Harlequin® Romantic Suspense.

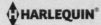

HARLEQUIN®

ROMANTIC suspense

UNDERCOVER IN COPPER LAKE
by Marilyn Pappano

A past he'd rather forget, a future he secretly longs for...

DEA informant Sean Holigan never imagined he'd return to Copper Lake and revisit the ghosts of his past. But bad memories aren't the only thing waiting for him. With their mother in jail, Sean's nieces are in the care of their foster mother, Sophy Marchand. Years and miles haven't erased Sean's high school memories of the young, studious Sophy, but she certainly has grown up. Beautiful and benevolent, Sophy represents a life, and love, Sean longs for—and one of three lives he must protect. Targeted by ruthless killers, Sophy and the girls depend on Sean... almost as badly as he depends on them.

Look for UNDERCOVER IN COPPER LAKE
by Marilyn Pappano in September 2014.

Available wherever books and ebooks are sold.

Heart-racing romance, high-stakes suspense!

www.Harlequin.com

HRS27886

ROMANTIC suspense

ONE SECRET NIGHT
by Jennifer Morey

*The morning after brings dangerous consequences in Jennifer Morey's next **Ivy Avengers** romance.*

After stumbling into the cross fire of a black ops mission, Autumn Ivy is saved by a dark, sexy hero—and swept away for a night to remember. Weeks later, she discovers her secret lover is soon to be a secret daddy, but what's more shocking is when Autumn tracks her mystery man right into the path of a killer.

Part of a famous Hollywood family, Autumn comes with paparazzi who threaten Raith De Matteis's hidden identity. But it's Autumn's news that puts the lone-wolf agent in jeopardy. Now more than his client is at risk. This time it's his woman...and his baby.

Look for ONE SECRET NIGHT by Jennifer Morey in September 2014.

The **Ivy Avengers:** The children of a famous movie director and Hollywood heavyweight, the Ivy heirs live anything but a charmed life when danger always follows them

Available wherever books and ebooks are sold.

Heart-racing romance, high-stakes suspense!